And All Our Yesterdays

Stories of Mystery and Crime through the Ages

Edited by

Andrew MacRae

DARKHOUSE
BOOKS

And All Our Yesterdays

All rights reserved

These are works of fiction. Any resemblance between events, places, or characters, within them, and actual events, organizations, or people, is but happenstance.

No part of this book may be reproduced or transmitted in any form or by any means, electronic or mechanical, including photocopying, recording, or by any information storage and retrieval system, without permission in writing from the publisher.

Copyright © 2015 by Darkhouse Books
ISBN 978-0-9908428-9-7

Published March, 2015

Published in the United States of America

Darkhouse Books
160 J Street, #2223

Niles, California 94539

Introduction

"Tomorrow, and tomorrow, and tomorrow,
Creeps in this petty pace from day to day,
To the last syllable of recorded time.

And all our yesterdays have lighted fools
the way to dusty death."

Macbeth, act V

It is with great pleasure that we present this, our second anthology of crime and mystery stories.

Within this book are sixteen stories that shake off the dust of yesterdays past. They are tales of mystery and crime, but they are also about people, place, and time. We may never achieve temporal travel, but words well-crafted can spark a light, and the glow from that light can illuminate our ever darkening past.

Historical mystery stories occupy a special rank in the taxonomy of the mystery genre. More care must be placed on setting and customs, as readers are quick to spot anachronisms and errors. In addition, the writer must be cognizant of, yet not a slave to, instead rather, a translator of idioms and word usage of the era.

In the course of this anthology, the reader will be taken back to medieval England, to France of a few centuries later, to frontier America, and elsewhere and when. Knaves and cutthroats will scheme and plot. Heroines and heroes will struggle to persevere. And always, ever always, human nature will out.

And that is the common thread woven through this collection of stories from disparate places and times. Human nature, at its best and at its worst, is on display in these tales, each a morality play, a cautionary tale, or perhaps simply good entertainment.

In closing, wistfully recalling words from another introduction, itself lost in so many years, return with us now to those thrilling days of yesteryear…

Andrew MacRae
March, 2015
Niles, California

We begin our collection with a story from shortly after the American Revolution and New England. A young man finds himself in trouble when he returns to his hometown. Daily life may change through the decades and centuries, but motives remain the same.

Ms Inglee knows her era. As a living history museum interpreter and guide, she has driven oxen, plowed a field with a horse, and written with a quill pen.

The Devil's Quote

By KB Inglee

Norton, Massachusetts, Spring 1799

"Iccarus Norton, you are under arrest for the murder of Doctor Benjamin Bacon."

I reined Medusa up in front of the two official looking men who faced me. One, I had never met, the other was Rob Freeman, my friend.

"Doctor Bacon is dead? How? When? Murder?"

Memories like snowflakes chilled my mind. I had been seventeen when my father sent me to study medicine with Dr. Bacon. Though I had been with him only a year and a half and left under less that happy circumstances, I respected him and was shocked and saddened to learn of his death. Slowly, I realized that I was at being accused of his murder.

Rob cast me a glance that told me to hold my peace for the time being. Then he turned to the officious man at his side, awaiting instructions. This was a relationship of subordinate to superior.

Father had written me that Rob had taken the job of sheriff's deputy at the New Year.

"Come along, young man." The sheriff was large of stature and forceful of will. Not a man to cross.

In spite of Rob's warning, I sputtered more questions. Both men regarded me with stony silence.

"Might I at least stop at my parents' house, since we ride by it?"

Rob glanced at the sheriff who finally nodded his assent. My parents lived on the Mansfield road just north of the Center.

My mother was sitting on the porch in the sun, knitting. She looked like she had been there for some time, waiting for her prodigal son.

The two lawmen tipped their hats to her. I rode up to the porch but stayed firmly planted on Medusa. My guards held their mounts steady in the road out of earshot. They didn't seem worried about my fleeing across the fields behind the house.

My mother spoke softly. "Do as you are told. Your father will see to your welfare." Had she expected this?

She glared at the two men who were to take away her youngest son. "Iccarus has been on the road from Boston for the last three days," she called to them. "I'm sure that will be easy enough to prove."

She turned to me and said, "Let me take your horse, son. Your father is out for the morning. I will send him to you as soon as he returns. Let us know if you need anything."

In spite of her apparent calm, I could see her heart was breaking. Such fortitude was not the least unusual for a Yankee woman who had lived through the War of Independence not so many years ago.

I hopped down off Medusa. I handed the reins to Mother, kissed her on the cheek, grabbed my bedroll, and turned to leave. I found I was looking forward to the adventure ahead. It would be easy enough to prove I had been elsewhere at the time of the murder. The first step was to find out where and when the murder had taken place.

It was a short walk to the town hall. Though they did not bind me, Rob rode beside me with the Sheriff in front of him. Were I to run, they could easily lay hand on me.

The cell was not much more uncomfortable than my previous night's lodging at the inn in Mansfield. It afforded a great deal more privacy, though it was damp and smelled of mold. The major difference was that the door here was locked against my escape. Two windows gave me access to the outside world, one in the door and one in the wall, both tiny and barred. A miniscule window above the bed, a few inches above the ground, looked into the back yard and was obscured by the vivid green of the spring grass. I would have preferred a view of the street. The room itself was three paces wide and four long. A rough wooden bench was both sofa and bed. A tin bucket served as the necessary. The writings of my predecessors adorned the walls. Good reading if my book failed me.

They let me keep my pack containing a warm blanket, a box of writing materials, and the book I was reading. As long as they fed me, I had everything I needed.

I arranged my belongings in a homely fashion and sat for a minute or so before curiosity got the better of me, as it usually did. I rose to read the messages scribbled on the walls. They were, as you might have expected, bible verses, snatches of love poems, sets of initials. They must repaint regularly since nothing there was more than a year old.

Hang the shiref

HBW Christmas Day 1798

I wil lift up my eyes unto the hils

One in particular bemused me. It was inscribed with care on the wall by the head of the bed.

> *There is nothing that keeps men out of Hell, but the mere pleasure of God.*

D'l B September 1798

It was an apt enough quote to find on a prison wall, but there was something disturbing about it. I remembered it was part of a sermon by Jonathan Edwards, but it was misquoted somehow. The signature put me in mind of my friend Daniel Bacon. But why would he have written it here? He was an upstanding young man. When I gave up my situation as apprentice to his uncle, Dr. Bacon, Daniel had continued on. Both of us would be doctors by now if fate had not diverted me.

I was still wondering what had become of Daniel when my father arrived.

"How did you get yourself into this situation?" he asked. He was a staunch believer that each man is responsible for his own destiny.

I shrugged and said, "As far as I can tell, I did nothing. Getting out, on the other hand is within my grasp if I can get a bit of help."

"I will do what I can. What do you need?"

"I need to know when and where this murder, if it was a murder, happened. I cannot prove I was elsewhere unless I know the when of it. I need to know how it was committed, and who found the body. I need to know if Becca was there, and how she feels about her husband after these several years of marriage. Does she benefit from his death in any way? That should do for a start."

Becca. I had been in love with her once. Her betrothal to my teacher and mentor, Dr. Bacon, had torn both relationships asunder.

"I can give you the where and how of it now; the rest I will have to look into. Doctor Bacon was found by his wife and Rob Freeman mid-afternoon yesterday. He was in his consulting room with his throat cut, face down at his desk in a pool of blood."

"Well, murder then. The murderer must have been marked with his blood," I said.

"So might anyone who attended the body," my father pointed out.

Father and I spent a few minutes discussing my recent commission, which had kept me in Boston since my last visit home in the autumn. I told him of my difficulties finishing the memoir I was writing for a prominent businessman who thought too much of himself.

"I have another bit of work for you once you find a way out of your current predicament." Clearly he expected me to do so.

"Medusa likes a good rub down in the morning and a crust of bread or two in the afternoon." He agreed to take good care of her. He fully realized she was the single entity dependent on my welfare. He had given her to me after looking at every horse south of Boston, and I suspect he thought of her as his ally in keeping an eye on his wandering son.

"Who is this man, the sheriff? He is not from here?" I asked.

"No, he held similar positions in Kingston, and towns in Connecticut and Rhode Island. Seems to stay about two years and then move on. He ran for the post saying he was the perfect law man for the scientific age, and since there were no personal ties, he would be impartial and fair. There's not a lot of crime in Norton, but he keeps order well. Has a wife and five children and lives in a fine house on Howard Street. Rumor has it that his wife has some money of her own so he can do as he chooses."

"Do you think he can be trusted? I would like not to hang for this. I need someone who is open to my ideas. You and Mother have too much interest in the outcome to have an objective view. I can't talk to Rob, since he may be implicated."

Father seemed startled when I said this.

"You said he found the body. I saw stains that might be dried blood on his shirtsleeve. He knew I was coming to town today. Who better to take the blame for him?"

"You would accuse your best friend of murder?" Father's disapproval was clear.

"Not without more proof than a stained sleeve. I would like to be honest with the sheriff."

Father thought for a bit before he answered.

"Some people here think he is the best sheriff we ever had because he brings in so much revenue. Others think he is too harsh and accuses people wrongly. I have never had dealings with him but I have talked to others who have and they are not always satisfied. I would take care, son. Perhaps I am the only one you should trust for now, given the circumstances. You are dependent on the care of Rob and the sheriff for your bodily needs. I would not trust my fate to them, as well."

Father looked at me in silence for some time, as if trying to decide to tell me more. At last he said, "It won't hurt for me to take a ride over to Mansfield and talk with the innkeeper."

I told him where I had spent the night. We parted with his promise to return with any additional information.

I was reading the inscriptions on the walls once more when Rob arrived with my dinner.

"The life of a wanderer appears to agree with you, Iccarus," he said, handing me the bowl of steaming stew with a large slice of brown bread on top. One sniff of the rising essence from the bowl made me aware of how hungry I was.

"I enjoy it. I like the variety it affords." I told him of some of my adventures. "The settled life seems to have been good for you."

"I farm a small parcel of land near the Barrowsville mill pond, and working for the sheriff brings in a bit of cash. I can't complain. A wife would be just the thing. I'm not much of a housekeeper and my mother doesn't seem to want to care for me the way she once did."

I asked about the people I had expected to visit this afternoon. Both Jack and Eli had married girls from another town whom I didn't know. When I asked about Daniel, he glanced at the wall behind me and said "Take care, Iccarus. You are suspected of murder and in the hands of the law." His warning chilled me.

I gave a meager try at extracting information from him. "Is this meat from your own farm?" I asked. I touched the rust stains on his cuff that I had noticed that morning.

"We haven't butchered since the winter." He seemed not in the least suspicious of my reason for asking. "The meal is from the Sheriff's family, probably leftover's from his own table."

"Is the sheriff a good man to work for?" I wanted to know more about my captor.

"He can be harsh. Some of the young men in the town say he accuses them unfairly of things they didn't do, but the town coffers are growing from the tolls and fines he collects." There was an uncomfortable pause. At length he continued. "On the whole the town is satisfied. He has been fair to me. But sometimes I think he goes a bit far.

"Once or twice…. No, when you are out of here we can share an ale and talk about it, but not now."

Rob remained steadfast in his decision not to discuss his job or the murder with me.

Never mind, he had given me a few tidbits and I had other sources of information.

I opened my book and spent the afternoon in London, courtesy of Mr. Fielding. My next visitor was a surprise. Becca Bacon. I said the name over in my head. She would have done better to marry me and become Becca Norton. And I might have stayed in town and become the rising star of medicine. I had been seventeen. Now I was a wise old man of twenty-two.

Still, her appearance at the door of my cell set a shock through my body that distressed me. She had not changed in the intervening years. She was dressed in a cream colored silk gown, with a strange concoction on her head that was half bonnet, half chamber pot, with ribbons everywhere. The height of fashion, no doubt.

For the first time, I saw what I had been spared: marriage to a woman aping a turkey in mating season. She fiddled with her gloves and shawl, moved the ribbons about and generally presented herself to me as though she regretted the evening she had told me she was to be wed to another.

I waited in silence for her to speak.

"It was hard for me to come to such a dreadful place," she said. She seemed unable to look me in the eye. Her gaze moved across the wall behind me as though she were reading what was written there.

"No harder than it is for me to be here." I had not meant to be so sharp with her. "Why did you come?"

"It is said that you killed my husband," she said.

"That is most unlikely since yesterday I was on the road from Boston. I doubt that I shall hang for the crime."

She lowered her eyes, and ran the fringe of her silken shawl through her fingers. When the silence fell over the edge into unbearable I repeated, "Why did you come?"

"I thought you might help me."

"Help you by hanging for a murder you committed?"

She jerked upright and finally looked me in the eye.

"I did not kill him. Somebody did, and I know it wasn't you. Find the person who did it. For yourself, if not for me."

"From a prison cell? I hardly think so."

Her expression softened, perhaps at the memory of what we had been.

"Very well," I said. "Tell me what you know."

She described the scene much as my father had. I knew she could not have drawn the knife across her husband's throat. It was far too personal and too bloody for someone like her. She could have inspired someone to do so. She was hardly the picture of a grieving widow.

"Who found him?" I asked. It was hard to think of Benjamin Bacon in past tense.

"Rob and I came in to find…" she glanced at her hand as though she could see the blood on her fingers.

"Why was Rob there?" I asked.

"He had cut himself and was seeking medical attention." Becca had never been a good liar.

"Does his death leave you destitute?" I asked.

"Not at all. The house reverts to his brother but there is some money, and a small house near Attleboro that is mine until my death. I am young enough to find another husband with ease and well enough off to make me a desirable choice."

"Do you have children?"

"None," she lifted her chin slightly as though daring me to probe that particular subject. I left it.

"And Daniel, is he well?" I asked to lighten the mood some.

She was silent for some time, but I knew she had heard me, because her face took on the sad expression I would have expected of her when she spoke of her husband.

"Dead. Since September." She glanced around the cell as if seeing it for the first time. If it was possible for anyone so fair to become paler, she did so. So he might have written it after all. But why here?

"Take care, Iccarus," she said. Another warning?

She seemed relieved when Rob came to show her out. He glanced at her and then at me as though wanting to ask a question. Perhaps he wondered if he needed my permission to court her. At length he took her hand and led her up the stairs and out of my sight.

Had I seen what I thought I did? When only their feet were visible on the stairs, they turned to face each other for a moment then continued the climb to the street level. So Rob was, indeed, a suitor.

Next came the sheriff. "I'm inclined to believe your parents' tale of your having been on the road for three days. The big flaw I see is that you could easily have arrived early afternoon yesterday, made a stop at Bacon's and gone back to Mansfield for the night. Rode in here big as life and all innocence this morning."

I felt my stomach tighten, but when I said nothing, he went on. "I expect your cooperation, young man. Dire things have been known to happen to people who are uncooperative."

Had he, like Rob, glanced at the quote behind my shoulder? There must be more to it than I had thought. Or was I letting my imagination carry me away from the truth?

I pondered what his visit meant as I watched him climb the stairs. I had met lawmen in other towns who enforced their will by intimidation. This felt more sinister. There wasn't much he could do to me since this is my town, not his. I was known to be of good character and I had no doubt that the residents would back me if I had any trouble. Would they not?

I was becoming uncomfortable with this place. At first it had seemed like a lark, but now I was trying to prove that my childhood friend and the woman I had loved were killers. The writings on the wall had made me realize how serious my position was. The air was growing colder. I was beginning to feel something deep in my soul. Fear.

At sunset, Rob brought me a meager plate of steamed vegetables and a small chop. We eyed each other with suspicion but spoke not a word. After my delightful repast, I sat in the growing darkness and considered my plight.

When it was too dark to pretend I was reading, I prepared my bed. I took off my coat and waistcoat and rolled them into a pillow. I was glad of my warm blanket. I set the book and the writing box on the floor by the leg of the bench that was my cot, and settled in for the night. I lay listening to the late evening sounds of the town settling for the night and thinking of ways to prove that Rob and Becca had committed the murder to free her for his embrace. Ere long Morpheus claimed me.

I awoke in a panic sometime before dawn. I lay still and tried to remember where I was and what frightened me so.

Slowly everything I had learned the day before came back to me. No one had said Daniel died here, but everything I learned pointed to it. Had Dr. Bacon been killed because he knew why his nephew had died? Was I in the same danger as Daniel? I trusted the town to see me through this. Daniel would have, too.

I knew in a flash of inspiration what was wrong with the quote on the wall. The writer had omitted the word "wicked." God keeps the wicked out of Hell, but someone else condemns any man, guilty or not. The pieces fell into place like the time I had mended my mother's favorite plate after I had dropped it.

Daniel… Snatches of our lengthy discussions along the banks of the Wading River came back to me. We fancied ourselves the only educated men in the village. "The devil can quote scripture," he had said, "but in his own way."

I felt that Daniel had been warning me all those years ago. I reached down and touched the writing box, some four inches square and more than a foot long. It contained an ink well, a roll of paper and three pens. Enough to write a confession.

I pulled on my boots and lay back down, covering myself with the blanket. I slipped the writing box under the cover. I didn't have to wait long.

"Wake up, Mr. Norton." I heard the jingle of a chain and the clank of keys as the sheriff opened the lock. I didn't move. He was by my bed in a single step. The light in the hall outside the open door made his body a dark and lurking presence.

"I let you keep the writing box because I knew you would need it." I locked my fingers around the box and waited.

When he was close enough I pivoted into a sitting position. Using the momentum of my upper body, I swung my box with all my might, aiming for his left temple. I made an awkward con-tact but it was enough to send him against the wall. I flew out the door, slammed it shut behind me, and turned the key he had conveniently left in the lock. Then I fled up the stairs.

The sight of a man running through the center of town without his coat and trousers at sunrise startled more than a few inhabitants.

"Father, I may have killed the sheriff. If not, he will be along for me soon. I believe he intended for me to write a confession saying I killed Doctor Bacon. Then he was going to kill me in a way that would look like I had taken my own life out of remorse. He intended to find my body and announce the murder solved."

"Like Daniel," he whispered.

Rob and his father were waiting at the town hall for us. Within the hour we had been joined by the minister and a few other men of importance. The sheriff stood by the door with his arms folded, scowling at the gathering. I myself, dressed in my brother's ill-fitting clothes, was forced into an armchair and closely guarded by Mr. Moody, the blacksmith.

The sheriff was fierce and angry, his eyes wild and his hair in spikes. The men, less than resolute in pressing my case, shuffled about and seemed diminished in front of the sheriff's bluster.

Only my father and Mr. Freeman, Rob's father, seemed truly interested.

"John Dawson, what is your response to Mr. Norton's accusation?" said Rob's father. It was the first time I had heard the sheriff's name spoken.

"Preposterous. Why would I do such a thing? I am sworn to uphold the law."

"It would not be the first time someone died in the jail after signing a confession." said Mr. Freeman.

"Doctor Bacon's nephew got hisself arrested for breaking a store window. Found him in the morning with a rope around his neck and a signed confession on the floor by the body," said Mr.

Moody, sotto voice, for my ear only. "Confessed to setting the Clark's barn on fire and killing their stock."

These were the crimes of a wayward youth, not an up and coming doctor.

I was no great orator, and in ill fitting and uncomfortable clothes and forced to remain seated, I was a poor substitute for one. But my life depended on what I said next. I pointed to the sheriff and said in a voice I was sure the minister would envy, "You killed Daniel in the cell, just as you intended to kill me. You killed Doctor Bacon when he threatened to expose you to the town."

Rob spoke up next. "You were going to make Iccarus take the blame for the murder. Dr. Bacon was his mentor and friend. We would never have believed it."

"Not so!" the sheriff's denial was explosive. "I had nothing to do with either death. You have no way to implicate me. And no one is going to believe a farmer and an itinerant over an elected officer of the law."

Rob reached into his coat and retrieved several pages that looked as though they had been torn out of an almanac. "Icaruus and I found these in your office before my father went down to let you out of the cell. I can vouch for the fact that they are in Doctor Bacon's hand. They were torn out of his journal when you killed him. Daniel and the doctor had discussed Daniel's trip to the towns you had served before coming here. These pages list the crimes you are thought to have committed. Never murder, but enough to put your veracity in question and your fitness to serve. There is blood on them. They are proof that Daniel did not take his own life for petty wrong-doings."

To my great surprise Rob's demeanor changed. He stood tall and spoke with authority.

"You, sir, are under arrest for the murder of Daniel Bacon and of his uncle as well."

Rob nodded to Mr. Moody who left off guarding me, to take the sheriff by the arm and hustle him off to the cell that had so recently been mine. Moody returned in a few minutes and handed me my clothing and bedroll.

"You knew all along," I said to Rob, "and you let me sit there to meet my fate?"

"You were quite safe. Moody was in the building and if you had cried out he would have been there at once. Becca and I tried to warn you to take care. Neither of us could say anything outright, for fear the sheriff would overhear.

"I had been carrying bits of information to my father for some time. He talked with Doctor Bacon about Daniel's death. That's when the doctor told father about Daniel's journey. Kingston wasn't the first town he left in a hurry, but no one had any solid information about why. Only suspicion. Some people are not willing to ruin a man's reputation on speculation."

That afternoon I attended Dr. Bacon's funeral with my family. We joined Rob and Becca at the grave as it was being filled. In the conservative togs of her deep mourning, Becca looked more elegant than she had in her expensive and colorful garb.

Becca Freeman, not a bad name at all.

Let's jump forward two hundred years for our next story, written by Jack Bates. It's a grittier tale, set in a world of swift and sudden violence. Dennis Bascom, the town of Haslett's only pugilistic pharmacist, does not seek trouble but trouble has a way of finding him on its own.

Mr. Bates is a two-time Derringer nominee. His children's book, "The Santa Spy" received the Best Holiday Book award from the Literary Classics and Book Awards Committee.

Sunday Morning

by Jack Bates

Sunday morning and Dennis Bascom, Haslett's only pugilistic pharmacist, sits on the curb in front of his drug store. The rising sun shines on his bald head. Bascom feels each tiny drop of sweat pop out of his pores. He's tempted to wipe the sweat away with his hand. Hell, he even raises one to do so but then he stops.

He's got blood on his hands. Literally and figuratively.

Down in the store's cellar there's a couple of Detroit goons who paid him a visit late last night and it wasn't to fill a prescription. They said they intercepted his barrels of rum coming across the river from Windsor, and if he wanted them back, he'd have to pay them a finder's fee.

Extortion fee is what you mean, Bascom said.

That's when the guns came out.

They weren't out long. Bascom had boxed at the University of Michigan on a scholarship. Did fairly well, but his heart wasn't in it. He didn't care much for the violence. He had street smarts and book smarts and he knew that if he kept putting on his gloves, his brain would turn to putty.

The first gunman had a glass jaw. One punch sent him staggering into the trajectory of hot lead flying from the second gunman's pistol. Slug after slug after that struck the concrete bricks of the basement. The gunman tossed the empty heater aside and reached for his second piece.

Bascom grabbed a crowbar from the top of a crate of acetylsalicylic acid and embedded the hook end into the second guy's skull. He had to put his foot on the guy's face to wiggle the bar free.

Bascom spun around, the crowbar clutched in his hand. He put the flat end into the little hollow below Glass Jaw's Adam's apple.

"Where's my rum?"

"We ain't got it, mister."

"Why'd you say you did?"

"Bix and me was in a joint couple nights ago. Heard these guys talkin' bout shipments. One of 'em said 'That place in Haslett brings in the dough, don't it?' That got us thinking. " The man spat out blood.

"You thought wrong, pal. I'm strictly local."

"Jesus," he gasped.

"You'll see him soon enough."

"Can't you get me a doctor?"

"You're gut shot, buddy. You're going to lose a lot of blood inside you before you die. But you're gonna die."

"Aw, Jesus."

"Now what did these guys say?"

The gut shot guy groaned. He rolled on his side. Bascom hooked him with the crow bar and rolled him back onto his back.

"Tell me," Bascom said. He hit the guy in the knee with the crowbar.

The man wailed. "Christ!" He clutched at his knee with bloody fingers.

"What. Did. They. Say?"

It was getting harder for the man to talk. "They said… they said they're coming to shake you down. Said taking it from you small guys is a snap and all they have to do is tell the boss you were short on your payments. They're off the hook and the boss sends his torpedoes to deal with you." Blood seeped out of the corner of his mouth and down his cheek. "I don't want to die like this."

"You and your friend didn't give two shits how I was going to die. You came in to do your business. I knew someone was going to die and it wasn't going to be me."

When the dying man spoke again it was barely a whisper. "We just needed money, mister. That's all." The gut shot guy's breathing slowed. His eyes followed something in the exposed floor joists above them. And then they stopped moving altogether. They stayed fixated on the overhead beam until they stopped seeing anything.

Bascom recalls his turbulent night as he sits in the heat of the morning sun. He didn't get his shipment of rum. There are two dead men in his cellar. The Smokehouse Boys are sending someone to teach him a lesson for skimming he never did, and the only two guys who could attest to that can't because they're lying dead in the cellar.

'Christ,' Bascom thinks. 'Jesus Christ.'

As if his Sunday morning couldn't get any shittier, Jace Witherspoon, the sheriff of Haslett, is driving up to the curb where Bascom's sitting. Bascom scoops up handfuls of dirt from the washboard street. He covers his hands in the dust.

Bascom stands on shaky legs. Another reason he quit boxing. Over-exertion weakened him. All he had was a right hook and a pretty good jab. What he lacked was a knockout combination. He could just never close it out, which is one of the reasons he used the crowbar the night before.

Bascom puts a hand on the brass doorknob. The blood and the dust leave prints on the surface. Before he can get inside, the sheriff's car squeaks to a stop. It's parked at an odd angle when Bascom turns around. Sheriff Witherspoon steps out of the car.

"You're open early," the sheriff says.

"That a crime?" Bascom asks. He is surprised by the thinness of his voice.

The sheriff laughs. "I think you know it's not, Denny. You feeling okay?"

"Yeah. It's the heat, that's all." He puts a hand over his eyes to block the sun. "Sun is really hot this summer."

"You cut yourself?"

Bascom looks at his raised hand. Fresh blood drips out of the dirt covering his palm. "Yeah. Guess I did. I was busting up crates down in the cellar—"

The sheriff's eyes snap wide. He reaches for his revolver in the hip holster. Bascom freezes in front of the door. Sucker punched, he thinks. He could never anticipate his opponent's move. All he ever did was react.

Bascom kind of regrets leaving the dead guy's gun below.

"Sheriff, I can explain."

Witherspoon coldly raises his revolver.

Bascom presses himself against the brick and glass of the building next to his pharmacy. He leaves bloody palm prints on his neighbor's storefront window. A dead faced mannequin in a fur coat smiles at him. He thinks it's the last woman he'll ever see.

It's Sunday morning and Dennis Bascom is about to die. He silently confesses to a life sized wooden doll.

'I was never strong enough,' he thinks. He closes his eyes.

From out in the street the sheriff fires his Smith and Wesson revolver. When the echo fades and the air clears of gunpowder, Bascom turns around. He finds the gut shot goon lying on his back inside his pharmacy. The crowbar lies next to him on the black and white tile floor. Sumbitch crawled up the stairs to finish what he came to start.

"Who is he?" the sheriff asks and Bascom says he doesn't know. Tells him, he and another man showed up last night after closing to rob him. When the sheriff asks if the second man is still below, Bascom tells him he is and he's dead.

"Like this fella was dead?" the sheriff asks.

Bascom says nothing.

"I'd better take a look. Oh, take it easy, Denny. We've all been turning a blind eye to your blind pig."

Bascom follows the sheriff into the cellar, the crowbar in his hand. The second man is still lying there dead.

The sheriff looks at the skull then back at Bascom who is still holding the crowbar. "You keep a piece, Denny?"

"No. Why?"

"The guy upstairs was gut shot."

"By this guy." Bascom points at the dead guy with the crowbar.

"Gut shot is the shittiest way to die," the sheriff says. "At least that's what I've been told."

"I sucker punched the gut shot guy, and he walked into this guy's gun path. So gut shot guy dropped and before this guy could shoot me, I whacked him."

The sheriff holds out his hand for the crowbar. "Evidence," he says.

Bascom looks at the tool before he hands it over. Witherspoon takes out a hanky and uses it to hold the crowbar. He lays it on a round pedestal table behind him.

Witherspoon squats next to the body to search the pockets. "Not a lot in there." He pulls out a handful of coins he slides into his own pocket.

"Gut shot guy said they needed money."

"Well, we all need money." Witherspoon looks around the makeshift speakeasy before he smiles at Bascom. "Guess that's why you sell rum after the drug store locks up."

"Guess it is."

"You know, Denny. What I said about turning my cheek away from what you do here?" Sheriff Witherspoon retrieves the gut shot guy's roscoe from the floor. He doesn't point it at the pharmacist but holds it at his own side.

Doesn't matter. Bascom recognizes what's happening. Witherspoon has been watching the people come and go. He knows that somewhere in the cellar is a cigar box full of cash. It's not a lot of cash but in these Hooverville days, a guy needed to take what he could get any way he could.

It's why there's two dead guys in his pharmacy and there's about to be a third.

It's Sunday morning and on the day of rest, when the Son of God is there to comfort, to cleanse one of his sins, the sheriff is planning on getting away with murder.

The pharmacy was being robbed and Witherspoon showed up in time to confront the two men who killed Dennis Bascom. Witherspoon shot one. The other struck his gun hand with the crowbar. Witherspoon struggled with the crowbar wielding man until he wrestled away the crowbar and swung it into the man's temple.

"Where's your stash?"

Denny lifted his chin. "It's behind the bar."

"What's it in? Pickle jar?"

"Floor safe."

"What's the combination, Denny?" Witherspoon drops down behind the bar and Bascom thinks, 'Dumbass.'

He should have had Denny open it.

Bascom rattles off three digits. The sheriff whistles as he opens the safe then adds a surprise note or two at the amount of money tucked away inside it. This allows Bascom to grab the crowbar. Witherspoon stands up as Bascom swings the crowbar at the back of his head. The sheriff falls to the floor but it doesn't stop Bascom's blows.

It's Sunday morning and Bascom is tired from all the bullshit he's had to deal with since midnight. He's hot from the unseasonably warm summer. His rain of blows slows until the crowbar drops from his hand. It clangs on the floor.

Witherspoon's head is a pulpy mess.

He takes the money out of the safe and puts it all into a waxy paper bag that he rolls closed. He doesn't have a lot of time. It's Sunday morning and the churchgoers will be leaving the Presbyterian service, and the Baptist revival, and taking last communion at St. Josaphat's. He wants to be on the road before all those congregations crowd his pharmacy for a King Cola and a bag of penny candy.

He takes the gun Witherspoon was going to use to kill him and goes upstairs.

There's a young woman staring at the body of the gut shot man. When she hears Bascom step into the room, she looks up. He knows her. She's the Susalla girl. Just turned twenty. Her brother died over in Flanders's Fields. Gassed.

He knows her name is Jenny. She comes in every Sunday to buy a pack of cigarettes and a pack of chewing gum before her parents get there. He knows he shouldn't sell cigarettes to her. She's very pretty in her Sunday best. Jenny forces up a smile. The bottoms of her eyes are watery.

"You gonna kill me too?" she asks.

It's Sunday morning.

Time to repent.

Bascom lays the gun on the counter. He's got enough blood on his hands.

"Go," he tells her.

"I won't tell anybody it was you, Mr. Bascom."

Bascom looks up at her young, pretty face. She's twenty. He's just turned thirty. But now there would always be this between them. Death would always be there between them.

"I said go."

The Susalla girl runs from the drug store. He knows the first thing she'll do is tell whoever is listening. It's all over for him.

He picks up the gun.

He picks up the gun and—

He picks up the gun and the bag and he runs. He runs out to the sheriff's still-idling car and he gets in it and he drives away even though he barely knows how to operate the damned machine. He's got enough money and he's got a car and he's got two fists that with the right kind of gloves and the right kind of coaching boxing can take him to places he would have never seen standing behind the drug store counter.

It's Sunday morning.

Jenny Susalla stands in the road in front of him. A cigarette hangs from her lips. She stares defiantly into the car. He hopes he can stop.

"Take me with you," she says.

"You're just a kid."

"I'm twenty. I don't want to be here anymore. Take me with you."

He's not strong. All he does is react.

"Get in."

Jenny Susalla gets into the car. She rides with her hands folded over her lap. At the south end of Haslett a truck passes them. There are two men in the front. Three more men ride in the back. The men in the back hold baseball bats. They are not dressed for a game. It's the Smokehouse Boys looking to bust up the pharmacy.

Ten miles outside of Haslett, Dennis Bascom dies in the cool waters of the River Raisin. He dives under, lets out a heavy breath, and floats just below the surface. All of the blood and grime and sin washes off. He can feel the flow of absolution carry him closer to the end of this world. When his lungs scream for oxygen, he pushes himself out of the water gasping. He pulls in hot, humid air. A new breath fills his lungs. A new life fills his soul.

It's Sunday morning and Dennis Bascom dies in a river alongside a road just outside of Calgary, only to be resurrected.

He'll choose a new name.

He'll choose a new home.

He'll choose a new life.

Jenny swims up to him. She presses her naked body against his. Her teeth chatter in the cold water. He holds her close, rubs her back, kisses her open mouth. He wants to make love to her but she needs to understand what life will be like with him.

"Jenny," he says.

It's all he gets to say.

A truck pulls up next to the sheriff's car. Three men get out of the back. Two men exit the cab. All five of the men walk down to the riverbank. A hundred years or so ago this river was the scene of a major battle. The river has a history of violence. Bascom moves in front of Jenny. He feels her hands on his back.

One of the men from the cab of the truck calls out.

"Bascom?"

"Who's asking?"

"You know who we are."

Jenny lays her face against Bascom's back. Bascom's hands get heavy. It's what happens when he knows he is going to win a fight.

The second man from the cab steps forward. He reaches inside his jacket.

Jenny puts her arms under Bascom's, puts them over his chest. She kisses his back.

The man pulls a bundle of bills out of his jacket. He drops it on the dirt.

"Mr. Steinbrook has heard of your losses," the man says. "He wishes to reimburse you for your troubles."

Bascom looks at the bundle. It's more money than he had in his safe. With that much money his new life—their new life would begin nicely.

Jenny whispers in his ear.

Bascom nods to her and tells the men on the shore, "Tell Mr. Steinbrook I appreciate his gesture but I'm not—we're not going back to Haslett."

"That's a lot of lettuce laying there," the first man says.

"You guys keep it," Bascom says.

"Mr. Steinbrook gave it to you."

"And I'm giving it to you."

The five men looked at one another. The man who dropped the bundle of cash picks it up. He nods his head at the truck. His four companions head back to it. The man with the cash turns back to Bascom.

"Was that your work back there?" he asks.

Bascom nods.

The man laughs. "Mr. Steinbrook said you were a helluva fighter."

It's Sunday morning and Bascom remembers carrying packages as a kid for Mr. Steinbrook. Remembers the day Steinbrook called on him and his family to say the University of Michigan was giving him a scholarship to box.

Only there was no scholarship. Steinbrook had paid for everything.

"Hey," Bascom says. "Tell Mr. Steinbrook—" But he doesn't know what else to say.

The man nods. "He knows. You'll be all right, Bascom. Ma'am." He tips his hat and joins the others in the truck. They drive off bickering about their bonus.

"I'm cold," Jenny says.

Bascom carries her from the river. They dress behind the car. Once inside, Jenny Susalla lays her head on his shoulder.

They'll have a good life, Bascom thinks.

Is that too much to ask on a summer Sunday morning?

The passage of time can cover many sins. However, in this next story a woman learns that even a half-century of deception can wash away and leave truth exposed.

The prolific Mr. Bracken is the author of over eleven-hundred short stories. His stories in the crime and mystery genre can be found in Ellery Queen's Mystery Magazine, Mike Shayne Mystery Magazine, and many anthologies.

Beneath Still Waters

By Michael Bracken

My husband and I spent a hot, dry summer Saturday sorting through several boxes of clothing destined for the local women's shelter, ensuring that my mother had not left money, jewelry, or important documents in the pockets of her various coats, sweaters, and slacks. By the time we finished, Bob and I had collected $3.12 in loose change and had located the watch my father had given her the Christmas before he passed away. The next day I presented it to my mother at the extended care facility where she had been since the first of February.

She took one look at the watch after I pressed it into her hand and then thrust it back to me. "I don't want that damned thing."

My father had given her a gold-plated, rectangular-faced, bracelet watch with a butterfly clasp, and it must have set him back several hundred dollars. "What's wrong with it?"

"He didn't buy it for me," she said. "He bought it for *her*."

"Her?"

"Look at the inscription!"

I turned the watch over and examined the back. Engraved in barely visible letters were the words, "For Ducky. Forever."

I asked, "Who's Ducky?"

My mother said Ducky was a female dog who had seduced my father years earlier, though she used more colorful words in her description of the woman. Her shouted profanities caught the attention of an aide, who stepped into the room to ensure my mother was not in distress.

"It's my fault," I told the aide. "I've upset her."

After I slipped the watch into my pocket, I turned to my mother, apologized for what I had done, and added, "But I didn't know."

"How could you?" she asked. "We kept it from you all these years."

"Why?"

"She gave your father something I never could."

"What could she possibly give him that you couldn't?"

"You—" she began. She turned away. "You wouldn't understand."

I wanted to know more about Daddy and Ducky but felt certain that prying would only further upset my mother. That she was lucid that afternoon was a gift I dared not squander, so we spoke of other things—people, places, and events from her past that were anchored in her memory in a way that more recent events were not—until all that remained were a few words about the weather. I asked if she remembered a drought as severe as the one Texas was experiencing that summer.

She did.

"I was ten when it started and they'd only just finished the reservoir the year before," she said. "Without it, the town might not have survived until the rain returned in the spring of 1956."

The reservoir had filled to capacity by the time my parents began their senior year of high school, and during subsequent years had become a boon to my parents' west Texas hometown as a popular destination spot for boaters, fishers, and other water sports enthusiasts.

My husband was still working in my mother's garage, sorting through all the hand tools my father had left behind and my mother had never touched, when I returned from the extended care facility on the other side of Waco. I told Bob what had happened.

"That must have come as quite a shock."

I handed my husband the watch and pointed out the engraving on the back. "My father had an entire life I know nothing about."

"Maybe it's better that way," Bob said. "Maybe you'd best leave the past in the past."

"I can't," I told him. "I have to know who this woman was and what she meant to my father."

My husband repeated his assertion that my thirst for knowledge might best be left unquenched, but he didn't interfere when I continued searching for answers to my questions.

I knew my parents had married the summer following high school graduation and had immediately moved to Waco so my father could begin his undergraduate studies at Baylor University. My mother, a newborn affixed to her hip, had made their one-bedroom, off-campus apartment as much of a home as she could under the circumstances. Were it not for my grandparents' support, they could not have accomplished much as teenaged parents in the late 1950s, but I knew little about their early life and had assumed my parents' reluctance to speak of it stemmed from the apparent shotgun nature of their wedding.

After my mother's reaction to the watch and my discussion with Bob, I approached cleaning her home—a two-story Georgian on Austin Avenue my parents purchased the fall I began my undergraduate studies at the University of Texas—with renewed vigor, determined to learn more about my parents' early life and about the woman my parents knew as "Ducky."

I finally found a clue two weeks later, when I discovered my parents' high school yearbooks in a box in one of the guest room closets. I smiled when I saw what my mother had written in my father's senior yearbook—"Yours Forever!!"—and I flipped through the pages, amused by the way west Texas teenagers had dressed in the 1950s.

My parents were members of the same class, so I examined their senior photos before flipping through the following pages. I almost missed it, and I'm not certain how it caught my eye, but after the last senior photo was the note:

Not pictured

Elwood Anderson

Angela Duckworth

I found my mother's yearbook from the previous year, when my mother, father, and Angela Duckworth were juniors. Angela and my mother could have been mistaken for sisters when they were teenagers. They had similar features and similarly shaped faces, a common enough occurrence in a small town with a limited gene pool, and for their junior pictures they'd chosen the same clothes and had their dark hair styled identically. I knew Angela was the woman I was seeking when I saw what she had written in my mother's yearbook—"What's mine is yours"—followed by her signature: *Angela 'Ducky' Duckworth.*

More than fifty years had passed since Ducky had signed my mother's yearbook, so I expected a cold trail from the 1950s. I carried the yearbooks home to study and the next day went online. I searched various social media for women named Angela Duckworth, easily eliminating from consideration the few I found as being either too old or too young to be the woman I sought.

I contacted the high school they had attended only to learn that the original building had closed in the 1980s when the new high school was built, that none of the records from that far back had ever been entered into the school district's computer system, and that the paper records were stored in an offsite facility that no one ever voluntarily visited.

"What about class reunions?" I asked the woman who had taken my call. "Someone must be in charge of class reunions."

"Maybe," she said. "We do try to keep track of the reunions. What class?"

I told her the year my parents had graduated and she put me on hold. A few minutes later she came back with the name and the phone number of Maisie Wilcoxin, the woman still living in town who had organized a class reunion several years earlier.

I dialed Maisie's number. After she answered, I told her I was looking for one of her high school classmates named Angela Duckworth.

"I haven't heard that name in ages," Maisie said. "Why are you looking for her?"

When I explained that I was Cletus and Geneva's daughter, she seemed surprised to learn they'd had a child. I told her that I was trying to find Angela because she had been my mother's best friend.

"Maybe when they were younger," Maisie said, "but not by the time we graduated. They were barely speaking when Angela left school in the middle of our senior year."

"She graduated with you, didn't she?"

"Technically, I suppose she did. I heard the school let her finish her last semester by correspondence."

"Why would they do that?"

"She—" Maisie hesitated before continuing. "Things were different back then. Angela went to live with a sick aunt her last semester. That's what they told us when she didn't return to school after the Christmas break, but we learned later that wasn't the truth. Angela was in a family way, and back then girls like that weren't allowed to attend school. They treated her condition like it was an infectious disease."

"Angela was pregnant her senior year?"

"Yes, dear," Maisie said. "I believe that's what I said."

"What happened to her?"

"Well, Ducky—that's what everyone called her back then—never returned, her parents moved away within the year, and no one's heard from her since."

I didn't correct Maisie by telling her that my father had maintained contact with Ducky.

"Your parents have never been to a reunion, either," Maisie said. "All these years and not a word about either of them until your call. The sixtieth is coming up soon. Any chance you might convince them to join us?"

I told her about my father's fatal heart attack a few years earlier and about my mother's losing battle with Alzheimer's.

"That's a shame," Maisie said. "We've lost so many others these past few years. I'm so glad to know Geneva has you to take care of her, especially because she thought she would never have children."

I thanked Maisie for her time, gave her my cell phone number in case she thought of anything else she could tell me about Ducky, and ended the call. I was no closer to finding my father's mysterious other woman than I had been the day before.

When my husband returned home from work that evening, I listened to him complain about the months-long drought turning Texas lakes into mud puddles before I told him about my telephone conversations earlier in the day.

"That puts a new twist on things," Bob said as he changed from his suit into jeans and a T-shirt. He had finished cleaning out my mother's garage by then—adding some of my father's tools to his tool chest and selling the rest—and we planned to visit my mother for a little while that evening before returning to the task of cleaning out her home.

Her condition had deteriorated, and she couldn't tell me anything she had done that day. Memories of the past came more easily to my mother, so we listened to her stories about swimming at the reservoir and about my father taking her there at night to watch the submarine races.

My husband was slow on the uptake. "There were submarines in the reservoir?"

My mother blushed. "Of course not!"

We left my mother with her memories and returned to her house. We'd heard so many stories of older people hiding valuables that we took care to open every teapot and thumb through every book before realizing that my mother hadn't hidden large wads of cash or fistfuls of jewels. The most valuable things we discovered were in a pair of chests we found in the attic that contained mementoes from my mother's past.

That night we carried the chests down from the attic and began a close examination of their contents, spreading everything around the otherwise empty living room. We discovered my father's letterman jacket from playing six-man football, a poodle skirt my mother had worn to the homecoming dance her senior year, programs from school plays and sporting events, report cards, photographs, and scrapbooks.

One entire scrapbook filled with faded and fragile newspaper clippings, obviously maintained by my mother, was dedicated to my father's accomplishments. He'd been an honors student and one of their small town's star athletes. In news stories about high school football games, my father's name was often paired with that of Elwood Anderson, especially game-winning touchdown passes from my father to Elwood. Elwood's name was absent from news articles my father's senior year and I returned my attention to my parents' yearbooks, where Elwood was listed with Angela Duckworth as "not pictured" their senior year.

A photo album my mother had kept was crammed full of photographs of her growing up, from her first baby photo to her first steps to her first day of school. Only after my mother had entered school were there gaps in the pages where photographs had been removed or defaced. Many of my mother's handwritten captions below those missing or defaced photographs had been scratched out and most were no longer readable. The few that I could decipher convinced me that my mother had, in one way or another, removed her childhood best friend from her scrapbook.

By the time my mother reached high school many of her photographs included my father, and several included other friends and classmates, including a boy identified in my mother's handwriting as Elwood Anderson. Just as in the newspaper stories and the yearbook, there were no photos of Elwood Anderson once my parents reached their senior year.

A few days later I touched my mother's shoulder. "Mama, do you remember Elwood Anderson?"

She turned her head and looked up at me. "Elwood?"

"Elwood Anderson," I prompted. "He was daddy's friend. He was your friend, too, wasn't he?"

"Elwood ran away."

I couldn't get anything more from my mother so I called Maisie Wilcoxin again, told her we had spoken several weeks earlier about Angela Duckworth, and asked about Elwood Anderson.

"Elwood ran off the weekend before our senior year began," she said. "He drove off in that big old DeSoto of his and good riddance to him."

"Why's that?"

"None of the girls liked him. He was always a little too fresh," she explained. "Going out to the reservoir with him meant wrestling an octopus."

"If Elwood didn't graduate with you, why is his name in the yearbook with the senior class?"

"I don't know, honey," she said. "You'd have to ask your daddy that. He was editor of the yearbook."

Because my husband's business depended heavily on farmers and ranchers, he tuned into the 10 p.m. news every night to watch the weather report and get updates on the impact the on-going drought was having on the state. I paid little attention beyond my fascination with the things uncovered as the water level of various Texas lakes and reservoirs receded: television sets, fossils, handguns, sunken boats, several automobiles and pickup trucks, a piece of the space shuttle Columbia, which disintegrated during re-entry in 2003, and the original site of the little town of Bluffton.

Every so often the evening news featured a report about a decades-old missing person case resolved when receding water revealed human remains once hidden by a liquid grave. I paid little attention to the news reports until Maisie Wilcoxin phoned to tell me a 1943 DeSoto had been pulled from the deepest part of the dried-up reservoir in her hometown, and that a body had been found in the passenger seat, the back of its skull crushed.

"I think they found Elwood Anderson," she said. "He drove a DeSoto."

I went online to read the newspaper articles about the discovery of the DeSoto and the body it contained, but learned little more than what Maisie had already told me.

My father had left nothing behind, or my mother had destroyed anything he had left, that could lead me to Angela Duckworth. Though not a search engine novice, I had never used the Internet for much beyond maintaining Facebook connections, watching YouTube videos of LOL cats, and killing time surfing home decoration sites.

I used my free time—what little of it there was between work at the bank, cleaning my mother's home, and daily visits to my decreasingly cognizant mother in the extended care facility—to search for anything I could find about my father's secret relationship. I first discovered where Ducky's parents had moved when they left town, and soon after learned where they were buried. Later, I found the name of the home for unwed mothers where Ducky had been sent, learned that she had given birth to a daughter, and discovered that immediately after giving her child up for adoption had legally changed her name.

During the following weeks I used various websites to track Ducky through the years, from Texas to California to Illinois and back to Texas. I finally found her in Galveston, about a three-and-and-half hour drive southeast of my home near Waco, and every source of information to which I had access led me to believe I had located the correct woman.

Ducky had no email or social media accounts that I could find. I found a landline phone number for her, but ultimately decided that what I wanted to know had to be learned in person.

By then we had finished clearing all of my mother's things from her house, so one Saturday I left my husband supervising repairs prior to listing it for sale, and I drove alone to the Gulf coast.

Mid-afternoon I checked the address against the paper in my hand and then climbed the steps to the porch of a small bungalow. I leaned into the bell and a moment later a prematurely balding woman wearing a loose-fitting muumuu and carrying a Foley catheter bag opened the door and stared at me suspiciously.

I asked, "Angela Duckworth?"

Her eyes widened in surprise. "You're not the home health nurse, are you?" she said. "No one's called me that in ages."

I explained who I was, told her how I had learned of her existence, and showed her the watch that had upset my mother so.

"You look just like your mother when she was your age," Ducky said. I didn't think to ask how she knew what my mother had looked like in her 50s, because Ducky held out her left arm and showed me the watch my father had given her that same Christmas, a duplicate of the watch he had given my mother. She removed it and handed it to me to examine. Only the engraving was different. "For Geneva, with love forever."

"He mixed them up," Ducky said, "and gave us the wrong watches."

"You knew and yet you still wear it?"

"He often gave us identical gifts," she explained. "It was easier for him that way. This was the only thing he ever had engraved and he must have forgotten to check the watches before he wrapped them."

She pushed open the screen door and invited me inside. After she pushed aside a pile of papers from MD Anderson Cancer Centers, we sat at her kitchen table.

"When I saw how my gift was engraved," she said, "I knew your father would have hell to pay from your mother."

"Why would my father send you gifts?"

"Because he loved me, in his own way."

"You were having an affair with him?"

Ducky shook her head but didn't elaborate, so I changed tactics.

"You left school because you were pregnant," I said. "Was the baby my father's?"

"Everyone thought the baby was his, even your mother," Ducky said, "but it wasn't. Your father and I were the only people who knew it wasn't."

"So whose was it?"

She didn't say, telling me instead that she had been raped, and she described the act in unexpectedly graphic detail. "Your father happened upon us just after the young man climbed out of his car and hit him with a roundhouse punch that knocked him down. Your father pulled me out of the car and helped me straighten my clothes before we realized the young man's head had struck the car's bumper and that he would never be getting up. Cletus gripped me by the shoulders and stared into my eyes. He made me promise I would never tell anyone what happened that night and that he would take care of everything. Your father's family had money and could have hired the best lawyer, but that's not what happened. I don't know what your father did, but no one ever saw that boy or his car again. Everybody thought he had run away."

Ducky hadn't named her rapist, perhaps fearing that naming him would make it all real and not just a bad, half-forgotten memory, but I had to ask, "Was it Elwood Anderson?"

She nodded and then continued. "I tried to put that evening out of my mind, to pretend that it never happened, but a few months later I realized I was pregnant, and soon I couldn't hide my condition. Everyone thought the baby was your father's and he never denied it, even though he was engaged to your mother. Your grandparents—both sets—had the money to buy their way out of any problem, and my pregnancy, though potentially embarrassing to both families, solved a problem they never publicly admitted to. They gave my parents money to send me away."

"They bought your silence?"

"Not my silence," she said. "Something more."

I leaned forward. "What?"

"You mother and I were best friends, but we were never of the same social class, and your father certainly couldn't marry down." She added, "You father knew that as long as his parents believed the baby was his, they'd ensure that it was well cared for, and they've certainly done that."

"So you put your baby up for adoption?"

"She went to a good family," Ducky said. "Your father saw to that."

"And Elwood?" I asked. "What kind of car did he drive?"

"A DeSoto," she said. "It must have been ten years old by then, maybe older."

I told Ducky about the 1943 DeSoto pulled out of the reservoir near her hometown and about the body with the crushed skull found in the passenger seat. "It won't be long before police identify the body."

She looked away for a moment. "We were kids," she said. "We didn't know any better."

"There's no statute of limitations on murder," I told her. "What happens if the police figure out what happened?"

Ducky looked at me. "What can they do?" she asked. "Your father's gone, the cancer's going to take me soon, and Elwood's got no people left to mourn his loss."

"But my mother—"

"Even though we were best friends through high school and shared everything," Ducky said, "your mother and I never shared this."

"My father never said a word to her, either. All along she thought you were having an affair."

"Cletus was only protecting her," Ducky explained. "To tell your mother what had happened and to expect her to keep our secret would make her an accessory after the fact. I don't know how he did it, but your father took care of everyone." She looked me straight in the eye and repeated. "Everyone. Don't mess that up."

We talked for a few more minutes and then Ducky walked me to the door. "You've turned out to be a fine young woman," she said. "Your parents must be proud."

My mother didn't recognize me when I slipped into her room the following day and sat in the chair beside her bed. I took her hand and told her everything I had learned about Daddy and Ducky and Elwood Anderson. "She said Daddy took care of everything and that the baby went to a good home."

I didn't realize until I finished that a tear had escaped from the corner of my mother's eye and stained the pillow beneath her cheek. Maybe she understood more than I realized.

My mother passed away a few days later, her house sold the following week, and we used the money to pay for her funeral and her remaining medical expenses. I thought that was the end of the story until a breast cancer scare several months later had me examining my parents' medical records. I was surprised to discover that my mother had never given birth because she had Mayer-Rokitansky-Küster-Hauser syndrome and had no uterus. Maisie Wilcoxin's surprise at learning my parents had a child and Ducky's insistence that my father had taken care of everything finally made sense.

Would it have been better to leave the past in the past, as my husband had once suggested? Maybe, but I would never admit it to him because I had no plans to tell anyone what I had learned.

That night I examined the yearbook photos of Ducky and my mother—their identical hairstyles, similar features, and similarly shaped faces—and then I looked in the mirror.

I did, indeed, look like my mothers.

Back in time once again, and to the era of the French voyageurs, fur trappers and traders in northern Great Lakes. The memory of some men lives on in legend, some in infamy. Terrible Fingal McKay does both.

Mr. Mallory is the co-author of two novels about Snake Jones, a zoologist sleuth. Readers may also recognize him from the short stories he has had published in many anthologies.

Terrible Fingal McKay

By Michael Allan Mallory

"This next item is one of our treasures," Alison, the tour guide said, indicating a small display case positioned in a place of honor. On the wall behind it was a large mural of an expansive watery land-scape by a wooded shoreline. Fifteen visitors gathered around the glass box. Low-intensity light illuminated the exhibit: a slightly rotted wooden handle attached to a chipped flint headpiece that rested on a cloth of red satin.

"This tomahawk dates from the late 1700s," Alison explained, "and was excavated not far from where we're standing. It may not look like much but it's the star player in a sordid drama of larceny and murder."

She paused to gauge their interest. This was her favorite part of the tour. She never tired of telling the story. "It belonged to a Scottish fur trapper named Fingal McKay. McKay was a noto-rious troublemaker, an opportunistic thief and bully, a man universally disliked by everyone in the territory. One reference calls McKay 'terrible—'"

A skeptical dark-haired boy raised his hand.

"Yes? You have a question?"

"I thought Indians used tomahawks," he said.

"They did. Many of the voyageurs and fur trappers who worked the Great Lakes at this time also adopted them as weapons, just as they copied the canoes of the native people. They knew a good technology when they saw it," Alison added with pride. She was one-sixteenth Ojibwe and enjoyed this personal connection to the exhibit. She waited to see if the boy had a follow up question. He seemed satisfied by her answer and remained silent. Good. Although she was there to answer questions—and questions meant her audience was engaged—she didn't like interruptions at this point in the narrative. She was on a roll. In a previous life, Alison had been theater arts major. Working at the museum gave her the opportunity to use her neglected storytelling skills.

She lowered her voice for dramatic effect. "This tomahawk is on display for several reasons. It represents a common tool-weapon used during this time period and it's rare to find one this old in such good shape. Another reason it's featured prominently in the exhibit is its association with the old trading post that was near this site, and for its association with Fingal McKay, who used the artifact in what many believe is his most insidious act. Murder."

That piqued their interest as it always did. Alison edged closer to her audience, now hanging onto her every word. "Exactly what happened remains a mystery, although we have a fairly good idea…"

• • •

A birch bark canoe skimmed across the lake surface. Seven powerful pairs of shoulders dug short paddles into the water at a grueling forty-five strokes per minute. After nearly an hour, the pace was getting difficult to maintain, yet it was one the rugged voyageurs of the *canot du nord* lived by. Or perished by.

Philippe Larpenteur, the steersman, stood at the rear of the long canoe, angling the long steering paddle to keep them parallel with the shoreline of the great freshwater lake the Ojibwe called Gichigami, and known to the French as *Superieur*. He reveled in the late summer sun on his face, the cool breeze, and the sensation of skimming across open water. Like many of the frontiersmen who rowed the great chain of lakes and St. Lawrence River, he wore a white cotton shirt, breeches with leggings, a sash, and a red toque that covered his shoulder-length hair.

"It won't be long now." Brule, who sat in front of him, glanced over his shoulder and grinned. Homely as a bulldog, the young Quebecer's excitement was infectious and made Philippe smile in return. Brule had spotted the landmark. A crooked cedar atop the tall sandstone cliff meant they were within five miles of Dusard's trading post. Five miles from making camp for the day.

It was a hard day's paddle from Grand Portage. Like Brule and the rest of the crew, Philippe looked forward to a restful evening before continuing an eight week trek home to Montreal. Another long season, longer than most, he thought. He'd been making the arduous journey for over a decade and, for the first time, he found himself growing weary of it. While he loved the beauty of the land and water, at thirty years old, he knew his time working the canoes was coming to an end. Theirs was a job for young men with strong backs that could tote ninety pound packs across wilderness portages. The past two seasons had left Philippe with achy joints and sore muscles, though he'd never admit that to anyone. He had worked hard to become a steersman and he knew others coveted his place in the canoe. Yet he could no longer deny that these journeys were taking a toll on his body. A winter cozied up by a warm fire with a tankard of spiced rum was an image he kept in his mind for persevering.

Brule had not been the only man who recognized the crooked tree landmark and its promise of an end to the day's labor. With new vigor the crew stroked the paddles and sang a rowing song.

"Be quiet!" Etienne Clement's raised hand called for silence. The bowman's profile was turned toward Philippe, a perceptive face tempered by experience and hardship, a strong chin, a long black sideburn beneath a felt hat with a broad flat brim, a white neck cloth tied loosely round his throat. Eyes that had seen much of the beauty and evil of the world gazed intently landward.

They all followed his gaze.

An overturned canoe rested on a grassy outcrop a hundred and twenty yards away. A man was bent over it, repairing the birch skin with a strip of spruce root. The man, aware of the passing group of men, stood and faced them. Burly and large, he was clothed in animal skins and dark leggings. Wild rust-colored hair cascaded around a bearded face. Bellicose eyes glared silent warning. Even from this distance there was no mistaking his message. If that wasn't enough, he now held a flintlock musket across his body.

Fingal McKay.

They all knew who he was. They had seen him often enough and were wary of him. Nearly everyone who traded goods on the north shores of *Superieur* and the Northwest Territories knew of the Scottish fur trapper. McKay's treachery blew far like a November gale. Disagreeable and vile-tempered, he was a pariah among good men, an unconscionable thief who stole from the traps of other trappers. Philippe and his crewmates first encountered McKay two seasons ago near Fond du Lac. Their canoe was tangled in the submerged branches of a fallen tree. McKay, passing in the distance, saw their distress but paddled on, breaking an unwritten code by not offering assistance to his fellow travelers.

Fingal McKay looked after only himself.

Clement gave an order to paddle and the crew muscled their way along. Philippe was glad to leave the unpredictable trapper, so easily sparked to violence, in their wake.

Before long, Dusard's trading post appeared on the horizon. Philippe steered them towards a wide inlet with an open, flat beach. The crew back-paddled until the canoe edged in the last yards. Clement stepped into the knee deep water and guided the craft around rocks and obstructions that might tear the delicate bark skin. A few yards out he signaled for them to unload. Philippe disembarked and, with a heavy cargo bag punishing his lower back, waded to shore. Brule and the others followed. After the canoe was empty, several men carried it onto the sand and turned it upside down. Philippe removed his sopping wet moccasins and wool stockings and wrung them out before putting them back on. The men began to set up camp as Clement motioned for Philippe to follow. Philippe's feet settled in the soft sand with each step as they strode along the narrow beach, a pleasant sensation after hours of standing in the canoe.

The trading post sat on a stubby peninsula that overlooked the endless freshwater lake. In design, the building was three interconnected log structures, constructed out of the plentiful white pine and bur oaks around them. Standing on the open lawn stood Dusard himself, a short, rotund man in a red flannel shirt and buckskin breeches. He paused in the act of chopping firewood to greet them. A wide, impetuous mouth stretched into a warm welcome.

They had known the trading post owner for many seasons. Philippe forced a smile. He could barely stand the man. Dusard had an inflated sense of self-worth and never tired of elucidating how the Montreal agents were fools for not appointing him as the manager for the North West Company fur brigade.

"If I, Jean Baptiste Dusard, were in charge, the trading company's wealth would double!" he was fond of saying, which he often did, and to the same people. Repeatedly. Jean Baptiste Dusard could be tiresome.

For his part, Clement nodded politely, as if this were the first time he'd heard of this injustice and not the fifteenth. Etienne Clement, who had briefly studied for the priesthood, and who had the required patience and listening skills of the confessional, let the trading post proprietor spout for a minute before changing the subject.

"Your knowledge of the trade is well known, Dusard," Clement said with the skill of a diplomat, adding a secret wink toward Philippe. "In fact, I have use for it now. The rest of our canoe brigade left Grand Portage after us. They should arrive before dusk. We'll need supplies. I have a list. Pemmican, smoked fish, and wild rice are at the top of it."

"*Bien.* You always plan ahead, Clement. Not like that mutton-head LaSalle. You know him? Dyspeptic-looking fellow with a big nose. Wears a beat up blue worsted hat. Thought he was clever by taking on three extra pelt bundles. Left him with little room for supplies. He's gambling on making good time back through the lakes. 'You can't eat pelts if you get delayed,' I told him. Would he take my advice? *Au contraire.* Dismissed me summarily. Summarily!" The garrulous trader spoke in a voice as coarse as a wood rasp drawn across a rough sawn board. It almost hurt to listen to him. "Come," he motioned for Clement to follow, "let us smoke a pipe while we discuss this list of yours." From inside his red shirt he withdrew a clay pipe.

Clement gripped the other's forearm, stopping him in mid-turn. "We saw McKay."

The affable smile disappeared, replaced by concern. "Where?"

"As we came in. Five miles west, I'd say."

Dusard turned his head and spat on the grass. "That scoundrel's been looting traps again. Louis Marignac caught him two weeks ago. They fought but McKay was too big, too much for little Marignac. McKay is part demon! Broke Marignac's arm!" Dusard's bulging eyes grew large. A sense of incredulity edged his voice. "He even got into my storeroom last month. I chased him off before he took anything, but only because my rifle was pointed at his fat head."

"You were lucky," Clement remarked. "McKay fights with no mercy. He'll kill you without a second thought."

"The Ojibwe and Cree won't deal with him. He has no honor, they say. A man like McKay poisons the well for the rest of us." Dusard, gazing at the land and business he had built up over the years, let out a resolute grunt. "He doesn't frighten me. I'd hoped he'd left the area, but if he returns I'll teach him a painful lesson."

Boastful talk from a blowhard, thought Philippe. Easy enough to say when the Scottish fur trapper was not present to hear you. Dusard seemed to understand the delicacy of the point, and after a second thought leaned in slightly. "However, I'm grateful you and your men will be staying the night. I doubt even McKay would dare try anything with a full brigade of voyageurs encamped here."

Clement gave a curt nod. "You would think so. But this is Fingal McKay. As you said, the man's a demon. Demons do not fear ordinary men."

Dusard, a rarity for him, had nothing to say.

As the two men ambled toward the trading post, Philippe signaled that he would join them later. He detoured toward the adjacent field, drawn by a friendly wave from Madame Dusard. The young Ojibwe wife of the trader sat in a sunny clearing on the grass where she laced leather bindings to the ash frame of a snowshoe. Snowshoes, blankets, and moccasins were among the items she made for sale.

"Bonjour Nokomis." Philippe indulged in using her given name rather than the more appropriate Madame Dusard. She was considerable younger than her middle-aged husband, could even pass has his adult daughter. Clad in a fawn-colored deerskin dress decorated with dyed porcupine quills and beadwork, her supple frame sat with an easy elegance. Her long black hair glistened in the sun. At his approach, her face filled with the warm, guileless smile of her people.

"Bonjour Monsieur Larpenteur," Nokomis replied in a voice as sweet as bird song. Although she smiled at him, it was muted by social convention. She should not show improper attention to a man who was not her husband. "Has it been a good season for you?"

"It has. We have many pelts." He laughed as he remembered something. "Unfortunately, this may be the last journey for my moccasins." His moose-hide footwear was worn thin in patches and there was a small hole along the side of one.

"*Nom de Dieu!*" Her slender hand flew to her mouth. An endearing chortle erupted in spite of her effort to suppress it. "Your poor moccasins won't make it to Montreal. You need new ones." Nokomis jumped to her feet in an energetic, graceful motion and signaled for him to follow her.

Philippe Larpenteur was well aware of her position as a married woman and the rules of propriety between them, yet he was quite willing to let the delightful Ojibwe woman help him pick out a new pair of moccasins. After all, it was her job to assist her husband's customers, was it not? And, truth be told, after nearly ten weeks in the exclusive company of rugged, boisterous men, it was a delight to hear a woman's laugh, to be in her presence. Although he had a low opinion of the corpulent, long-winded trader, Philippe regarded his native wife with high esteem. Long ago Clement had told him Nokomis was the niece of a local chief and that her marriage to Dusard was part of an elaborate arrangement to improve commerce between the French and Ojibwe people. How Dusard had managed to pull off his coup bewildered Philippe. Perhaps he had underestimated the abilities of the trader.

Before the sun sank to the top of the trees, the remaining freight canoes appeared and put in to the encampment. There followed a lively evening of food and drink and pipes of tobacco, as well as colorful stories shared by crackling fires. The long day at the paddles made the men ready for sleep soon enough, yet for Philippe sleep did not come easily. His mind was restless. Restless from what, he did not know. Eventually he drifted off in a fitful slumber when a sound insinuated into his awareness. It penetrated beyond the lapping of lake water against the shore, behind the song of crickets.

Faint voices raised in anger.

His eyes flashed open. The sound came from the direction of the trading post. Trouble? Only one way to find out, he knew. Probably nothing, but he had to be sure. He pulled aside his blanket and got up. New, soft-soled moccasins let him step quietly by his sleeping crewmates, as well as smoldering campfires whose orange hot embers provided little in the way of illumination. Philippe approached the trading post with caution, drawn by the flickering candle light from a side window, aware he could be walking toward a danger he was ill-prepared to handle. Wary eyes searched the forest beyond the dim glow for movement, into darkness as black as the Devil's heart. He drew in a deep breath to calm his nerves. Instinctively, a hand wandered to his sash for the assurance of his knife and tomahawk.

He edged closer to the window from which the glow from the candle emanated. Philippe pressed his back against the rough-hewn logs to conceal himself in the shadows and dared to peer through the glass. He made out the plump shape of Dusard in a nightshirt gesturing angrily toward his Ojibwe wife.

It was nothing, a quarrel between man and wife. Philippe released the breath he'd been holding. He should go and let this private matter play out.

But he didn't move. Curiosity kept his feet in check. That and concern over what the mercurial husband might do.

Suddenly the door swung open. Candle light burst into the darkness. Philippe nearly jumped out of his skin.

He was completely visible now.

If Dusard walked out, Philippe would be caught in an awkward situation. He inched back toward the shadows and was relieved when no one emerged.

"Understand your position," Dusard's raunchy voice bellowed from inside. "You are my wife, my property. I will not stand to have you make a cuckold of me!" The last he added with dramatic flourish.

Madame Dusard, clutching a blanket around her, spoke in a voice accustomed to such rants. "Dusard, you are a drunken oaf. What you say is not true."

"I know what I saw. You and Larpenteur are up to something. I can tell."

Eh? Philippe was all attention now. This was about him? His ears burned to catch every word.

"I'm your husband. Your job is to obey me. Obey me or take your leave—and as you are, with the clothes on your back!"

"I'm tired of your threats, Husband. If that is the choice you give me then I'll go. And gladly."

She walked defiantly towards the open door. Dusard swore and lunged toward her with a swipe of his meaty hand.

The young Ojibwe woman jumped aside. She shot him a derisive look. "I am Nokomis, Daughter of the Moon, member of the Muskrat clan. In my tribe no girl ran faster than I. You think you can catch me you fat old man?"

The door had closed after Dusard released it but had not shut completely. Open a crack, it was enough to let their voices filter out. Looking through the window, Philippe saw the trader raise a threatening fist. This time Nokomis stood her ground, her face and posture filled with contempt. However, instead of striking her, Dusard snatched a small clay pot from a nearby shelf and flung it. Nokomis raised her arms to cover her face. Shards of pottery fell to the floor. At the same moment Dusard raced toward her. For a heavy man he moved surprisingly fast. Powerful, rough hands gripped her by the throat. Nokomis kicked and pounded at him to no avail.

Not wasting a second, Philippe charged through the doorway, grabbed two handfuls of Dusard's night shirt and, with every ounce of strength in him, wrenched the fat man off her, then slammed him hard to the floor.

Philippe's cheeks burned as he stood over him. "Don't lay a hand on her!"

Murder was in Dusard's eyes as he climbed back to his feet. "*C'est mon, affaire!*"

It didn't matter to Philippe; he was making it his concern. His fist ached to silence the drunken lout. Yet before Philippe could do anything, Dusard went berserk and charged at him. The two men traded blows. Younger and stronger, Philippe got the advantage initially but Dusard fought like an enraged bear, and Philippe's lower back, sore from long weeks in the canoe, seized up against the savage onslaught. The hesitation let the other slam a bulky shoulder into Philippe's chest, sending him tumbling hard against the bedpost. He sank to the floor blinded by the pain. Through the blur he saw the other reach for on object on the floor boards. Philippe's knife had fallen out during their struggle. Dusard snatched it up and lurched toward him. Philippe attempted to move when his back refused him. With a grimace he angled away as the knife came slashing by. Wide open eyes watched the razor-edged blade just miss his face.

It wouldn't miss forever—

An explosive crash startled him, an eruption of sound and wood splinters. Philippe marveled as Dusard collapsed to the floor to reveal Nokomis standing behind him, in her hands the remains of the snowshoe she'd cracked over his skull, a head as dense as granite, it seemed, for Dusard climbed slowly back to his feet. Swearing a guttural oath, he lumbered toward her, the knife aimed to kill. Nokomis backed away, astonished the man could still walk, so astonished she forgot to run. Liquored up and full of rage, the trader was unstoppable. Philippe feared for her life. Through the pain he propped himself up, knowing he'd never get to them in time, so he did the only thing he could; he ripped the tomahawk from his sash and took aim.

The flint axe head landed squarely and deeply in Dusard's back.

At impact his body reared upright with a violent jerk. For a few seconds he remained vertical before he dropped hard like an overstuffed bale of wild rice.

Then there was nothing.

It was a strange, uneasy silence as Philippe studied the fallen trader to see if he would rise up once again. A tense moment turned to relief as it became clear that Jean Baptiste Dusard would never get up again.

When the knot in his back failed to cooperate, Philippe used the bedpost to hoist himself to his legs.

Nokomis hurried over to assist. "You're hurt."

The distress in her voice was a balm to his suffering. "I'll be all right. What about you?" For the first time he'd noticed the marks on her neck, marks left by brutish paws of her husband. Without thinking he took her hand, and was pleased when she did not withdraw it. Her soft brown eyes lingered on his. Not a word was exchanged but much was said, and in the meaningful silence of that moment an understanding passed between them.

"What will you do now?" he asked.

"I don't know."

"Will you stay and run the trading post yourself? Return to your people?"

She gave a shrug, unable to answer, overwhelmed at events too recent to sort out.

The door banged open and they both turned with a start at the clamor.

A dumbfounded Clement stood on the threshold. "Merde! What treachery is this? Philippe, explain yourself."

Nokomis stepped forward. "Monsieur Larpenteur risked his life to defend me. Dusard was drunk. We were arguing. He would have killed me if Monsieur Larpenteur had not intervened."

Clement contemplated the tomahawk blade wedged in her husband's back. "Intervened is somewhat of an understatement." He listened to the others recap what happened. When they finished, he scratched a black sideburn thoughtfully. "Dusard was an insufferable oaf at times, but this"—Clement gestured to the corpse—"could cause problems for the two of you."

Philippe and Nokomis shared a apprehensive glance.

Ever the planner, Etienne Clement snapped his fingers, sparked by a new thought. "I know! What went on here doesn't have to be known. We'll tell a different story."

Philippe was taken aback. "Shouldn't we tell the truth?" He was an honest man with a code of honor.

"People don't want the truth," Clement replied, "they want a story they believe, one they like. And we shall give them one." His eyes flashed with inspiration. "Fingal McKay did this. Understand? You did not kill Dusard, Philippe, it was McKay. Dusard caught him in the act of stealing, and the two men fought. You got here too late. That's McKay's tomahawk in his back. McKay knocked you down and ran off." Clement was emphatic, "*It was McKay.*"

Although he didn't like being untruthful, Philippe cared less for the alternative, that he might be punished for killing Dusard while trying to save the life of Nokomis. He had little faith in faraway magistrates with no knowledge of the rough and tumble life on the frontier. And McKay was the perfect scapegoat. The man already was known as a thief and blackguard. He'd even been spotted in the area that same afternoon. The idea, he had to admit, was appealing.

A noise from behind made Clement look over his shoulder. He turned back, agitated. "You agree to the plan? Be quick, the others are coming. They'll be here shortly."

Philippe looked to Nokomis who gave a complicit nod.

"We're agreed." Philippe stuck out a hand toward Clement. "*Merci, mon ami.*"

Clement plucked the knife from Dusard's lifeless hand and returned it to its rightful owner. "We're agreed on our story then. McKay killed Dusard and fled. You can never tell anyone the truth," he warned.

They agreed.

"The murder of Dusard was a turning point for McKay," Alison wrapped up. The faces of the tour group were a mixture of amusement and fascination. "Until that moment his bullying and thievery had been tolerated because he was a menace no one wanted to take on. This was the last straw. Trappers, traders, voyageurs, and settlers demanded something be done. Of course when McKay's confronted with the crime he denies any involvement. But criminals always do that, don't they?" she added with thick sarcasm. "After the killing there are a few scattered sightings of him but McKay soon makes himself scarce. One account has him relocating to Saskatchewan where he drops out of history. And so it was one throw of a tomahawk—this very tomahawk—that cemented the legend of Terrible Fingal McKay."

A smattering of polite applause followed and the erstwhile theater arts major took a bow. One person, she observed, had not joined in on the applause. A tall, pinched-faced woman looked back with a dubious expression. "This was a hundreds of years ago," she said in a reedy voice. "How do you know that's what really happened?"

Alison pounced with a ready answer. "I'm glad you asked. We owe the story of Jean Baptiste Dusard's murder and Fingal McKay's role in it to the granddaughter of his widow, Nokomis Dusard. In the 1870s a newspaper editor in Thunder Bay was doing a story about early settlers. He'd heard inklings of this story from a friend and contacted this direct descendant of Madame Dusard for the family's version."

The tour guide motioned them over to a nearby case in which hand-written documents were on display. "We have the actual letter here."

"Which one is it?" A small girl in a print dress looked over after squinting inside the display. "There's nothing here from a Dusard."

"You won't see one. Nokomis had no children with Dusard. She remarried," Alison explained in a tone dismissive of any significance to the new union. "The letter is from her granddaughter by her second husband. It's at the bottom on the case, the one signed by Abigail Larpenteur."

Our next story takes us far deeper into the past, to 14th century France. Though distant in time, human nature will always foster hucksters, con men, and bamboozlers — and death is never far away.

Ms Norwood believes in listening to her characters, letting them construct and solve the mystery. Some of the characters appearing in this story will be showing up in two novels currently in development.

Water into Wine

Loraine Norwood

Enscribed in the Chirurgia of William of Oxford
St. Cecilia's Day
1326

So begins the tale...

I

Halybutte the Dwarf is dead.

He was an irritating, self-righteous, troublesome creature, but no man deserves to die as he did.

If I believed in Heaven, which I decidedly do not, I would say he dances, pain-free, among the angels.

That is, if I believed in angels.

The little dwarf belonged to a troupe of players selling useless medicinal remedies to the gullible. Acting on the stage with him were jugglers, a beautiful young woman named Serafina, a monkey named Pettipaw, and the leader of the troupe, Robertus Medicamus.

Long ago, when I was young and green and full of piss and vinegar, Robertus, then known as Robert of St. Albans, and I were students at Oxford. We studied together, drank, chased the same bit of skirt, and wandered from village to village begging for money in order to pay our masters for the next session of schooling. We enjoyed each other's company. But as soon as we earned the right to the title of *physicus*, Robert of St. Albans changed his name to Robertus Medicamus and flew the coop, rambling the wide world over as a thief, entertainer and magician. Along the way he gathered other players to entertain the crowds. One of them was the dwarf Halybutte.

I, on the other hand, practiced medicine and surgery in London and other parts of England where my skills were requested. My curiosity regarding that most miraculous of machines, the human body, led me to investigate its inner- workings, a course of study that required corpses. All of this was done in secret, of course, as the Church has forbidden dissections. Fortunately cadavers are easy to come by in London, especially among the poor who cannot pay for burials.

I met Robertus again, by chance, some years later as he and his players joined me aboard a little cog sailing for Marseilles. Also traveling with me were my son Gerard and my apprentice and student Meg. From Marseilles we planned to travel overland to our destination, Montpellier, where I hoped Gerard would enter the medical school, earn the title *physicus* and begin his own practice. Meg, too, wanted to do the same in order to practice as a *physica*. As Montpellier does not accept women, I had not much hope for her.

In Marseilles we bought a horse and wagon. Robertus, who had been of a mind to travel to the lucrative markets of Paris, decided instead to join us on our journey. Truth be told, I wasn't anxious for his company. But Robertus insisted.

"You forget that I've traveled to these parts many times," he said. "I know the roads. I know the rivers where we can drink safe water. And most importantly, I know the inns where you can sleep without getting your throats cut."

"And why would you do this – go out of your way, take up your valuable time, when you could be fleecing the gullible in Paris?" I asked.

Robertus pressed a hand to his parti-colored surcoat. "I am hurt by the insult, sir."

"Don't play innocent with me, I *know* you."

"All right, then. You force me to admit to an ulterior motive."

"I'm shocked. You, an ulterior motive?"

Robertus ignored the jibe. "The truth is, Montpellier is a lucrative city for my profession. People travel there for their health because the weather is warm and pleasant. It is also a stopping point for pilgrims who walk the Way of St. James to the shrine at Santiago de Compostella. Pilgrims travel to the shrine for two reasons: either to be forgiven for their sins or to be healed from infirmities.

"Aha! There's the motive."

"Those who seek the grace of St. James are often infirmed and looking for a cure. They are more than willing to part with their money."

"Why not help them? Why cheat them when they are desperate?"

"Listen, my old friend, there is one immutable fact in this world: no matter how much we argue, we will never agree." He patted me on the shoulder, and I stiffened, sure that he was about to relieve me of my moneybags. "I say we call a truce. You practice your brand of medicine and I will practice mine."

As Robertus predicted, men and women on their way to Santiago de Compostela joined us in Arles. Many of the pilgrims, young and old, used a crooked walking staff for support. Some wore a scallop shell on their cloaks while others carried it in their hands or hung it from the crooks of their staffs. At night, the pilgrims took refuge in nearby churches or monasteries where they were given donations of water and food.

On the last day of our journey Serafina, the red-haired girl, beckoned to Robertus before he could pick up the reins and whip.

"Robertus, our feet are sore. We've had enough of the road. If Halybutte is allowed to ride, why can we not join him? Let us ride. Please?"

He sighed. "Get in then. We'll be in Montpellier by nightfall. The horse can take the extra weight for one day."

Serafina and the others whooped and hollered and were soon climbing over Meg and Gerard and stepping on my feet in an attempt to find a comfortable seat. Serafina insisted on a place next to my son. She shoved Halybutte aside, then yanked at the little monkey Pettipaw who was curled up on the wagon bench. Pettipaw squealed in surprise as she threw him into Meg's lap.

"May I sit next to you, fine sir?" Serafina asked Gerard, as she pressed against him, her thigh touching his.

Gerard smiled at her. "Certainly."

I may be getting on in years, but the parts of me that serviced a woman are not dead yet. Cupid's arrows do not escape my notice even when they are intended for my son and my pupil Meg.

During the long sea voyage to Marseilles that Serafina had pulled back Cupid's bow and was aiming squarely at Gerard. Meg, whose childish adoration of my son had grown to a deep respect and I believe love, was greatly pained by the woman's obvious flirtations. Meg was plain—and some say ugly—due to a disfigurement at birth that caused her right cheekbone to be misshapen and that eye to droop. She dressed in grey wool, her hair plaited and hidden within a wimple. Serafina's hair, unlike Meg's, was loose, her red curls flowing wantonly. She dressed in brilliant colors, her surcoats decorated with slashes to reveal a red or blue tunic underneath. Bits of metal and bells sewn to the surcoat glinted like sunbeams and jingled as she walked.

"Do you mind if I put my head upon your shoulder?" Serafina asked Gerard. She tossed her curls, releasing a tinkle of music from her costume. "They tell me that you are traveling with your father and sister."

"Father, yes. Sister, no. She is my father's student, but we are like brother and sister," Gerard answered.

Meg's crumpled face reflected her misery and I felt her heart break as if it were my own.

Serafina ran her hand up and down Gerard's arm. "I had no idea that you were a man of such power."

I chuckled while Gerard scowled at me. My son is thin as a fence post. He can pick up a feather quill and an book, but little more.

As the caravan drew closer to Montpellier, young Meg, who had never been outside her village until she joined me in London inquired about the scallop shells painted on the trunks of trees and signposts.

"What do the shells mean?" she asked. "Why do the pilgrims wear them?"

"Those who have made a pilgrimage wear the scallop shell as a badge of completion," I explained. "It's a symbol of St. James, the apostle who was beheaded in Jerusalem. His body was sent by boat to Galicia where he had preached the gospel, but it was lost at sea. Later it washed up on shore, but by a miracle it was undamaged."

My son Gerard snorted in derision at the story, but Meg's eyes grew wide and her mouth formed a stunned Oh.

"The body was protected by scallop shells that covered it," I added. "James was buried in Santiago de Compostela, along with the scallops, and soon his grave became a shrine."

Meg regarded the dozens of pilgrims who formed a ragged line, voyagers suffering afflictions of the body, cripples, those who were sick at heart, diseased, and despondent, all walking beside the happy sinners who chattered like magpies. Some of the pilgrims wore three or four scallop shell badges.

"They must have great faith to make such long journeys," she said.

"Either that or they believe anything they are told." Gerard rolled his eyes in the direction of the travelers.

I laughed at my son's quick wit. "You sound more and more like your blasphemous father every day."

Halybutte, whose crooked little legs couldn't bear the daily walking required by our journey, had been riding in the wagon since the second day. He had listened to the endless theological and philosophical discussions bouncing like juggler's balls between me, Gerard, and Meg. Suddenly he sat up and pointed his finger at me.

"You are a learned man, but your mockery is not wanted here," he said.

"What? Am I not able to speak my mind? Or is that forbidden on this journey?"

"You mock the beliefs of these people and you belittle the miracles of Our Savior. God's judgment will be on your head."

"You dare to lecture me about God's judgment?" I snapped, "You, a scheming dwarf who tricks people out of their money and sells them false cures?

"I have already received God's judgment, have I not?" Halybutte punched his crooked legs and winced at the pain. "I have lived with my affliction, faced the mockery of many, yet I dance on the stage so that others might laugh. This is the body God gave me, just as that is the face God gave *her*." He swung to Meg and pointed at her sunken cheek, where bones had refused to grow from birth, and the drooping eye that seemed to slide into the hollow.

Meg's face grew flushed and she sucked in her lower lip.

"Leave Meg out of this," Gerard and I shouted in unison. Mistress Meg had been my apprentice and student for so many years that I confess I often failed to notice her disfigurement. I was much more concerned with her medical skills.

Halybutte sat in silence for a moment and then sighed. "Pardon, mistress, I did not mean to pain you. I suspect you have received many hurts in your life, but with a face such as yours you have a lifetime of hurts before you." He turned to look at me. "As to you, these people do not deserve your scorn. They have faith, something which is obviously foreign to you."

"Oh, I have faith," I said. "I have faith that the sun will come up in the morning and go down in the evening."

"I can only hope that God sees fit to lift your black humour before your death. Perhaps then you will enjoy life among the living."

"And I hope, little man, that you will keep your sermons to yourself for the remainder of the journey. Thankfully Montpellier is not too distant."

Halybutte muttered under his breath. "Uneasy lies the head of a heretic."

"Gentlemen, gentlemen," Robertus interrupted. "Let us not quarrel among ourselves. We are all tired and anxious for this journey to end. We want to sleep in a comfortable bed, have a warm bath, be rid of our fleas and lice." He clicked to the horse to pick up her trot. "But look here, see the road ahead of us?" He nodded toward a section of cobbles that rose out of the dirt path. "That is the old Roman road. The men who built it have been moldering for hundreds of years, their disagreements long since forgotten, their gods long since vanished."

"Robertus, you should have been a philosopher," I said. "Or a bard. You have a silver tongue in your mouth."

"Ha!" Robertus laughed. "Why do you think Fortune smiles upon me?"

Later, as the light faded and the warm afternoon began to chill, Robertus announced that we were crossing the Lez River. He pointed ahead of the wagon. "There is Montpellier."

A mountain of hewn stone loomed ahead. The city walls stretched far to the right and left, topped every fifty feet or so by a tower whose cone-shaped roof provided shelter for the guards walking the parapet.

"The city is built on two hills surrounded by the walls," Robertus said. "Steep narrow streets. And crowded. We'll go through the gate and—"

"And find food and shelter," I interrupted.

"I know just the place," Robertus said. "The Herbaria market."

Following our entrance through the Gate of St. Giles, where the female players waved and flirted with the guards, we rode through a labyrinth of narrow winding streets. Merchants called to us offering sugar and spices, the finest leather, embroidered textiles, cloth from Bruges.

Our progress was slow owing to the many passers-by, some of who cursed at the wagon and then laughed as Halybutte the Dwarf raised his tunic and offered his bare bottom in reply. Several times a street ended suddenly as a building loomed ahead and what appeared to be alleys to the right and left turned into dead ends. When that happened, the entire party had to scramble out of the wagon while Robertus backed the horse. Pettipaw offered his aid by jumping on the poor creature and pulling its tail, all the while chattering encouragement. Fortunately the creature was exhausted and not inclined to protest.

Pettipaw offered his aid by jumping on the horse and pulling its tail, all the while chattering encouragement.

"I thought you said you had been here before. Do you know where you are going?" I grumbled to Robertus.

"Have faith," Robertus answered and cast a sideways glance at Meg, muttering to her, "Not an easy thing for him to do."

Finally the narrow street emptied into an open-air square.

"Herbaria," Robertus announced. "I'll stay with the wagon. Find what you need, but do it quickly. The light is going."

One week later I found myself at the same square watching in rapt but disgusted attention as Robertus sold elixirs to unsuspecting men and women desperate to cure their aches and pains.

Halybutte couldn't know it, but that would be the last afternoon of his life.

II

All morning I had been lecturing Meg and Gerard on Plato and Aquinas so that they might pass their entrance exams to the *Schola Medica* in Montpellier. Their faces went from terrified attention to the heavy-lidded *ennui* of students overcome by tedium and sleepiness. At that point I called a halt to the lecture and announced we would go for a walk, return for a mid-day meal, and resume studying.

I set a swift pace, my long legs churning ahead of them so that they had to work hard to climb the steep Rue St. Pierre. We turned left through the streets of leather workers and drapers and, side-stepping the tables of cloth and leather goods, walked uphill to the Herbaria Market. A huge crowd had gathered at the market square and blocked our way.

"What the devil?" I asked and peered over the heads of gawkers to see what drew their attention. "Ah, speak of the devil. I might have known."

"What is it?" Meg asked and stood on tiptoe in an effort to see.

"Robertus and his players."

"Oh, may we stop, Master William? Please?"

"We have work to do. You both are woefully lacking in—"

"Please, father," Gerard joined in. "We won't stay long."

I relented. "A few minutes only. I'll be walking in the market." My first impulse was to ignore Robertus completely, but I changed my mind. I'm a tall man, and big to boot, which helps when you want to elbow your way to the front of a crowd. I landed on the first row, adjacent to a makeshift stage, where I could see better.

With Robertus, seeing was *not* believing for he performed all manner of tricks that defied natural law. In between deceits, his players entertained the onlookers. They played music while Serafina danced, the pieces of metal, glass, and mirror sewn to her surcoat flashing in the sunlight. Then Halybutte tumbled about on stage, stood on his hands and waggled his feet in the air, and allowed himself to be thrown between two jugglers as if he were a ripe melon. He made lascivious gestures to the women in the audience. As the beautiful Serafina sang plaintive love songs, Halybutte sidled up to her and pretended to copulate on her leg, like a dog in heat. This brought loud guffaws and set the crowd in a good frame of mind. A happy crowd is a buying crowd or so says Robertus.

When Robertus returned to the stage, he strode to the edge where men, women and children waited with upturned faces. He was dressed like an outlandish bird from a strange country. His yellow leggings were criss-crossed with strips of blue silk and his tunic, a bright brocade of blue and green, sparkled in the sunshine. On his head was a jaunty felt hat of deep green. A peacock feather had been thrust into a red and gold band that encircled the crown of the hat. On his shoulder sat his constant companion, the little monkey Pettipaw, dressed in red and gold leggings.

Without a word Robertus threw up his hands and a fine powder floated toward the crowd. Then there was an ear-splitting bang and a flash of fire. Women screamed and ducked, but the fire quickly disappeared. Pettipaw chattered at the women in front who laughed in embarrassment.

"My good ladies and honorable gentlemen," Robertus was saying, "now that I have your attention let me ask you if you are acquainted with the story of how the Lord Jesus changed water into wine?"

The crowd nodded and murmured assurances that they knew the story.

"I'm sure some of you must be thirsty. If I had wine, I would share it with you. But wait… perhaps I can yet… Halybutte, if you will, bring me a goblet of water."

A hush fell over the crowd. A woman standing next to me, leaned over and whispered, "I've seen him do this before. He turns water into wine. 'Tis a miracle."

"I wouldn't expect anything else from that scoundrel," I said and the woman scowled at me.

Halybutte had returned to the stage and carried a goblet of clear glass, filled to the rim with water. Robertus announced a miracle was about to happen.

The crowd grew still. No one spoke as they waited in anticipation. Robertus held the goblet aloft. He waved his palm across the top of the goblet and muttered a prayer to the heavens. Halybutte scampered around Robertus's legs and jumped for the goblet, crying out that the water was still clear. The crowd strained to hear Robertus's words over Halybutte's chattering.

A man in the front row shouted, "Admit it, Robertus, you have failed. You are an ordinary man. Only Jesus can turn water to wine."

Robertus swatted at Halybutte as if he were a bothersome fly. As he did so, the crowd gasped. The water was pink. Then red. Then burgundy in color.

Robertus grasped his chest and hung his head, as if the effort of changing the water had exhausted him. He staggered toward the crowd. "You, sir. Yes, you… the man who did not believe me. Come here and taste this. And bring your wife as well."

The man started forward. His wife held back, shaking her head, but slowly the man coaxed her onto the stage.

I recognized the man and woman. They were dressed as country folk and wore wigs, but they were players in Robertus's troupe, skillful actors who had fleeced the good people of York, sailed with us to Marseilles, and walked behind the wagon from Marseilles to the marketplace.

Robertus held the goblet out to the man. "Drink this," he said. "And then tell me whether you think I am a fraud."

The man raised the goblet to his mouth. He sipped. Licked his lips. Looked at Robertus in surprise. And then drank deeply.

"Wait friend, leave some for your lady."

Laughing along with the crowd, the man handed the goblet to the woman, who also drank. She returned the goblet to Robertus and then covered her mouth with her hands as if she could not believe what she had just tasted.

Robertus gave the goblet to Halybutte who sat at his feet and then held up his hands to the boisterous crowd. "Are you certain that you drank wine and not water?"

The man and woman nodded their heads. "Yes," they said in unison.

A great roar rose from the crowd. Women screamed and clasped their hands as if in prayer. Someone from the back yelled that a woman had fainted—no doubt another shill—and Robertus strode from one end of the stage to the other as if trying to get the crowd under control. Pettipaw jumped off Robertus's shoulder and ran to Halybutte who was rubbing his calves as if to knead a cramped muscle. The monkey grabbed the goblet from Halybutte's hands and the dwarf tickled the monkey and pulled at his tail.

"Now my good people, settle down, settle down," Robertus said. "I show you this talent of mine not to scare you, but to demonstrate that my wares are mysterious…" He paused and waited for quiet. "…mysterious and divine. My medicines are blessed." He looked to the sky as if he and the Almighty mixed drugs together at the mortar and pestle. "And they are available only to you, my friends. Only to you." He waved an arm to his right where Serafina was holding a basket. "Tell the lovely Serafina your ailment and she will be glad to help you. Please have your coins at the ready—we have many suffering people who must be served."

People began to line up, docile sheep ready to receive the communion of cures.

"How does he do it?" the woman next to me gasped.

"As you said, good woman, it is *indeed* a miracle."

She must have had some doubts due to the tone of my voice for she scowled at me again.

At that moment someone to the left of me screamed. A woman's voice, piercing, terrified, ear-splitting, descended to a choked garble. I followed her outstretched arm and pointing finger to the stage where Halybutte was shaking and quivering, foam oozing from his parted lips. Pettipaw sat astride his chest, screeching and tugging at the bells sewn onto the neck of his tunic. Halybutte caught my gaze and held it. The hair on my arms lifted as if a spirit walked over my grave.

Pushing the gawkers aside, I rushed to the tormented man who not five minutes before had been tumbling about on stage. Pettipaw yelped and ran into the crowd as I knelt by Halybutte's side. I reached under his tunic and put my hand on his chest. His heart was beating wildly, out of rhythm, yet with such rapidity that it threatened to burst his ribcage.

"Halybutte," I yelled, "can you hear me?"

Something flickered in the dwarf's eyes. He put his fingers to his lips. "Bur…ning. Cannot feel…"

"What happened?" I asked. I put my ear close to his lips to listen to his breathing, which was swift and shallow.

"Wine," he rasped. He twisted his head to the left where the goblet lay shattered on the stage.

Pettipaw sidled up to the suffering dwarf and then put his face against the man's cheek. Halybutte whispered something to the little monkey that I was unable to hear. Pettipaw leaned over and licked the bubbling foam from Halybutte's lips.

"Get on," I snarled and pushed the monkey away.

I glanced around as Gerard and Meg reached Halybutte's side, but it appeared Robertus and his players had disappeared. The crowd was pushing against us in an effort to see and the little monkey, frightened by the commotion of babbling voices and pressing arms and legs, left Halybutte and crawled into Meg's lap.

I examined the dwarf's fingers. They were cold, as were his arms and legs. I held both his hands and let go. His hands dropped to his sides like stones thrown into a pond.

Strange, I thought. *It's as if he has no feeling in his arms and legs.* His lips were blue. He gurgled in agony and once again stared at me, as if imploring me to help him. But I was at a loss. I have attended many dying people in my years as a *physicus*, but never one who was dancing one minute and frothing at the mouth the next. Perhaps he had a falling sickness and had hidden it from us during the trip. Perhaps he had—

The next sound caused my heart to freeze. Meg was screaming in terror. The riotous crowd fell silent. I turned my attention to her and watched as her face lost all color and her lips grew white with fear. My apprentice for years, Meg had dissected cadavers and tended all manner of wounds. Nothing had ever frightened her. Until now.

Lying in her arms, limp and lifeless was Pettipaw. His face was wrenched in a grimace, his lips coated with the same white foam that clung to Halybutte's mouth.

Upon seeing the dead monkey, Halybutte the Dwarf shuddered and inhaled his last breath.

III

I must admit I was excited at the prospect of dissecting a monkey. I've dissected pigs of course, every medical student has done that in an effort to learn about the human body, although my experience with cadavers has taught me that a pig's innards bear little resemblance to a human's. The medical masters would disagree, clinging as they do to what they read and what is forced upon them and not what they see. As to the monkey, I quieted my excitement, concentrating first on the corpse of Halybutte. I had spirited his body away from the crowd at the market by pretending that he was still alive and in need of care. I shouted at Meg and Gerard to follow me and to bring the monkey as well. They ran behind me, oblivious to my destination, but thankfully keeping their concerns to themselves.

I had by chance visited a tanner across the river only the day before the incident at the market to inquire about renting a space near his stall. The craft of tanning was so malodourous due to the urine used in the process that they were placed outside the city walls—and thus outside the quivering nostrils of most townfolk. The building the tanner showed me was ramshackle and hidden at the end of a path along the river. I thought it would do quite well. To get to it, any curious visitor would have to pass by the suffocating vats of urine. The stinging smell of piss was as good as a starving mastiff roaming the property. And no one would notice blood dripping into the river, especially with the tanning vats downstream. In order to ensure privacy, I told the tanner that I was investigating new methods of softening leather and needed secrecy to keep my techniques from being stolen. But I was satisfied that not even the most foolhardy man would quench his curiosity by visiting us.

I raced across the bridge and past the tanner's vats into the little shed where soon Halybutte was splayed on a table like a roast suckling pig at Christmas. Meg washed the body and Gerard made the first incision using the knife I carried on my belt. There was no time to return to our lodgings for dissection instruments.

I expected to see Halybutte's heart in a twisted, convoluted mass. I was shocked therefore to see a heart that was healthy and moreover a normal size. I had thought that his organs would match his stature. He was stunted, therefore his organs would be the size of a child's. But that was not the case. He was normal in every respect on the inside. His exterior was a different matter.

"I cannot find anything that would have killed him," I said to Meg and Gerard. "I don't understand."

"Is there anything in his mouth?" Gerard asked. "He complained of burning."

I investigated his mouth then opened his neck with the knife and found more foam in his gullet. "Just like Pettipaw," I murmured.

I touched the man's hands and was reminded of my sense at the market that he had no feeling in his arms and legs. It was intuition only, but my instinct told me I was right.

"Meg, did you notice anything peculiar about Pettipaw?"

She glanced at the monkey's corpse lying at the opposite end of the table. "What do you mean?"

"Did you notice anything unusual about his hands and feet?"

She reddened and dropped her eyes, as if in embarrassment. "I'm afraid I was terrified, sir. I shouldn't have screamed. It won't happen again."

I waved off her apology. "No need to feel that way. I was terrified as well." I moved to the end of the table and picked up Pettipaw's left leg. "What I mean is… were there any signs of movement in the monkey's hands or feet?"

She thought for a moment and then brightened. "I remember now. I lifted his little feet because they look so human. They would have made me laugh, that is if the circumstances had been different. But his foot dropped on my lap as if he couldn't hold it up. Almost as if he were dead from the waist down. Also, now that I think of it, it was peculiar that he didn't put his arms about me as he always did." She reached toward the monkey's face. "Then the poor little thing started to choke."

I slapped her hand away from Pettipaw's mouth. "Don't touch it!"

"What is it?"

"Poison."

IV

The Cygnet, a tavern where Robertus had lodgings for himself and his players, was located outside the northern wall past the stalls of the laundresses, women with ruddy cheeks and chapped hands whose clamorous voices carried above the beating of wet washing.

Noise assaulted us as soon as we stepped over the threshold. The tavernkeeper, greeting me with a hearty slap on the back, gestured to a table where Robertus and Serafina already sat waiting. The other players sat behind them in the corner. When Serafina spotted Gerard, she called out, arms extended. He walked to her, a little more lightly in his step, and Serafina crushed him to her chest.

"Oh, I have missed you, Gerard," she squealed in her lilting accent. "Why do you not come to see me at the market? And now we are traveling again, and I shall think of you forever." Her thick hair, twisted in a gold chignon held every color of autumn, but her eyes, a startling shade of green, seemed to promise not the cool of an autumn morning but the sultry heat of a summer afternoon. Serafina caught sight of Meg and nodded, but her lips twisted into a sneer.

Gerard, cheeks red, apologized for missing her performances. "I'll come before you leave," he promised.

The tavernkeeper brought lamb stew and a hunk of brown bread with fresh butter for Gerard and Meg. I was not hungry and waived away the food. I wanted to concentrate on the task of ferreting out Halybutte's killer, not on dinner.

Serafina, arms lolling across Gerard's chest and shoulders, nibbled on his ear lobe while he ate. My son, I noticed with amusement, had been transformed, swayed by the attentions of a pretty girl and the inevitable response of the *membrum virile*. He was no longer a human being. More like a slobbering wolfhound enjoying a belly rub.

Meg speared the lamb with such force that the point of the knife went through the trencher bread and stuck to the table. She jerked it loose and with the piece of lamb balancing precariously on the end of the knife, threw the meat into Serafina's trencher, causing the broth to splash onto the girl's dark green surcote.

"Oh, *Mon Dieu*," Serafina yelped, "I bought this only yesterday at the market."

"Meg," Gerard shouted, "you've ruined Serafina's fine dress."

"I thought she needed to nibble on something more hardy than your ear," Meg spit in return.

Gerard borrowed a cloth from the tavernkeeper and wiped at the wet spot which blossomed in the valley between Serafina's legs. She smiled and murmured something about his kindness.

I turned my attention to Robertus, thinking it time to focus on Halybutte's death. "You and your group seemed to mysteriously disappear today, once Halybutte grew ill."

"Nothing mysterious about it. The crowd was unruly. I feared for the lives of my players."

"You didn't show the same concern for Halybutte."

Robertus came halfway off the bench. "What are you getting at? So the dwarf had a fit of falling sickness. It happens. What of it?"

"Surely you know."

"No, I do not and I'm tiring of whatever game you're playing at."

I paused and stared at each one of the players, including Robertus. "Halybutte is dead."

All seemed to register shock, but then again these were seasoned actors used to playing out emotions on the stage. I tried a second surprise.

"And so is Pettipaw."

That got their attention. Immediately their hands flew to their mouths and the women began to cry. Robertus, whose chin was quivering, shook his head as if in disbelief.

"How?" he asked.

"The same way Halybutte died. Poison."

"Poison?"

Everyone began talking at once, but I made a motion to quiet them. No need to let the entire tavern—and thus the entire town—know what I suspected.

Robertus lowered his voice. "What kind was it?"

"Why don't you tell me?"

"How should I know what poison was adminstered? And why do you keep talking to me as if I am suspected of such a heinous crime? We may have differences of opinions about medicine, William, but I assure you I am not a murderer. A scalawag, charlatan, purveyor of rubbish to the gullible, yes, but not a murderer."

I walked past Robertus to the players at the other table and held each of them in my gaze. The husband and wife who pretended to drink from the "wine" dropped their heads and suddenly found the tabletop fascinating.

"You two were the last to drink from the goblet before Halybutte, and yet here you are, still alive. How do you explain that?"

They shook their heads. "We don't know, sir," they said in unison.

The wife added, "I was the last, sir. And there weren't nothing in it but water and a little wine—from the sponge that Robertus drops in—to make it change color."

I could hear Gerard exclaim behind me, "So that's how it's done! A sponge soaked in wine and then dried, dropped in the water and *voila!*"

"Therefore the poison had to be dropped in the goblet after you drank from it."

"That's correct," Robertus said. "And I couldn't have done it because I was still before the crowd."

I pointed to the wife. "Well, perhaps she did it after she drank the water."

"No, sir!" she cried. "No such thing." She grasped her husband's shoulder and shook him. "Tell him, tell him. I couldn't 'ave done no such thing."

"No, sir, she didn't," the husband said. "And even so, why would she want to kill the dwarf? He was a prick most days, but that's no cause to kill 'em."

"And if anyone has a motive, it's *you*," Robertus chimed in.

"Me?" I asked, genuinely puzzled.

"Yes, I heard you arguing with Halybutte in the wagon. About being a heretic. Suppose you were afraid that Halybutte would denounce you to the bishop? That might be a reason to do away with him. I've heard the bishop's dungeons are dark and deep."

"That's ridiculous," I spat. "I don't fear the bishop any more that I feared Halybutte's so-called Hell."

"Master William," Meg hissed. "Be careful, sir."

Gerard joined in as well, apparently fearing for my corporeal being, if not my soul. "Father, sometimes you go too far. There are ears everywhere."

Robertus, not to be outdone, turned his attention to another suspect. "And what about Meg? Anyone could see she was jealous of Serafina."

Meg's eyes went wide with fear. She didn't deny Robertus's accusation, but asked, "What has that got to do with Halybutte?"

"And what of Serafina herself?" I shot back at him. "Perhaps the dwarf was not content to pretend to copulate with her. Perhaps he attempted it and she got rid of him."

It was Serafina's turn to shake with fear, but with a temper to match her ginger-hair, she jumped to her feet and screamed that I was a devil to think of such a thing.

"Well?" I was guessing, but her response made me wonder if there was truth to my suggestion.

"And suppose he did try? A good kick in the arse is all it took to make sure he never crawled in my bed again. When it came to that little runt, I could take care of myself. Besides, what about the little monkey? Why would I want to kill Pettipaw? I'd take him to bed sooner than Halybutte."

Everyone began to talk at once, suspicions being cast as wide as a net in a fish pond. I held up my hands to silence the babble of accusations.

"To answer your previous question, Robertus… the poison was *Aconitum napellus*. Aconite."

"Aconite?" The color drained from Robertus's face.

"Yes. And if I'm not mistaken, you were treating Halybutte for pain in his legs, isn't that correct?"

"Yes.

"With aconite?"

Robertus hesitated then dropped his voice. "Yes." The players gasped and he rushed to continue. "But only in very small quantitities. Sometimes as a tincture and sometimes mixed in water with ginger or licorice if the pain became too great… but just in the smallest of drops… and only from the root, never from the flower."

"Root, flower, stems… it doesn't matter," I explained. "All of the plant is deadly."

I turned to Gerard and Meg. As students of medicine, it was vital that they understand. "Aconite is known as monkshood because of the shape of the flower. It can reduce fever and pain, just as Robertus said. But while the advantages are great, the disadvantages are greater. It is deadly, even in small quantities. A fatal dose by mounth causes burning of the lips and tongue, just as Halybutte tried to tell us. Vomiting and salivation also occur—witness the foaming at the mouth. The heart beats without rhythm, shaking wildly. And paralysis sets in, affecting the arms and legs. Death can occur in minutes or days. A truly terrible way to die."

Robertus, ashen-faced, looked shaken but perplexed. "But how could he die from aconite in the goblet? I hadn't given him a dose today. And if no one here did it, then who?"

"Ah," I said, admittedly savoring the moment. "Perhaps it is better to say 'what' especially as creatures are not considered to have souls."

"What do you mean?"

"I believe that your closest companion, the creature who never left your side, watching you each day as you went about your business, including taking care of Halybutte, thought he would mimic your compassion by dropping the aconite into the goblet. He knew that Halybutte always drank the rest of the water in the goblet while you spoke to the crowd. He probably saw the dwarf rubbing his painful legs and did what you would do… administered the medicine to make the pain go away."

Robertus dropped his head in his hands. "And not knowing any better, he touched the aconite with his paws."

"Yes. Meg noticed when he climbed into her lap that he was unable to put his arms around her as he would have done. His hands were limp. In addition he licked the foam from Halybutte's lips, which was lethal."

"Poor little monkey," Meg whispered.

V

On the way back to my lodgings to retrieve my dissection tools, I encountered bands of craftsmen playing musical instruments and dancing. Masons, butchers, bakers, dyers, drapers, and blacksmiths, dressed in the finest livery, pounded drumskins and sang to announce their approach on the street. And then I remembered... it was St. Cecilia's day... a day to celebrate music and dance. Surely had the little dwarf lived, hewould have joined in, running between the musicians' legs, causing havoc and laughter.

Crossing the bridge to the tanners' quarter, I sighed and wondered if Halybutte knew what had killed him before he died. Did he know Pettipaw had given him the aconite-tainted drink? And did Pettipaw, seeing Halybutte fight for breath , know that he had killed him?

Once safely inside the shed, I sewed up the dwarf and dressed him. Tomorrow I would let it be known that he died of a paralysis of the heart, not uncommon in men of his stature whose organs are the size of a child's. No one would be the wiser because all accepted such a notion. Only Meg, Gerard, and I knew the truth. I would deliver his body to Robertus for burial at the Cemetiere de St. Marie in the morning.

It suddenly occurred to me... Halybutte's final whisper... could he have forgiven the little monkey? Halybutte's faith was strong. Certainly stronger than mine. I couldn't fault him for absolving his murderer.

I, on the other hand, looked forward to the first incision running from the monkey's neck to his tail. While I couldn't absolve him, I could listen to his confession... one organ at a time.

So ends the tale... Amen.

Our next tale returns to this country and a more recent age, the time of homesteaders attempting to tame a wild and unforgiving land. A young girl named Sookie learns several lessons about life and death over the course of the seasons.

Ms Miller is the author of the Frankie MacFarlane, Geologist, mysteries. Her most recent novel, Chasm, was recently released from the Texas Tech University Press.

Bury the Secrets Deep

by Susan Cummins Miller

"All families have secrets, things they don't share with the neighbors," Pa said, as we put the shovels away in the barn.

I read the warning behind the words. But I was a questioning child, for better or worse, usually the latter. "The circuit preacher says, God knows everything, even our thoughts," I said. "So is anything really hidden?"

Pa rinsed his hands in the wash bucket. The water turned brown, but grit still outlined his fingernails and clung to the grooves in his skin. He grabbed a stiff brush and tried again, saying, "God keeps secrets too, Sooki."

I puzzled on that for a moment, standing in a patch of sunlight that carried little warmth. "Like, um, what happens next?"

"And why we're here in the first place. There's gotta be a reason."

"Even for the Decker boys?"

Pa's face got dark, reminding me of the shadow crawling across the moon two nights ago. He threw the brush in the corner, stepped out of the barn, and spit in the wet dirt of the yard, leaving the question hanging, leaving me to work things out on my own.

That eclipse had brought things to a head. Ten hours after the moon reappeared, my sister Acey went into labor. Couldn't be happenstance, Ma said as she started the owlshead stew. She used Granny Jenn's recipe, the one thickened with mesquite flour, and flavored with green chiles and chunks of prickly pear. The stew doesn't have any owl parts in it, head or otherwise, so while we were cutting up beef for the big cast-iron pot, I asked Ma about the name. She said her family had always served it on *Día de los Muertos*, the Day of the Dead. Young as I was, I knew that seeing an owl or hearing it's cry meant someone was going to die soon.

All morning I savored the aroma of cooking stew. But by the afternoon the smell was making me sick. Or maybe it was due to Acey's carrying on.

Town's far away—maybe twenty miles, if you draw a straight line across the caprock. But the dirt road zigzags like a lightning bolt around barb-wire fence lines, windrows, and arroyos, making it more like forty. Too far to go for a doctor, especially with a storm bearing down.

The clouds had arrived in the wee hours, pushed by a wind that didn't pause to say howdy. Never does, here on the Llano. It just drives on like a thirsty herd hell bent for the Pecos. But something stopped the clouds that morning. While I was weeding the kitchen garden and picking a few straggling beans for the stew, those clouds piled up, turning the color of green split peas. I knew what that meant.

When Acey started her moaning, I thought at first it was the wind, till I went inside to set the table for dinner. The storm hit an hour later, as Pa and my brother Ben headed back out to tend to the cattle. The wind drove the rain horizontal, and the cows naturally turned their rumps to it and went looking for a drier place to hunker down. That meant they huddled in the low places where the flashfloods could catch 'em.

I asked Pa if I could saddle up and go with him. The howling of the storm was easier on the ear than Anna-Christie's caterwauling. Pa patted my head and said maybe next year, when I'd turn twelve. I watched him and Ben ride off, wondering how many stupid cows they'd save, and how many the storm would take, and if we'd still have a ranch when the skies finally cleared.

I was almost done with the washing up when Ma called me into my bedroom. I'd never before seen a woman in labor. I was little when Ma lost the twins. After them, she was done with childbearing. I helped Pa birth calves and colts, but they never put up a fuss, at least not the way Acey did. It was enough to put me off the process entirely. Ma said I might change my mind when I was older.

I couldn't imagine changing my mind in the next three years. Acey was only fourteen, after all. But then, she didn't plan on having babies—at least, not before she found a husband. All that changed last winter, when she got cornered by the Decker boys. She was bringing in Bessie, the milk cow, from a patch of grass we'd found on the far side of Cemetery Hill.

Them Deckers left my sister there, more dead than alive. She crawled as far as the graveyard atop the hill, where the chinkapin oak grows. I found her just as the sun set, and hoisted her on the cow's back. Bessie shied at the blood smell. We started downhill, Bessie's bell swinging and clanging like the iron bells in Ben's favorite poem. Acey's groans fell into the rhythm, and I recited Poe's lines to drown her out and calm myself:

> *In the silence of the night,*
> *How we shiver with affright*
> *At the melancholy menace of their tone!*
> *For every sound that floats*
> *From the rust within their throats*
> *Is a groan...*

The trip home seemed to take forever, but it must have been worse for Acey. And for Pa. He carried her into the house, left her in Ma's care, then picked up his ax. Ben did, too. I heard them splitting wood for a time, and then nothing but silence. Ma said that sometimes men just have to be alone with their anger.

Acey didn't leave the house for weeks, except to go to the outhouse or work in the kitchen garden. And even then, Pa, Ben, and I had to build up the garden wall so no one could see her. It was stupid. Who'd see her? We don't have any neighbors closer than ten miles out.

I liked helping Pa build the wall. Being outdoors was like rock candy, hard and bright and sweet. In the house I had to share a room with Acey. Before the evil visited her, she was fun. She'd make up stories, and we'd act them out. Sometimes she'd read me to sleep. But when she woke up the day after the attack she asked me to nail a blanket over the bedroom window. After that, no light got in, no light got out.

That was the last favor Acey asked of me. When she found she was with child, she settled in, stolid as old Bessie, to wait for the day she could get rid of the thing growing in her belly. The "memory made flesh," Ma called it. Pa and Ben didn't talk about it at all.

The men were out with the cattle when the baby arrived. He had a crown of black hair, ten fingers and toes, and skin the blue of my sister's eyes—on account of the cord being tight-wrapped around his neck. Ma and I tried and tried to breathe life into him, until finally we were too tired to go on. I remember how quiet it was in that room. The only sounds were the wind shaking the rafters, the rain splattering against the windows, and the fire crackling under the owlshead stew.

Acey wouldn't even look at the baby. She just lay there, eyes closed, a little smile on her face. I'd forgotten what her smile looked like.

Ma wrapped the baby's body in a white blanket that had been mine when I was little. She ran her hands over the soft flannel, as if it were full of treasured memories. Tears seeped out of her eyes and ran down her cheeks to plop on the blanket. The last time I'd seen Ma cry was when I brought Acey home that winter night.

Ma held out the bundle to me. "Bury him," she said. "Bury him deep, Sooki."

"Where?" I'd never been asked to bury a body before.

"Next to the twins."

I did it right then, wanting to be out of that house, even in a storm. The rain had softened the ground a mite. I dug and dug and dug, shoveling out dirt, using a pail to scoop up water. It didn't seem right to bury someone in a muddy grave, but I did what I was told. I didn't want to go back inside to my mother's tears and my sister's smile.

But when I finished the job and dragged my wet body back to the house, my sister had stopped smiling. She was the color of parchment paper. Ma couldn't stop the bleeding. I didn't know bodies had so much blood. By four o'clock, Anna-Christie was gone. She'd whispered I love you to Ma and me, right there at the end, her voice hoarse and threadbare as the rag rug on the floor.

Ma prepared the body. I couldn't stand to stay inside another minute. I grabbed the breaker bar, a sledgehammer, gloves, and the shovel, and went out to start digging a bigger, deeper hole right next to the baby's plot. I needed the breaker bar to get through the caprock. I needed the storm to cover the sound of Ma's keening—and to wash away my tears. Thunderclaps and the ringing of hammer on breaker bar reminded me of ghouls tolling death knells on Poe's iron bells:

> *And the people—ah, the people—*
> *They that dwell up in the steeple,*
> *All Alone*
> *And who, tolling, tolling, tolling,*
> *In that muffled monotone,*
> *Feel a glory in so rolling*
> *On the human heart a stone…*

My heart surely had a stone on it, one big enough to press all the air out of my lungs. But I kept hammering and digging. The storm grew so fierce that only hanging onto the shovel kept me upright. I heard the arroyo rumbling with flood, rocks crashing and tumbling down the bed. If Pa and Ben hadn't found and driven the cows to high ground…

I was torn between wanting to help the living and preparing the grave for the dead. I kept thinking how Pa and Ben didn't even *know* about Acey or the baby boy, the one who was already in the ground—the one who hadn't lived long enough to be named.

A flash of lightning outlined Pa and Ben herding cows toward the hayfield. We'd finished haying last week, but hadn't yet had time to plow the stubble into the ground. If the cattle collected there, where there was grazing, Pa might have a chance to keep them from scattering again, keep them out of the arroyo.

The men circled the herd, cutting and darting after breakaways, bunching the cows tighter and tighter, until finally, the lead cow was too tuckered to bolt. By then I'd taken the hole down nearly six feet. I collapsed on the dirt pile and pulled off the gloves. Bloody blisters covered my palms. I hadn't felt a thing. My back, arms, and shoulders ached, too, and I was ravenous.

I gathered up my tools, thinking about that stew. The next clap of thunder came right with the lightning. My heart and body jolted something fierce, and everything went black for a minute. Maybe longer.

When I was conscious again, I found myself on my back, looking up into that old chinkapin oak. Half of it was on the ground. The scar was black and smoking. My palms, too.

"What am I gonna do with you?" Acey said. She was sitting above me on the low climbing branch she favored, dressed in her Sunday-go-to-meeting dress, swinging her legs, and smiling like that Cheshire cat in the Alice story. "You oughtta know better than to hold onto metal in a thunderstorm."

I tried to answer her but my throat was paralyzed, same as my body.

"You dug us nice resting places, Sooki. Real nice." Acey looked down at the bundle in her arms. She was cradling Baby No-Name, blanket and all. "He deserves a marker, don't you think? Your nephew. The first grandchild. None of this was his fault. You can name him Will, after Pa."

I managed a nod, which was a good sign, but she wasn't there to see it. I was alone with the rain hissing on the burned tree, the wind rattling the leaves, and an owl, hooting in the copse by the river. Acey never spoke to me again.

The storm moved away as slowly as strength returned to my arms and legs. The moon rose over the Llano and laid a path to my feet. When I sat up at last, the cows were black dots bedded down in the hayfield. I heard Pa's horse snicker as he and Ben crossed the arroyo. The flood had passed.

But that gullywasher unearthed secrets, too. This morning, checking on the herd, I found bones littering the slope below the hayfield. No skulls, but lots of human bones and tattered clothes. Insects and burrowing varmints had been at them. The leftovers were scattered from here to yonder by rillwash and coyotes.

I knew right then why Pa and Ben had gone out the night Acey got hurt. They tracked the Deckers down and made sure they couldn't hurt any other girl. Didn't bother to give 'em a proper burial, just put the bodies in a cut in the caprock and caved in the sides. They hadn't counted on the hundred-year-storm.

I rode home for Pa and Ben. My bandaged hands were too sore to dig any more graves. We bagged those bones, took them to the family cemetery, and buried them outside the fence. Unhallowed ground. No marker. Served them Decker boys right for what they did to Acey...

Pa came back into the barn and put a hand on my shoulder.

I stopped mucking out Bessie's stall and looked at him. "Does Ma know?"

"She's had enough sorrow for one lifetime, Sooki."

I put a finger to my lips. He nodded, accepting that as a promise. Family secrets would stay buried deep.

We lost a quarter of the herd in that storm, along with Anna-Christie and little Will. But not the ranch.

I kept that promise, too, till Ma, Pa, and Ben passed. Now, I take grandchildren up to the old oak and tell them the story, show them my scarred palms, and point out the names painted on the gravestones.

And I tell them how that day was the last time Ma or I tempted Fate by cooking owlshead stew.

Keeping with the frontier theme, a flatboat on the Mississippi provides the setting of our next story. A pair of young men learn that sandbars and submerged stumps are not the only dangers that lie waiting around a bend.

Mr. Lauderdale has had a life-long interest in the subject of this story, and he paints a compelling portrait with his words. This story was previously published in Lissette's Tales of the Imagination.

The Flatboat

by Kevin Lauderdale

"Abe, Abe! Wake up! There's someone on board!"

Abraham Lincoln opened his eyes. It was dark as pitch inside their flatboat's little cabin. Each of its four walls had a small hole that served as a window, and one of the walls had a large hole for a door. Through all of them Lincoln saw only darkness.

"It's the middle of the night, Allen," Abe muttered.

"I heard some rustling noises," said Allen Gentry, trying to whisper. "I think there's—Look!" Through the window at the far end of the cabin Abe saw something—someone move.

Abe shook his head to clear his mind, nodded, and then pointed towards the door. The two nineteen-year-olds crawled out of the cabin on their knees, their buckskin breeches sliding across the wooden deck.

The flatboat was built of new poplar, and as they crept, its warm smell rose up from the deck. The boat was essentially a giant raft with a knee-high wall running all the way around, and the shelter at one end. The wall was there to keep the many barrels of all sizes they carried from falling into the river. On other flatboats, it also would have served to corral animals.

Outside, the night was partially illuminated by a half moon. Cottonwood and cypress trees dripped with Spanish moss. The boat traveled solely at the mercy of the river's current, relying on Abe and Allen to steer her away from snags, sandbars, and occasional thick tree roots that played havoc with travel on the Mississippi River. As they had every night, they had moored the flatboat to the riverbank, tying her to two trees. The necessity of rest after a hard day's steering aside, only a fool would travel the river when he couldn't see what was ahead of him.

There was nobody else with them at the stern of the boat. Abe raised himself to his full six-foot four-inch height and looked over the shelter's roof. At the boat's bow a handful of Negros in tattered clothes were pulling at the ropes and trying to tip over the larger barrels in order to roll them onto land. He saw four aboard and another three on the land, arms outstretched, ready to receive the goods.

Looters! Trying to steal their cargo of pork, tobacco, corn, and sugar.

The deck of the flatboat wasn't very large. The miniature plank wood cabin that was their shelter was barely big enough to contain Abe when he lay down inside it. The whole boat was only "threescore and five by sixteen," as Allen's father, and Abe's boss, James Gentry had said.

The robbers didn't appear to have weapons, but one was attempting to cut through a rope with a sharp rock. Abe and Allen didn't have guns, but they had a good set of knives that they used to gut fish and cut salted pork. Unfortunately, those were sitting in a box at the boat's bow, right at the feet of the raiders.

With his long, brawny build, Abe was the best wrestler in Spencer County, but he couldn't tackle seven—or even three or four, once he and Allen divided the band. Allen wasn't quite as brawny as Abe, nor anywhere near as tall, but he could probably account for himself well enough. All they needed were weapons.

Abe looked around for something, anything. Behind him was the thirty-foot oar they steered with, but that weighed a good three hundred pounds. Even he couldn't wield that. But just a few feet away lay two smaller oars they used to take them in and out of the river's flow. A good six feet long and cut from stout oak, they would make formidable clubs. Abe pointed, and they each grabbed one. Allen went starboard. Abe went down the port side, creeping all the way. He carefully stuck his head around the cabin's wall.

The men worked without speaking, moving carefully and quietly.

"Blazes take you!" yelled Allen as he sprang out from his side of the cabin, swinging his oar. The men all roared something that Abe didn't understand. Allen's oar made contact with the nearest man's chest, and he collapsed on the deck. The three men on shore turned and started running into the dense swampland, while the two nearest Abe lunged at him. He turned his oar horizontally. That deflected one of them, but the other, a man nearly as tall as Abe, rushed past him and slashed into his forehead with the pointed rock.

"Blast!" shouted Abe, feeling the jagged, hot shot of pain. He turned to face his attacker and was pummeled in the back by the other. Abe crashed to the deck but quickly turned himself right side up.

The man with the rock moved to leap onto Abe, who instinctively used a wrestling move. He put his feet up, caught the robber, and then rolled backwards pitching the man back over his head. His fellow raider gave him a hand up, and they too made for the shore.

Rounding the cabin walls again, Abe saw that Allen and remaining would-be pirate were trading punches.

Abe grabbed the man's arms from behind and locked them behind his back. "Off!" he yelled, turning and all but throwing the man ashore.

"Get the guns!" shouted Allen.

Guns? Allen knew they didn't—

Suddenly, the man who Allen had first hit with his oar was on his feet, turned, and jumped back to the shore, joining his comrades. Oars and fists were one thing, but the threat of guns was another altogether. The men fled into the darkness.

Maybe that was the end of a simple crime of opportunity, or maybe they'd be back armed. In any case, it was time to put as much distance as possible between their flatboat and the thieves.

Abe and Allen crouched, hands on their knees taking deep breaths.

"Cut the cables," said Abe, reaching down and opening a knee-high pine box. He pulled out two knives and gave one to Allen, who quickly made it to the opposite end of the boat.

Allen hacked at his rope while Abe did the same. In seconds the frayed ends of the lines fell to the deck.

Using his oar, Abe pushed against the shore with all his might. Allen did likewise, though to less effect. Still, it was enough to get them out of leaping distance from the riverbank. They moved to the center of the flatboat and within minutes had negotiated it into the middle of the Mississippi, where it began moving down-river.

At night, the Mississippi's four- or five-mile-an-hour flow was undisturbed by other boats, but the dark made sandbars and other river snags nearly impossible to see. Allen lit a lantern. It wasn't much help, but it was something.

"We'll just trust to Providence for a few minutes to get us a little further away," said Abe, "and then we'll tie ourselves to the other side of the river. Somehow I don't think they have a boat."

"What do ya' reckon, runaway slaves, most likely?" asked Allen, joining Abe in the stern where Abe steered.

"I can scarcely credit it," said Abe. Never before during the nearly three months, and more than one thousand miles, that he and Allen had been steering the flatboat from Indiana down towards New Orleans, had anyone tried to loot them. "They must have been mighty desperate."

"Yeah, I guess so," said Allen.

Neither of them had ever seen a slave—escaped or otherwise—before. Indiana was a free state. Abe wondered if the robbers had been trying to get there or somewhere else free. Then he wondered if any of the politicians in Louisiana who favored slavery had ever tried it themselves.

Suddenly he felt sorry for the men who had attacked them. They were Negroes, but they could just as easily have been white. But for the accident of Lincoln's birth, he could have been one of them. And but for his father owning a tiny piece of land, an old horse, and a worn plow, he practically was one of them. The poor and the desperate came in all colors. You would have to be pretty desperate to raid a flatboat. The pork might have fed all of them for a few days, but if they wanted to sell the tobacco, they would have had to drag the bales some distance to the nearest town. And what would anyone who didn't run a general store do with a barrel of sugar?

"Here," Allen handed him a bandana. "You took a mighty knock to your forehead there, just above your right eye."

Abe wiped his head. "This too shall pass away," he said.

"I dunno about that. I think it's gonna leave a scar."

"Well, it can't be any worse than what Nature's already graced me with," said Abe with a chuckle. "Might even be an improvement."

"Any luck with that fishing line yet?" asked Abe.

He was sprawled out on the flat roof of the boat's cabin reading while Allen steered the great oar behind him. The work was so demanding on their muscles that they took turns, working in one-hour shifts. Both of them ached from last night's fight, making the duty particularly unpleasant. Allen had drawn the short straw; the first shift.

Allen looked down over his shoulder and took his corncob pipe out of his mouth. "Doesn't look like it. Not a bite."

Abe sighed. He was getting tired of the hardtack and salted meat they had brought as provisions, and he could sure do with some catfish. The Mississippi was supposed to be teaming with them around these parts, but they hadn't caught any in three days. Abe wondered if had something to do with how close they were getting to New Orleans. The bigger the city, the more water traffic he saw. Maybe all the flatboats, not to mention the paddle-wheel steamboats, were stirring up the water and disturbing the fish. They were just a little past Baton Rouge now, which meant they were less than one hundred miles, only a couple of days, away from their final destination.

Abe looked up and down the river. This was a particularly twisty part of the Mississippi, and as it happened there weren't any other boats around in the small section he could see.

"How much longer?" asked Allen.

Abe looked at the white-faced pocket watch Allen's father had provided them with. "You've got another fifteen minutes."

"Well, you could do something else besides lay around reading, you know."

"Funny thing," said Abe, "my father taught me to work, but he never taught me to love it." He laughed. All the days he had spent in an actual classroom didn't even total a year, but he'd developed a powerful love of reading. His father didn't approve of it, bristling whenever he saw Abe reading while taking a break from his chores, and even once while plowing a field, a book propped up on the horse's collar.

Allen grunted. "What are you reading anyway?"

"*Aesop's Fables.*"

"Still? You were working on that a month ago."

"Not still, again," said Abe. "There was only room for a couple of my books aboard. And what have I told you a dozen times?"

"'The things I want to know are in books,'" said Allen in a suitably high-pitched imitation of his friend. 'My best friend is the man who'll get me a book I ain't read.'"

Lincoln laughed again.

As they made their way down the Sugar Coast of the Mississippi, they had done a little trading here and there, picking up some fresh fruit and fowl, but they had yet to encounter anyone with a spare book to trade. Abe was almost ready to tackle *Robinson Crusoe* for the third time on this voyage.

"Ahoy the flatboat!" came a call from the nearby shore. Abe and Allen turned. Where the river was slower and narrower, they were often greeted by folks on the bank. The caller was a man in a top hat and cutaway coat.

"Ahoy the land!" called Abe. "What town is this?"

"Bayou Goula!" The man continued to call through cupped hands. "Are you bound for New Orleans? Will you take a passenger there?"

Allen said, "Grab an oar, Abe, I'm steering us over."

"We're not really fixed for passengers," said Abe, reluctantly sliding off the roof. Allen's father hadn't specifically proscribed the boys taking on passengers, but he specifically told Abe that he wanted him to accompany Allen because he trusted him.

"Honest Abe," Mr. Gentry had taken to calling him, and Abe knew that meant not just that he himself wouldn't kill Allen and make off with the bacon, sugar, and corn aboard, but that he would exercise everyday good judgment, something the impetuous Allen sometimes lacked. Also, Abe had experience running a boat. He'd made a few dollars in his day ferrying people out to steamboats from the banks of the Ohio River. But he and Allen had not taken on passengers before.

Allen leaned towards Abe. "I know you're still stinging from last night," he said in a low voice, as he pushed and rowed, "but there's all the world of difference between handful of escaped slaves and one, well, obviously not an escaped slave."

Abe leaned into his oar. He wasn't sure. In at least two of Shakespeare's plays the Bard had warned against judging by appearances. Just because the man on the bank was white didn't mean a thing. So were those "half-horse, half-alligator men," Abe heard about on the river, rowdies like Mike Fink, who was so mean he had once set his own wife on fire for looking at another man. The sort of men who might try to loot them. Though, admittedly, that would be more difficult on the water than when moored.

"There's only one of him and two of us," said Allen. Looking Abe up and down to indicate Lincoln's tall stature, he added, "Two and a half, really."

Abe grinned. "All right."

Now that they were closer, Abe could see that the man's coat and shirt were rich and lustrous, with shiny buttons and deep greens and reds. He looked to be about 40 years old, with red hair and whiskers.

"Thanks for stopping, lads. I'm Avery Humphrey of New Orleans. I'm a lawyer down there." He reached into a pants pocket and pulled out four silver half-dollars that gleamed in the sunlight. "Will you take two dollars for my fare?"

Two dollars! A dollar each! Along with their fare back on a steamer, Allen's father was paying them eight dollars a month to steer his goods down to New Orleans. That was just a little more than twenty-five cents a day, which was what Abe's father hired him out for sometimes to butcher hogs or split logs into fence rails.

It was adding up to a full, three-month trip, but that twenty-four dollars wouldn't stay in Abe's pocket very long. Like nearly everything he earned, it would go to his father, Thomas, when he got home. But maybe he could spend that extra dollar on a book or two in New Orleans.

Abe nodded to Allen.

"Agreed then." Allen handed Abe his corncob pipe, and used both hands to help Humphrey aboard. "I'm Allen Gentry and this is Abe Lincoln, out of Little Pigeon Creek, Indiana."

Abe, who had been holding the flatboat steady near the land, now pushed off. "Howdy," he said.

Humphrey nodded to both of them. "Your servant, lads," he said warmly, handing Allen the coins.

"Have you heard any new stories, Mr. Humphrey?" asked Lincoln, steering with his oar. This was a typical river greeting. News, stories, songs, and jokes were almost as valuable as gold on the river.

Humphrey sat down on a low barrel and said, "I heard a good one about a hotel-keeper over in St. Louis who boasted that he never had a death in his hotel. Whenever a guest was dying, he carried him out to die in the gutter." Allen slapped his leg and Abe chuckled. "Yourself?"

Abe stepped out of the way to let Allen take control of the main oar and said, "Back home there was a feller who killed his parents jus' so he could come into his inheritance early. When he was tried for the crime he begged the court for mercy saying he was, after all, an orphan."

Humphrey snorted a laugh and looked around. "You fellows havin' any luck with your fishin'?" he said, pointing to the lines.

"Not a bite in days," said Abe.

"Bad luck. You ever go ashore and hunt some turkey or duck?"

"No, said Allen, "no guns—"

"As I thought," said Humphrey with a smile as he pulled a pistol with a long, curved wooden handle out of his jacket. He aimed it at Abe's chest, but spoke to Allen. "I'll take my two dollars back, boy, and then let's move over to that shore yonder." He pointed to the starboard riverbank with his chin.

"Never," said Abe. "I won't allow it." This would not happen. He had not come all this way only to lose everything this close to their goal.

Humphrey kept his pistol level. "You won't?" He laughed coldly. "I fought side by side with Old Hickory at the Battle of New Orleans. Don't test me, boy."

"Before I let you take this boat," said Abe, "I'll… I'll… blow it up first!" Where had that thought come from? Abe thought he'd better back it up with the strongest words he knew. Cussing usually reinforced things nicely. "I'll blow us all to Hell!"

Humphrey snorted. "With what? Ain't no gun powder aboard. I can see all you got is general mercantile."

"With," Abe looked around. There was the perfect barrel. He risked one long step away from Humphrey towards a barrel the size of a large piglet. Humphrey's gun stayed trained on Abe as he swept the barrel from the deck with one hand and held it up near Allen's still-smoking corncob pipe, which he still held. "With this *bauxite!*"

"Huh?"

Abe barely remembered where he had first heard that word. It was something they had discovered in France a couple of years back. It wasn't any kind of explosive at all. It was a rock, and they were extracting something from it. But it was a big deal now because now they had found it in Georgia, Alabama and Arkansas. He'd read about it in a newspaper he'd borrowed from a neighbor.

"What exactly is that?" Humphrey asked a little warily.

"Don't you know?" Abe feigned surprise. Because of his long face, he knew that when he opened his eyes wide, the effect was practically doubled. And twice as convincing.

Humphrey just scratched his chin and raised his gun, which had dipped a little, back up so it was level with Abe's chest.

Abe thought quickly. "It's only the biggest explosive known to man. Forget gunpowder. This stuff is ten times as powerful." He turned to Allen. "Right, Allen?"

"Oh, yeah. At least," replied Allen lamely, both hands on the oar and turning his head back and forth from the river to his friend. Abe knew he couldn't rely on Allen to come to his aid. If he didn't keep the boat safe, they really could be dashed to bits. If only some other boat would come by. But there was no one else within sight.

Abe said, "We're taking it down to New Orleans for mining."

"Lemme see," said Humphrey, stepping forward.

Lincoln held the barrel closer to him and waved the pipe threateningly over it. "Any nearer and I'll set it off."

Humphrey stopped. "You wouldn't dare." He gave half-hearted laugh. "You wouldn't kill yourself and your friend over these groceries."

Allen said, "Ain'tcha never heard of 'Honest' Abe Lincoln, mister? My friend here once worked a week to replace a book that got ruined by rainwater. He'd rather sink with honor than let a thief take his cargo."

Good work, Allen, thought Abe. Of course Allen knew that there wasn't any bauxite—whatever that was—aboard. But he almost sounded convinced himself.

"In fact," Allen continued, "so would I. This is my father's cargo. I'd rather go to tarnation than face him having lost it all."

Fine, Allen, thought Abe, but don't lay it on too thick.

Allen was more used to lying than Abe.

Abe loved to tell stories and was pretty good at making up songs and jokes. He wasn't above stretching absurdities even further than some of the more colorful anecdotes in *Quinn's Jests*. But telling an out-and-out lie was a whole different matter.

Part of him thought that it would serve him right if this watery highwayman didn't believe his lies. Abe's favorite parts of Reverend Weems' *The Life of Washington* were the early pages, where Washington's father took him into his arms for not lying about cutting down one of his Pa's cherry trees with a hatchet. Particularly interesting was how the elder Washington had said that parents might actually force their children to lie by punishing them for every trespass.

Abe planned to practice a little charity with his children. Likewise, he hoped the Almighty would forgive these lies, considering the circumstances.

Abe dropped the pipe and thrust the barrel at Humphrey's head. Humphrey, who most likely thought it was going to explode on impact, dropped his gun, screamed, and held up his hands to protect his face. The barrel crashed against his sleeves and bounced onto the deck, remaining intact.

Abe dove for the gun, grabbed it, and looked up at Humphrey's face from the deck. "'Those who live by the sword shall die by the sword'," said Abe as he slowly stood up, never taking his eyes from Humphrey's.

"Not hardly, boy," said Humphrey with a smile. "You see, that gun ain't got no bullets."

Abe pointed the gun skyward and pulled the trigger. A hollow click echoed through the air, and nothing else. He'd been bluffed! Abe tossed the pistol to the deck.

Humphrey lurched towards him, plowing headfirst into Abe. He destroyed his top hat, but managed to knock Abe flat on his back.

Abe was sore all over, but he felt he could still take Humphrey. Though he'd rather outsmart the robber and save himself the effort.

"Fine," said Abe, "you win. Take the bauxite! Just take it!"

Humphrey seemed to waver for a moment, as if he couldn't quite remember if the small barrel had been his original intention or not. He looked around, and Abe followed his glance. There was a huge, white, triple-deck steamer coming up the opposite side of the river as well as a flatboat nearing them. Morning traffic had picked up.

"Root!" yelled Allen, as he bore down on the oar, steering away from a huge gnarled root that rose up out of the river like a cat arching its back.

Seeing his chance, Humphrey scooped up the barrel and his gun, and then jumped overboard, landing on the root.

Abe, Allen, and the flatboat drifted on and away from the would-be looter.

"What was in that barrel anyway?" asked Allen.

"'Small-boned bacon.'"

"Herring?"

Abe nodded.

Allen nearly bent over laughing.

"Yep," said Abe. "That's a loss of a couple dollars."

"Not really," said Allen as he reached into his pocket. "We've still got Humphrey's two dollars." Abe grinned. "And even if we didn't, it would have been worth it."

"How so?"

"It's not every day I get to see 'Honest' Abe lie though his teeth and get bested in a wrestling match."

Historical Note: Lincoln and Gentry's flatboat voyage down the Mississippi in 1828, during which the fight at the start of this story took place and Lincoln received his scar, are historical fact. The rest of the story is fiction.

We now plunge back through time to medieval England. A headstrong young woman is determined to discover what has happened to her father, a knight at odds with a powerful lord. In her pursuit of the truth, will she find more than she bargained for?

Ms Sutorus is a self-described history geek and has the degree to prove it. She has been a finalist for numerous prizes, and her work has been published in numerous anthologies.

In The Midwife's Basket

by Caryn Studham Sutorus

Amaria stood in the doorway and watched her mother's delicate hands moving over the embroidery frame as if dancing, wood crackling in the fireplace the only sound in the small room, except at least three times a day when her mother would hear a door slam, and cry out, "Oh, it's William. Is he home?" And Amaria would have to reply that William still fought in Normandy with the king's brother. He would not be home for many more months. Her mother's face would fall, but then her eyes would glaze back over, and her fingers would resume their dance over the linen.

So Amaria had little fear her mother would question her absence for the afternoon. She crept into the kitchen, pulled on an old cloak, and slipped out of the house.

The rain alternated between mist and drizzle as she wandered the labyrinthine streets of Dirkby's village. In the seedier side of the town, she huddled under an overhang, taking refuge from the rain. An old man, swaying as he walked, barreled into a wooden door across the way, spilling tavern sounds and smells into the street until the door slammed behind him.

Amaria shuddered and continued on her way, skirting the muddy puddles dotting the roadway. In the second alley, she counted five stoops, took a deep breath, and marched up to the worn wooden door, glancing back down the alleyway before knocking. After a few minutes, the door creaked open. A wrinkled female face peeked out at her.

"What do you want?" The woman eyed Amaria with suspicion.

"I am looking for Roese, the midwife." Amaria gazed with trepidation over the woman's shoulder, into the darkened room beyond. The old woman beckoned her into the house. Its single room was cluttered, with a bed in one corner, a pitiful fire sputtering against the opposite wall, and shelves filled with different colored liquids and powders, and hung with drying leaves and herbs. A sweet odor clung to the rush mats, and Amaria realized that they were quite alone. This woman must be the infamous Roese, but she did not appear malevolent. She gestured for Amaria to sit on a wooden bench by the fire. Amaria silently complied, riveted by the unfamiliar surroundings.

"What brings a nice young lady like yourself to see Roese?" The woman studied Amaria, but it was not uncomfortable. Her gaze seemed to be diagnosing.

Amaria met her gaze. "I am the daughter of Sir Robert of Carswell."

Roese clucked with sympathy. "You wish me to help you find him?"

Amaria nodded. "I don't believe he would leave us. He would not leave my mother. She needs him. Something has happened, I am sure of it."

The old woman reached out her arms and motioned at the crowded shelves. "I make potions and draughts of every kind, but none possess the magic of finding people. I do not make magic, child. No one can do that."

"That is not why I have come." Amaria straightened up, her face burning. "I have reason to believe you can help me because of your connections. There are people who were angry at my father."

"Yes." Roese eased herself onto a bench in front of the fire. "Calling Lord Barwaithe a liar in public would be cause for death if your father was not of a privileged position. And the Abbot felt slighted by your father's accusations as well. Do you think there was retribution for his action against the new mill?"

"The new mill was a shameless plot by the Abbot and Lord Barwaithe to steal the livelihoods of my father's tenants. He was only defending his people."

"That may be so." Roese smoothed her coarse gown across her knees. "Lady Mathilde, the lord's wife, is my special client, and I purchase many herbs from the abbey's garden. You are a clever girl to come to me. Have you any other notions?"

Amaria took a deep breath, closing her eyes as she conjured up a dark figure in her mind. "There was a man who visited my father three times in the week before he disappeared. I never saw his face, and he never spoke, but just the same I would recognize his carriage and his walk."

Roese motioned at a basket in the corner. "Come then. I am bringing Lady Mathilde her sleeping draught this afternoon. You can come with me if you like, as my assistant. I will do the talking, you will do the listening."

Amaria's heart hammered as she picked up the basket with one hand and pulled the hood of her mantle lower with the other. "Do you think she will recognize me?"

"So what if she does? With your father gone and your only brother at war, it would be best for you to learn a useful trade."

The truth of the old midwife's words fell over Amaria's shoulders like a cloak of iron. Feeling small and trapped, she followed the woman out into the bleak afternoon.

Lord Barwaithe's manor house rose against the gray sky, a rambling structure of wood, recently added on with stone and fortified to resemble a miniature fortress. Even so, the gate was unguarded when the two women passed through. Amaria followed Roese up the wooden steps into a great hall, blazing with firelight but nearly empty, except for a couple of scraggly dogs fighting over a bone, and three children chasing each other across the hall.

"Where is everyone?" asked Amaria.

Roese pursed her lips and regarded the scene. "Perhaps they have left for a hunt. Lady Mathilde will have stayed back. Come this way."

She waved Amaria through a large doorway into the living quarters of the house. Climbing another staircase, lit by torches, brought them to a landing outside a wooden door. The midwife knocked, and the muffled sounds of a lady's voice replied.

"Please enter."

Amaria followed Roese in to an antechamber cluttered from floor to ceiling with colorful tapestries, cushions, and low tables. Lengths of cloth and skeins of thread stacked against the walls, and fire danced in the large hearth, warming the room with its orange glow. Lady Mathilde remained seated on a low bench, a tall but thin woman, wearing a fine violet wool gown crisscrossed by tooled leather belts. Her sleeves hung to the floor as she raised a hand in greeting.

"Roese, you are right on time." Her tinkling voice sang the words more than spoke them. Deep brown eyes gazed out at Amaria beneath her linen veil. Amaria's first instinct was to stand straighter, but then remembering her position, she hunched over instead, avoiding the lady's eyes.

"My Lady," said Roese, "I have brought your compound." She pulled out a sachet, bound with leather and a bottle.

"I'm afraid I require two this time."

"Two?" Roese shook her head and clucked. "I do not like to give you so much at once. This draught is dangerous."

Lady Mathilde frowned. "My husband has built up such tolerance over the years, I can no longer put him to sleep with one spoonful."

Amaria looked back and forth between the two women in alarm. Lady Mathilde drugged her husband? She observed the woman with wonder now, noting the strength in those bony fingers as she opened the extra sachet and retied the bundle. Lady Mathilde stood and crossed the room in three steps, her stride long to match her height. She pulled a bundle of coins from a carved chest and placed them in Roese's hand.

The lady met Amaria's eyes and reached out to pat her arm. "Dear child, I am sorry to hear of your father. He was a good man."

Amaria flushed. "Thank you, my lady, but I do not have any reason to believe he won't be home soon."

Lady Mathilde stepped back and shot a questioning glance at Roese, which served only to deepen Amaria's resolve to stay calm.

"Well then," said the midwife. "We shall leave you to your pursuits."

As Roese and Amaria moved toward the door, the midwife stopped short, her gaze fixed on something in the bedchamber beyond. Amaria stumbled into her, craning own neck to see what the midwife saw. But Lady Mathilde glided across the antechamber and stood in front of the door, blocking Amaria's view. She did not think it was her imagination that the lady paled as she met Roese's eyes. Did Lady Mathilde know her own husband was the chief suspect in the disappearance?

Before the door shut behind them, Roese called out, "Perhaps I shall come by in the morning?"

Lady Mathilde stayed the door with her hand. "That will not be necessary."

The midwife clucked and turned to face the lady. "Just the same, I shall be along this way. It would be no trouble to stop in, by myself." With a quick nod of her head, she turned back to the stairwell, leaving Amaria trailing behind her.

As they left the manor, the rain picked up, and Amaria huddled deeper into her reeking, thin cloak. "Why does she drug her husband?"

Roese sighed. "Her husband does not treat her well, especially when he is in his cups. For years I have been helping her calm him."

"So it is true that he is a violent man?"

The midwife nodded. "He is, indeed, a harsh and unfair man who turns to violence far too easily."

The dirt path that led from the Barwaithe manor to Dirksby Abbey was pocked and puddled, and Amaria's light slippers were soaked by the time they reached the wooden walls of the old abbey. Inside was a buzz of activity, as stone masons and builders scurried about, building a new chapel all in stone — new mouths to feed, new people to clothe, all of which led to the showdown over a new mill.

Roese pulled Amaria across the courtyard to smaller fenced area that contained the abbey's extensive vegetable and herb gardens. The old woman stopped to survey the rows of anise, chicory, fennel, and yarrow, her eyes satisfied at the bountiful harvest.

A young monk opened the door to the hut, bowing as he saw the women. "Greetings." His tonsured head bobbed up and down as he waved them into the shelter of the hut. The fragrance of drying herbs assaulted Amaria, and the smoke of a damp fireplace tickled her eyes, causing her to stumble into a rack of drying leaves.

"Sorry," she said, righting herself and re-spreading the basil leaves.

The young monk glared at her, his grey eyes sharp. "You are the Carswell girl, yes?"

She nodded. "I am."

Roese set down her basket and shook the raindrops from her mantle. "She is looking for information about her father. Perhaps you can help?"

"How would I know of her father's whereabouts?" The monk clasped his hands in front of his broad stomach, much too large for a man of his age.

"No reason, Brother Walf," said Roese. "You are close to the Abbott, and he was heard threatening her father. 'Tis no reflection on you, of course, but I thought, as a special favor, you might have information."

Walf cocked his head to the side, glancing back and forth between the fire and the door. "Young lady," he began, "your father was not popular with this abbey. In fact, the Abbott was set to excommunicate him for standing in the way of our mill."

"Excommunicate?" Amaria was aghast. "All he was doing was trying to preserve the ancient rights and customs of the Carswell people. We have a charter from the king."

"You have a charter from a dead king," interrupted the monk. "The Abbott is on his way now to the court of King Stephen to request a new charter."

"Oh and how convenient that my father is not around to contest his claim." Her anger boiled up and Amaria seethed, her hands clenched at her side.

Roese put a comforting arm around her. "It is indeed suspicious," she directed her words at Walf, "but our friendship has always been so dear to me, and your garden absolutely indispensable that I believe we can work through this mystery without anger."

Amaria turned away, cheeks burning as stared at the floor.

The monk walked over to the rack of drying herbs and began bundling them with twine. "As I said, the Abbott has already left to seek King Stephen's approval of the new mill."

"What day did he leave?" asked Amaria.

Walf looked up at the ceiling and bit his lip. "It was the day of that glorious sunrise, last Tuesday."

"My father disappeared on Tuesday." Fear and disgust pitted her stomach. "Is it possible he would have taken my father with him? Against his will?"

"Do you think your father would submit to that without a fight?"

Amaria shook her head, more bewildered than ever. She looked over at Roese. "Somebody had to have seen something, right?"

Roese had joined Brother Walf at the table where she counted out vials, trading for the raw materials on his rack. She smiled at Amaria. "Somebody always sees, my child. The truth always comes out."

Amaria watched Brother Walf closely but his face betrayed no emotion beyond annoyance.

"Perhaps if you pray for your father's sins…" he started as the women turned to the door.

Amaria shook her head. "Brother Walf, perhaps you would be so good to pray for him."

The rain had returned to a light mist as they headed back toward the village. If Roese noticed Amaria's tears, she did not say so.

"I believe that Brother Walf was telling the truth." Amaria pulled her cloak tighter.

Roese nodded. "I believe that as well."

"Then what next? Can we track down Lord Barwaithe?"

The old woman's voice lowered. "I would keep your voice down, my child. One cannot accuse the lord without evidence and support."

"But he's the only one left." Amaria flung out her arms, frustration building with each step.

"Open your mind wider," said Roese. "People are killed by all manner of bandit or robber on the road, even a wild animal might have found him, or he could have slipped in the river."

"He can swim," protested Amaria, but she knew Roese was right. Accidents happened. She could hear the rushing water of the nearby river as they neared the Carswell mill. "Shall we visit?"

Amaria barely heard the shouts of the miller's children as they played chase, so entranced was she by the magnificent movement of the great wooden wheel. The miller himself called out a greeting, pulling her out of her dark thoughts, centering her to their purpose.

"Miller," she said, "may I ask you a few questions?"

The miller motioned to one of his sons to watch the wheel and stepped outside to talk to the women. "How can I help you?"

"When was the last day you saw my father?"

Concern passed through the miller's warm blue eyes. "Ach, is he still missing, then? I'm sorry to say I haven't seen him since last Tuesday when they came by."

"They?" said Amaria. "He was with someone?"

The miller stroked his shaggy beard. "Yes, but the young man stayed by the roadside. I did not see who it was."

Amaria leaned forward, placing her hand on his arm. "It is so important for me to know who that man was."

"I have seen him about now and then." The miller shook his head. "But I do not know his name. He was about the same height as your father, but slight. He wore a fine mantle, but his head was always covered."

Amaria turned to Roese. "It is the same mystery man that I have seen. We must find out his identity." She turned back to the miller. "Where did they go when they left here?"

He waved toward the road to the village. It could have been anywhere — the Carswell House, the Barwaithe Manor, the Abbey… She sighed. The weight of her impossible task bowed her neck.

The miller's small voice pierced her clouds. "I'm very sorry, young lady, about your father."

She nodded her acknowledgement and allowed the midwife to guide her back toward the path to town.

"An inn, perhaps?" Roese said. "If there is a new young man in town, we could start checking at the inns."

By nightfall, a weary Amaria stumbled back to her house, grateful for the steadying arm of the old midwife.

"William? Is that William?"

She groaned at her mother's plaintive cry before answering. "No, Mother, it is just Amaria. William fights in Normandy still."

"Will you stay the night?" she asked Roese. "It is dark to travel back by yourself."

Roese smiled. "No one takes any care to disturb an old woman like me, but I should like to rest. Perhaps I will stay, but only until dawn. I have much to do on the morrow."

"Like visit Lady Mathilde again? May I not go with you?" Amaria sank onto the bench in front of the fire and pulled off her wet slippers as she regarded the old woman.

Roese stared into the flames, rubbing her arms. "I will go alone tomorrow morning, but I will visit you later in the day. If I learn anything new, you will know of it."

Amaria sighed and rubbed her forehead. The inns had been a waste of time. Dirksby was a small village. There were no new people. No one passing through had fit the description of Amaria's mystery man. She left Roese in front of the fire and entered her mother's solar, sitting beside her as she finished her work for the day.

When the tallow light faltered, Amaria walked her mother to the wide bed and laid her under its woven blanket, removing her own gown before climbing in with her. The rhythmic snoring cradled her tortured thoughts until she sank into sleep.

Screams woke her from a restless slumber. Light had barely begun seeping above the horizon when the shouts rang out. "It's the midwife!"

Amaria bolted out of bed, threw on her gown and rushed out the front door toward the small crowd at the end of the road. She stifled a cry, biting her fist as she looked down upon the sprawled form of Roese. The midwife's basket, overturned, lay just out of her reach, her mantle spread around her, not quite covering the red marks on her neck, as she gasped for breath, pale eyes bulging against her flushed features. Amaria sank to her knees, tears falling from her eyes as she pulled the old lady up into a seated position.

"What happened?" she whispered, rubbing Roese's back as the midwife wheezed and trembled in her arms, unable to speak.

Amaria scanned the crowd of shocked villagers, then turned to search the tree line. As the villagers began to rummage through Roese's basket, Amaria called them off. She crawled over and pulled it close to her, counting through the vials and bundles. Something was missing. But what was it? She rifled through the aromatic goods until a movement in the forest caught her eye.

Roese pulled at Amaria's arm, inclining her head toward the woods.

Amaria stood and dropped the basket. In the shelter of trees, dark cloth fluttered in the wind. Without thinking, she sprinted toward it, rushing through the damp fields as her gown swirled around her. She stopped and leaned against an oak tree, out of breath, scanning for another sign of life. Her heart pounded as she drank in deep breaths. A flapping sound at her left lured her deeper into the dark of the woods. And there, hanging on a tree branch, a muddy brown mantle swung in the breeze, empty. Amaria gasped, reaching out toward the abandoned cloak, hands shaking as she felt for the edge.

There was no one about. The empty forest hummed with the running of squirrels and buzzing of insects, but no human footsteps marred its peace, only Amaria's own heavy breathing. She pulled down the empty cloak. It was dry. Someone had just left it there, but she would have seen someone run out of the tree line, so she rushed deeper into the forest, looking for signs of life, for a path to follow.

She tried to control the speed of her breath and the tread of her slippers, silence and speed warring with one another. She hopped across a tiny creek, and skipped over a fallen log, following a path of broken twigs and matted weeds.

A blur of burgundy whizzed through the trees ahead. Amaria cried out and renewed her speed, now hearing the crash of underbrush as her mystery person ran away.

The height was as she remembered, the smooth gait was correct, but the clothing was all wrong. The stranger was not a young man after all. The person she chased through the wood wore a lady's gown. The figure ducked behind a tree and Amaria pulled up short.

"Who are you?" she called out. "I see you." Her heart pounded in her throat and she knelt down, pawing at the ground until she felt a broken stick. She brandished it in front of her, turning in a circle. "Come out."

The forest rumbled again as her mystery woman took off running back toward the road. Amaria cried out in frustration, leaping over logs and weaving through trees as she caught up. The woman looked back, her dark brown eyes filled with fear as Amaria jumped forward, tackling her to the ground. She groaned as their air left her lungs, then met the woman's wide eyes.

"Lady Mathilde?" she whispered. The scent of lavender and something deeper overpowered Amaria as she struggled against the agile older woman. Half a dozen vials had escaped from a sac around Lady Mathilde's waist, and she scrambled to reach for them.

"Get off me," Lady Mathilde cried.

Amaria brought her forearms to bear over the woman's arms, trapping her beneath her. "What were you doing in the woods? What did you do to Roese?"

"The old woman had no business asking after your father," she spat out, her face contorted with pain.

"My father? What does he have to do with this?" Amaria sat back and picked up a lavender vial.

Lady Mathilde snatched it back and wiped a stray hair from her face. Tears ran down her pale cheeks. "It was an accident."

"What?"

The world stopped around them, the birds silencing themselves and shushing the bees. Even the breeze slowed its whisper through the leaves. Amaria fought through the confused fog and pieced her words together. "You were the young man. You dressed like a man? But why? Why were you with my father?"

The pain radiating from Lady Mathilde's face answered her question all too clearly. Amaria gasped and shook her head.

"No. My father would never…"

"My husband would have killed him." Lady Mathilde closed her eyes. "It was the only way we could be together." She threw one of the vials against an oak tree, where it shattered into a thousand pieces. "Your father drank the wrong wine that night. He was not used to the draught, but my husband, he could drink four and feel no ill effects. He would just fall asleep and leave me free for a few hours, free from his evil words and hands."

Amaria's heart sank. The air thickened around her and all she could see in her mind was the figure of her father, walking carefree, next to the cloaked mystery man. Was he happy with her?

"You killed my father?" she whispered, tears falling now, soaking into her braids and wetting the collar of her gown.

Lady Mathilde covered her eyes with her hand and let her head fall back. "It was an accident. I would never have hurt him. I loved him."

The strangled cry that rose from Amaria's throat broke through the forest like a wild boar. She heaved her fist at Lady Mathilde again and again, gaining freedom with each thunk and groan.

"Enough!" In her struggle with Lady Mathilde, Amaria had missed the crunching of leaves and cracking of twigs as Roese, still wheezing, stumbled into the clearing. The midwife waved a trembling hand at Amaria. "Enough, child. Lady Mathilde will have many years to repent her sins."

Out of breath, Amaria staggered to her feet "You knew then? What did you see at Barwaithe Manor yesterday? Why did you not tell me?"

"I saw this." Roese held out the muddy brown mantle Amaria had seen hanging in the woods. "It seemed a bit out of place for a lady's dressing room." The midwife stepped closer to Lady Mathilde's cowering form. "I would not have exposed you, foolish lady. Who do you think they would have hanged for murder?" She held up her basket.

Amaria shook her head and pointed at the lady's bloody face, daring Roese to step any closer. "She must pay for her crime. She says my father loved her. Yet she poisoned him."

"But you heard her." Roese's voice radiated calm. "It was an accident. There will be no need to discuss it further. I do not wish to hang." The old woman crossed the clearing and picked up the stray vials of sleeping draught, shaking her head as she tucked them into her basket.

Lady Mathilde, gasping and sobbing, turned onto all fours and eased herself to standing. "Please, please. I would do anything to have him back. What can I do? What can I do?" She leaned against the tree, coursing tears leaving pale tracks down her bloodstained cheeks.

Breathless, Amaria stumbled back against another tree and raised her arms in grief. She gazed up at the sky, red streaks still glowing through the canopy of trees as the sun began its rise.

When she looked down, Lady Mathilde knelt at her feet and wrapped her arms around Amaria's legs.

The lady's eyes beseeched her. "He would not want us exposed. Please, do not besmirch his memory." She rose slowly, reaching out her arm and stroking Amaria's damp hair. "I will take care of you. He would want me to. Come back with me, and you will never have to worry about the future."

Amaria swallowed, finding it difficult to breathe as she searched the lady's wild eyes. She thought of her helpless mother, her absent brother, and the midwife's admonition that she learn a trade. The noises of the forest resumed around the trio, the chattering of squirrels and crunching of leaves making all of her thoughts difficult to focus on.

"Lord Barwaithe," said Roese, "Would he welcome her into your household? Should she not fear him?"

Lady Mathilde stepped back, a rueful smile creeping across her features. "No. She need not fear him. I will make certain of it."

Amaria creased her forehead, shaking her head in confusion. "But I thought he—"

"He will not be an accident." The lady spun around, holding her arms high as she let out a throaty chuckle.

The midwife pawed through her basket and pulled out two vials. "You will be needing these then." She handed them to Lady Mathilde and shot a warning glance at Amaria.

The girl's eyes widened, then narrowed as the wheels turned in her head. "Where is my father then? Take me to him."

Lady Mathilde shook her head. "He lies at the bottom of the river. No one will find him there."

She was wrong.

A week later, the bloated body of Amaria's father floated to the shore at the next village over. It was deemed an accident, mysterious only because the very next day, the bloated body of Lord Barwaithe also floated to shore. A mystery that baffled villagers even more was the strange pairing of the widow Barwaithe and Carswell's daughter. They lived together, with Amaria's vacant-eyed mother and the old midwife, in the Barwaithe manor house, running the old mill and the new mill, and running a side business in poison, so they say.

A luxury liner and the gilded mansions of New York City of the Jazz Age provide the setting for our next story. A refugee Russian countess feels safe at last among her new-found friends, but is she?

Ms Sutton is the author of the Newport Mysteries, novels set in Newport, Rhode Island, including Murder Stalks a Mansion, Gilded Death, and Keep My Secret.

The Empress's Pearls

by Anne-Marie Sutton

Natasha Telitsyn pulled the collar of her heavy sable coat close against her throat. The feel of the fur's familiar warmth caressing her skin flooded her head with memories. Memories she tried hard to push from her mind. It was no good remembering the past. It was gone forever. Sergei Vladimirovich was dead, along with her parents and her brothers. Everyone she loved had been killed in the Revolution. Was she lucky to have escaped? She had once thought so. But now, standing on the deck of the *Majestic* as it steamed away from the coast of France and into the dark Atlantic, she wondered. Five years had passed since those horrible months, and she couldn't yet go through a day without reliving them. The Bolsheviks hadn't murdered her body, but they had murdered her soul.

A figure stepped forward from the shadows.

"Countess?" the voice called and she turned toward the sound. It was one of the smartly dressed stewards who took such good care of the first class passengers. "You must be cold."

"Yes," she agreed, "I am. I should return to my cabin."

"We'll have a calm sea tonight. That helps for good sleeping."

Natasha nodded, but her thoughts for the night were uneasy. The dreams were waiting for her.

Lavinia Knox was settled in bed, a book in her hands, when Natasha returned to their stateroom. The young American wore a lilac bed jacket trimmed in lace, and her golden red hair, free of pins, draped beautifully around her shoulders.

"Natasha, darling. I was beginning to worry about you." Her bright blue eyes followed the slim dark-haired woman as she slipped off her fur and sat down at the dressing table. "Natasha, what's wrong? You're not still worried, are you? I thought I had convinced you that George can handle everything. My brother knows everyone in New York."

Natasha managed a weak smile. Living among the Russian exiles in Paris these last several years had been difficult. There were so many émigrés trying to make a living by any means, especially men who were only too happy to take advantage of a young Russian aristocrat without the protection of husband and family.

"You are too sweet to me, Lavinia, to take me to your home in New York. I don't know what I have done to deserve such kindness." Meeting Lavinia Knox at a soiree in Paris the previous month had changed the countess's very existence. The American heiress had immediately become her protector in society.

Countess Telitsyn picked up a small casket from the dressing table. The white enameled top of the delicate gold box was decorated with an image of the Winter Palace in St. Petersburg. She stroked the picture of the palace where the Emperor Nicholas and his family once lived. "And to give me this lovely box which reminds me always of home."

"I just wish you wouldn't use it for those awful sleeping powders," Lavinia said. "Once we get to New York, I hope you never need to take those things again."

———

A chauffeur-driven car met Lavinia Knox and her guest at the dock in New York City. From the back seat, Natasha watched the unfamiliar crowds and bustling traffic. She was amazed at how openly people stared into their big car, scrutinizing its occupants with frank and sometimes disdainful curiosity.

Lavinia showed no interest in what was going on outside the car's windows. "I can't wait for you to meet George," she said eagerly. "I'm betting he'll fall in love with you by the weekend." When Natasha looked startled, her friend exclaimed, "Don't be so worried, darling. My brother falls in love with every beautiful woman he meets!"

"He must be a man with great charm."

"Yes. So you must tease him. A real countess will be a feather in his cap."

———

The Knox home was an unassuming - to Natasha's eyes - brownstone on East 73rd Street, near the corner of Fifth Avenue. Accustomed to lavish palaces in old Russia, Natasha had expected her rich friend to live in a large mansion house surrounded by acres of parkland. Lavinia had pointed to where Central Park could be seen at the end of their block. But that was a public, people's park. Did the Knox family take their walks in such a place? Were they accompanied by servants? Natasha realized that she was going to have to get used to many new ways of doing things in America.

Her bedroom was on the third floor, a corner space with a large rounded window overlooking the street. The chauffeur brought up her luggage and Lavinia rang for a maid.

"I'll leave you alone for a while," Lavinia said as a hesitant pink-faced young woman in a maid's uniform entered the room. "George is at his club this afternoon, and I have a million things to do now that I'm back, after all these months abroad." Lavinia gestured to the maid. "Come on in, Bridget. Don't just stand there like a statue. Help Countess Telitsyn unpack."

Bridget scurried forward and Natasha handed her the luggage keys.

"Lie down and try to rest after you get settled in," Lavinia said. "We have cocktails in the drawing room at 7:30." She turned to the maid. "Bridget, be here at six to help Countess Telitsyn bathe and dress."

"Yes, Miss Lavinia," Bridget said, a definite Irish lilt in her voice. She had the two trunks opened and was reaching for the leather traveling bag.

"I will unpack that," Natasha said, moving quickly and placing a proprietary hand on the handle of the bag. "These are my private items."

"Yes, ma'am," Bridget said.

The fatigue of the long ocean voyage and the stress of her arrival in New York had made Natasha weary. After Bridget left, she took the gold box with the picture of the Winter Palace from her personal bag. The countess stared at it for several minutes before placing it carefully on her bedside table. As always, she ran her fingers across the surface as if she were saying good-by.

The pounding on the door was in her dream. Natasha could hear the voices in the corridor and the shouting.

"Wake up, Countess. We must get ready." The command was repeated over and over.

They must get ready. The soldiers were coming for the Imperial Family at four that afternoon, and everyone had to help with the packing. There was furniture and food and wine and so many household articles to be taken to the train, the family's destination still unknown. Only a few of the loyal servants and staff were to accompany them. Natasha had rushed to Empress Alexandra's boudoir where she found her and her four daughters furiously sewing jewelry into their corsets. Without a word Natasha set to work, the needle in her hand flying through the air as she grabbed diamonds, emeralds and rubies to insert into the fabric. Ropes of pearls lay on a table. The Grand Duchess Tatiana was threading them through her mother's undergarments. The Empress was crying.

"Countess, let me in." The knocking on the door had started again. "Please unlock the door."

Natasha cried out in her sleep. "No, no. Don't take the Empress."

With a start she sat up in bed, her heart pounding. Where was she? Her eyes fell on the gold box, and she knew that she was in the Knox house in New York City. She was alive, and everyone else was dead.

***

Lavinia was right. Her brother George was an attractive flirt. He mixed Natasha a cocktail despite her protestations that she didn't drink them. The martini was cool and stimulating, and she found she enjoyed its taste. But she would not be persuaded to have a second.

She was introduced to two fashionably dressed young couples, friends of Lavinia, and a distinguished older gentleman, Henry Janeway. At dinner, the women were curious about Natasha's background. They seemed not to know that there had been a revolution in Russia in 1917 and thus appeared to believe that she remained a countess in her home country. The men talked of money and Wall Street.

After dinner ended, Lavinia and the four young people began to make plans to go to a speakeasy. To Natasha's surprise, she was not asked to accompany them. After the revelers left, George invited her and Janeway into his study.

"Please sit down, Countess Telitsyn." George indicated one of the dark leather club chairs. Janeway remained standing.

George poured three snifters of cognac from a crystal decanter and handed them around. Feeling her nerves tightening, Natasha was glad for the drink. Her host sat down at the desk.

"I thought you would want to discuss this matter right away, Countess. Lavinia has explained your difficult financial situation." He gestured toward the other man. "That's why I've asked Henry to be here. He's an expert in jewels. An appraiser and also a dealer."

Natasha sipped the brandy.

"Countess? You do have the pearls with you? Lavinia said they never leave your side."

Natasha nodded.

"May we see them?"

"But first the story," Henry Janeway interrupted. It was the first time he had spoken. "These transactions are always better handled if I know the full history. The value in the market place can be so much greater."

"Ah, you are right, Henry," George said. "As always. Whoever will bid to buy these pearls will pay through the teeth to own a necklace which once hung around the neck of the murdered Tsarina of Russia."

Natasha shuddered, and George knew immediately that he had overstepped the bounds of good taste. He quickly apologized to Natasha, but added that what he had said was so unfortunately true, if poorly stated. Rich Americans were suckers for royalty. And this time George was careful not to say *dead* royalty.

———————————

As Natasha began her story, George refilled her glass. The countess spoke slowly as she described that last day at Alexander Palace and the frenzy of getting the Imperial Family ready to leave Tsarskoe Selo, on their train journey to Siberia.

"No one knew where they were going," she said tightly. "Nor if we would ever see them again." She paused. "And, of course, we didn't. They were murdered a year later."

"And when did Empress Alexandra give you the pearls?" Henry asked. "She did give you the pearls?"

"Oh, yes," Natasha said. "There was so much jewelry. Jewels were her favorite things. Everything was kept in large wooden cases that always traveled with her. That day..." her voice trailed off.

"It must have been difficult," George encouraged.

Natasha was staring down at the amber liquid in her glass as if she could look back in time.

"That last day," she continued, her voice becoming stronger, "her four daughters took what they could from the cases. But they couldn't hide everything on their persons. The Empress had a beautiful pearl necklace with three strands. She was often photographed wearing it."

Henry, looking pleased, met George's eyes.

"The clasp was made with diamonds in the shape of a large bow. I watched her hold the necklace and sigh. I think she knew she would never wear it again."

"So she gave it to you," Henry repeated impatiently. "It is important to establish the provenance for its sale."

"The Empress wanted me to have something to remember her by. I had been her lady-in-waiting since the outbreak of the Great War. My husband Sergei was a minister in the war office and stayed at the army's headquarters at the front."

Natasha reached into her handbag and slowly removed a leather pouch. She loosened its strap and shook a huge jumble of threaded pearls onto her lap. Taking hold of the necklace's glittering diamond clasp, the countess easily fastened the three ropes of pearls around her own neck. The longest strand hung down to her small waist.

"The necklace of Alexandra Feodorovna Romanova," she said with pride.

George whistled in admiration, while Henry squinted at the voluminous gold-hued pearls.

"They are beautiful, Countess," George said while Janeway took a magnifying glass from his pocket.

Natasha removed the pearls and handed them to him for a more thorough examination. The decision to part with them had been a hard one to make, but Natasha knew the Empress would have understood her need to survive.

At last Janeway looked up. There was a frown on his face, his jaw set in a scowl.

"What's the matter, Henry?" George asked.

"I think Countess Telitsyn is having a pretty game with us."

Natasha was confused. Perhaps she didn't fully understand the English language. "What do you mean, Mr. Janeway? This game?"

Janeway threw the necklace onto George's desk. "This necklace, which you say once belonged to the late Empress Alexandra."

"Yes. It did."

"No it did not. These pearls are fakes, and the diamonds are paste."

"That is not true," she said.

But in her mind Natasha knew it could be. Grigori Ivanovich. Against her will, he had taken the necklace to a Paris jeweler to be valued a few months ago. When Grigori returned he had not pressured her to sell it. Now she knew why.

Natasha felt dizzy. Her head was swimming, and her entire body suddenly felt leaden. She leaned forward in her chair. George Knox was immediately onto his feet, running toward the corridor.

"Bridget, Bridget," he shouted. "Oh, where is that damn girl?"

Sgt. Daniel O'Connell had been with the New York City Police Department for fourteen years. A thin, energetic man, he had a reputation as a problem solver. Sitting in the parlor of the Knox house on East 73rd Street, listening to Mr. George Knox explain the finding of his new house guest dead in her bed that afternoon was not engaging the detective's usual interest.

"It's such a tragedy," Knox said. "Countess Telitsyn sailed from Paris with my sister on the *Majestic*. They only arrived yesterday. Lavinia was quite keen to have her staying with us." He smiled slightly. "I'm afraid my sister is a bit of a snob, and well, a real Russian countess. You can imagine the social value of that." O'Connell made no remark, and George laughed nervously. "I'm sorry. That didn't sound the way it should have."

"Can we get back to the tragedy as you call it? Who found the body?"

"That's just it. We all did."

O'Connell raised his eyebrows at this. Now he was interested. "Can you explain what you mean, Mr. Knox?"

"We had people in for dinner last night, as I said, to begin to introduce her around. After dinner, Lavinia and several of the young guests went out, but the countess didn't want to go. I invited her into my study for a nightcap, and she accepted. But I could see that she was extremely tired, and I had Bridget, one of our maids, take her up to bed. That is the last I saw of her."

"Until this afternoon."

"Yes. Bridget took some tea to her bedroom this morning, and the door was locked. When she knocked, there was no answer. At first, it didn't seem strange. According to Bridget, the countess had locked her door yesterday afternoon while she was resting. I expect it is because of what happened to her in Russia. She lived through the Revolution and her family experienced much violence. Locking the door no doubt made her feel safe while she slept."

The police detective nodded. "But what made you decide to break down the door?"

"My sister became alarmed when Countess Telitsyn didn't appear for lunch. That's when she told me that the countess had some sleeping powders that she always took at night. Lavinia insisted she had a bad feeling. At first, I disagreed with her. I mean, how would we look, breaking into this woman's room if she were merely sleeping?"

"You had no key to open the door?"

"I wish we did. Frankly, neither my sister nor I ever lock our bedroom doors. It's so inconvenient for the servants. I wasn't even aware that the door to the countess's room had a key, but apparently it did have an old one, and Countess Telitsyn used it."

"And you are convinced she took these sleeping powders to end her life?"

"Lavinia said she had a full box of them in their cabin on the ship crossing the Atlantic." George Knox shifted in his chair. "Do you wish to speak to my sister? And to the maid, Bridget? They are both in the house."

"Yes," O'Connell said. "If Miss Knox can see me now. And, I would appreciate if you would give me a list of the names and addresses of your dinner guests."

"Why do you think Countess Telitsyn committed suicide, Miss Knox?" the detective asked, wasting no time getting to the point.

"Oh, why didn't I take those powders away from her? This is all my fault." Lavinia took out a handkerchief and dabbed at her eyes. "I thought coming here, making a new start in New York would be just what she needed to forget about the horrible things that happened to her in Russia. I should have realized how desperate she was."

"You met her in Paris, I believe?"

"Yes, the city is full of Russian émigrés. Princes, princesses, grand dukes, you name it." She looked at him with her eyes wide. "Would you believe some of them are waiters in restaurants?"

"Do you know where Countess Telitsyn got her income?"

"Natasha had been selling her jewels. They had been her mother's, and she was able to smuggle them out of Russia when she escaped. In Paris she sold the jewelry. But her money was running out."

"You mentioned a new start." O'Connell looked around the room. "Did you mean to give her a home here? What were her plans?"

"I really don't know," Lavinia said, shaking her head. "We hadn't time to discuss it. I believed that once she was here, things would work out. She was so lovely, so kind. Perhaps she would marry again." She began to cry. "She had become my friend. I wanted to help her."

Sgt. O'Connell ran his fingers over the splintered wood of the doorframe of Natasha Telitsyn's empty bedroom. Slowly he approached the bed where disheveled linen and a pillow lay on the floor.

"Well, Danny," he said out loud, "what happened here? Why did Her Highness end it all when she had some rich friends willing to take her in?"

O'Connell pulled on gloves and examined the gold box. It was a pretty piece and worth some money. He opened it carefully. Small scraps of paper with the texture and shape used in doctors' compounds filled the cavity. Poking to the bottom revealed no trace of any powders. Only the paper debris remained. The box would have to be tested for fingerprints.

"Sir," a small voice said. The policeman turned and saw a slight girl of seventeen or eighteen standing in the doorway. "Miss Lavinia said you be wanting to see me."

"You are Bridget?" The girl nodded, and he asked her to come into the room. "Tell me about last night, Bridget," he said, giving her an encouraging smile. "I understand you brought Countess Telitsyn up to bed."

"Yes, sir."

"And how did she seem?"

"I don't understand, sir."

"The Countess. Was she tired? What did she say?"

"I tink she was upset, sir." Like most native Irish speakers Bridget didn't pronounced the <u>th</u> sound.

"Tell me about that."

"She told me to leave, not to be helping her undress."

"And did you? Leave right away?"

"I did, sir."

O'Connell narrowed his eyes and looked at the door again. "Did you see her after she died?"

"Oh, yes, sir. I come with Baines, ta chauffeur. Mr. George wanted him to open her door. I be sent to get him."

"And Miss Lavinia was waiting here with Mr. George?"

"Yes, sir. She liked Countess."

"How do you know?"

Bridget pointed to the box still in the detective's hand. "She give tat to her."

"This box was a present from Miss Knox?"

"For sure it was. She bought it for her in Paris."

"Who told you this?"

"Countess. Isn't it grand? See tat picture of the palace on the lid? Ta king and queen of Russia lived tere."

"Do you know what was kept in this box, Bridget?" Bridget looked down and shuffled her feet. "Come, Bridget, this is Danny O'Connell from County Clare you're talking to. Don't be afraid to tell me what y'know."

Bridget slowly raised her eyes and swallowed hard. "I didn't tink she would be mad at me if I just looked inside it while she be having her baf last night."

"What did you see in the box when you opened it?"

"I tought tere might be rings," the maid said disappointedly. "Pretty jewels. But it were little papers full of powder."

"How many papers filled with powder?"

"I don't know, sir, how many. Lots of tem."

"And what else did you look at while the Countess was having her bath?"

Again, the young girl stared down at her feet. "Well, you being a copper, I guess you be wanting to know if she be having anyting wort stealing."

"And did she?"

"I want you to know, sir, I wasn't looking where I wasn't supposed to. I know she was fussy about her special bag, ta one over tere on the chair. She told me not to unpack it, and I never did."

"Fine."

"But Countess had taken a nap and her bed be needing straightening. I did it while she was in her baf, and tat's when I saw."

"Saw what?"

"A bag full of pearls. I know what pearls is."

O'Connell looked around the room. "Exactly where did you see this bag of pearls?"

"It were under her pillow."

The detective's steps were quick as he moved toward the bed. He picked up the pillow on the bed, but nothing lay under it. He pulled the bedding off the mattress and shook it out onto the floor. Again, nothing. The pillow lying on the floor hid no pearls. O'Connell got down on his hands and knees and looked under the bed. Bridget began to shriek.

"Stop that, girl," he commanded. "Stop screaming like that."

"I didn't take tem. I swear on my gran's grave. You have to believe me, sir. I didn't steal tem pearls. I'm a good girl."

"Calm down, Bridget," the policeman said, shaking the girl until she became quiet. "I believe you." He looked around the room. "And if they are in this room, I will find them."

But O'Connell did not find the pearls. He discarded his first instinct to question Mr. and Miss Knox about the matter. Either they didn't know anything about them.

Or they did.

And if they did, their failing to disclose the pearls' existence was certainly suspicious.

***

The next day Daniel O'Connell was at his desk, taking stock of the case of the untimely death of Countess Natasha Telitsyn and the disappearance of a bag of pearls she had carried with her from Paris to New York. Pearls which never left her side - except when she took a bath.

According to the coroner, a large dose of veronal had been ingested by the deceased. Small traces of the same drug were also found in the gift box presented to Natasha Telitsyn by Lavinia Knox in Paris. The locked bedroom door indicated that the victim herself had taken all the powders. Only her prints were found on the gold box.

Unless, he mused, the missing pearls had been the motive for her death. How many people knew she had the pearls? Had someone removed them from the scene of the crime in the confusion of finding her lifeless body? Lavinia or George Knox. Bridget or the chauffeur. All four had been in the dead woman's room.

O'Connell turned his attention to the guests who had been invited to dinner at the Knox house. Mr. and Mrs. Randall Barton, he a scion of the publishing house Barton & Sons, and Mrs. and Mrs. Conrad Templeton, the husband being a young stockbroker. And the middle-aged Mr. Henry Janeway, whose presence puzzled the policeman. Janeway owned an art gallery on lower Fifth Avenue.

Henry Janeway. O'Connell repeated the name, trying to retrieve something from his memory. Yes, fencing stolen art. That was it. Three years ago Janeway had been accused of handling stolen paintings. It had all been hushed up, the wealthy buyers embarrassed to be known as having been swindled. But among society in the city, Janeway's reputation had been tarnished.

Why had George Knox chosen him of all people to meet his sister's prized Russian countess? Well, was it so much of a leap to go from stolen art to stolen jewelry?

A visit to the Janeway Gallery seemed in order.

<hr>

Henry Janeway quickly admitted to O'Connell that he joined Natasha Telitsyn and George Knox in his study after dinner, where they shared not one, but two snifters of cognac. The discussion, the dealer explained, centered around painting, sculpture, and the unfortunate loss of so much valuable Russian art to the hands of the hated Bolsheviks.

"A lovely woman," Janeway added. "So enchanting. As all Russian women are."

"Did you also talk about jewelry?" O'Connell asked. "Surely a lot of that must have been grabbed by the Reds when the palaces and estates were looted."

"So I understand. But jewelry's not my line."

"No, it isn't," O'Connell said. Not jewelry. Just theft.

<hr>

It had been a sleepless night for the police detective, convinced as Daniel O'Connell had become that Countess Natasha Telitsyn had been murdered while she was a guest of Lavinia and George Knox.

He was certain that the countess had been given a large dose of veronal in the glasses of brandy she drank in the study after dinner. Tired and feeling weak, she had been helped to her bedroom by Bridget. Once inside, it must have taken all the Russian woman's strength to lock the door, undress and get into bed.

Even if she had managed to take her usual dose of the sleeping powders, that would not account for the large number of empty papers found in the gold box after the countess died. Bridget was definite that there had been a great many doses inside.

The detective concentrated. An idea was forming. According to the fingerprint report, only Natasha Telitsyn's prints had been found on the box of powders. But Bridget had said that she had opened it while the countess bathed. Why hadn't they found her prints? Now, at morning's first light, Danny O'Connell was sure he knew how the crime was done.

Lavinia Knox was easy to crack. Sgt. O'Connell's vivid description of the electric chair had its desired effect. The woman gasped in horror as he painted the picture of her arms being strapped to the death chair, her neck in its brace.

"It was all George's idea," she cried. "He made me do it. I wrote to him about the necklace. Natasha showed it to me in Paris and said that it had belonged to Empress Alexandra. Natasha had some fool appraise it for her in Paris for fifty thousand francs. That's less than $35,000! George said Henry Janeway knew people in New York who would pay the earth for such a necklace. At least $200,000."

"Why did you have to kill her? Why not just steal the necklace?"

"That was George's idea, too. To tidy things up, he said." Lavinia started sobbing. "On the ship coming over Natasha had terrible dreams. She often woke up screaming. I convinced myself she would be better off in another world. I can't believe I let him talk me in to this."

"Where are the pearls now, Miss Knox?"

"George has them in a safe deposit box at our bank. That night in the study, he and Henry told Natasha they were fakes. She was so upset she left the necklace in the study."

"But they aren't fakes, are they?"

"No, they're worth a fortune. Henry said so. The pearls are large and perfectly matched, and the diamonds are flawless."

O'Connell was silent, thinking of the young woman who had unwittingly agreed to stay in a New York townhouse where death awaited her.

"But, tell me, Sergeant. How did you know it was us? George said we had the perfect plan. Her death would be declared a suicide because when she was found dead all her powders would be gone."

"Ah, Miss Knox," the detective smiled. "But that is exactly what gave me the answer." Lavinia stared at him. "Your maid Bridget opened the box of powders on the night the Countess died."

"Bridget? I don't understand."

"The gold box intrigued her. She wanted to see what the Countess kept inside of it. Her fingerprints should have been found on that box along with those of Countess Telitsyn when we tested it." Lavinia looked confused. "And of course they weren't."

"Such a nice gesture, Miss Knox," O'Connell continued. "To give your new friend a fancy gold box with the picture of the Winter Palace on it. The countess was touched, was she not? Of course she wouldn't know that you had the jeweler in Paris make two identical ones. You switched your original gift with the second box while you were sharing the cabin on the *Majestic*, didn't you? The first box would have a perfect set of her fingerprints on it. All that remained was to store that one away and produce it in New York when her body was discovered, when it was time for you to make the second switch."

"I can't believe it," Lavinia said with dismay. "Did someone see me?"

"Change the boxes in the bedroom after Baines broke down the door?" O'Connell shook his head. "No. No one saw you. I'm sure your brother was diverting attention toward the countess while you replaced her full box of powders with the one from the ship, which you had filled with empty papers. You expected that Natasha Telitsyn's fingerprints would be the only ones the police found on the box, confirming that she took her own life."

"What will happen to George and me now?"

"That's up to the courts to decide, Miss Knox. My job is to give them the evidence to convict you."

"Will they believe you?"

"I think so. I've already telegraphed to the police in Paris to ask for their help in finding the jeweler who made the boxes for you. I'm sure they have begun their search."

Lavinia slumped in her chair. She had as good as confessed.

Back again through the swirling mists of time to mid eighteenth century France, where impoverished peasants labor and suffer and dream of revolution. What ought to have been a simple trip to the market becomes a perilous journey for a young widow and her son.

Ms Borchert draws her material and story ideas from a life-long interest in France and its culture, language, and wines.

Not Our Blood

by Debra Borchert

~1750~

I awoke to pale moonlight shining between the weathered slats of the lamb shed. My son lay on his mat of hay, his arms and legs sprawled like those of a colt, his blond hair covering his face. I brushed the curls from Étienne's eyes and smiled, remembering his remedy for the stench in our home. *I would rather smell my own hair than the sheep droppings, Maman.* No matter how hard I swept and scoured, still the odor of mouton lingered.

I got up, feeling an ache in my back, arms, and legs from the previous day spent picking fruits and pulling vegetables. Shivering, I wrapped my shawl about my shoulders, went out, and latched the door behind me.

A row of poplars cast shadows over the dew-laden meadow. At the top of the hill stood the house I had come to live in as a bride. My husband managed the estate and the workers well, for twelve years, until the drought and the last brutal winter. The Baron cared not that his tenants were starving, but my husband could not stand by and watch. The stores of the Baron's grain had begun to mold, and instead of allowing it to rot, he gave it to those who were starving. He did not know at the time, the terrible price he would pay for saving their lives. I ran my finger along the back of my neck, the spot my husband always kissed first when he came in from the fields. The hoot of an owl broke the silence.

Carrot fronds grew high in the kitchen garden. I planted them only three months ago, when the garden, too, had been mine. I slipped through the fence, pulled up two, and headed for the barn. If any people were watching, they would not accuse me of stealing, although I sometimes wished they would, if they did, the Baron would judge me guilty and hang me, like he had my husband. But there was Étienne. No, they would see that the widow was feeding the carrots to the horse that had also once been hers. Before I entered the mare's stall, I broke off the roots and shoved them into my apron pocket. She munched the fronds as I led her out of the barn and hitched her to the loaded wagon.

I returned to the shed, knelt, and shook Étienne. "It is time to leave."

He groaned. "It is still night."

I pulled back the blanket, more holes than wool. "We go to Paris today."

He pulled it back. "I am tired. I picked all day."

"As did I."

"I do not want to go to Paris."

"Monsieur Gois is very kind to lend us the mare and wagon." I poured weak ale into our cup and took a sip. "We will sell much more there than at the village market. With the extra money we can rent a room in town and not be sleeping in a lamb shed." I took the blanket and folded it. "Now get up."

He sighed and heaved himself up like an old man. Only ten, and already he was only a head shorter than me. I held out the cup. He drained it, placed it in the iron pot, and dressed.

We walked to the wagon packed with baskets. My aching muscles reminded me of every *haricot*, *courgette*, and *aubergine* I had picked and loaded. Étienne stumbled and stooped to retie the rope that kept his shoe on his foot.

I tried to sound cheerful. "At least it is not raining and there is no mud." He nodded and took a peach. I grabbed it. "They are for sale."

Dark circles surrounded his blue eyes. "I am hungry, Maman."

"We need every sou for firewood this winter, or we shall freeze." I reached into my pocket and handed him the carrots.

"I will gather wood from the forest myself." He straightened his shoulders.

"And the Baron will be hanging you, as he did your father."

Tears rose in his eyes.

Why had I reminded him? I bit my lip and handed him the peach. "Just one."

We climbed up onto the bench. I gripped the reins and urged the mare forward.

Étienne slept through the three-hour journey. As we crested the last hill, I looked to the east and my breath caught. Beyond, the Seine reflected golden-pink light, making Paris look like she was wearing one of the queen's jeweled gowns. Before Étienne was born, my husband often brought me to the Paris market. I smiled, remembering that our son had been conceived in this very wagon returning on one of those late, sweltering evenings.

We joined eight wagons already waiting to pay their taxes at the Saint Martin gate. A guard reached into our cart, shoved baskets, and tossed bunches of radishes about. I held my breath and my tongue. Bruised fruit would not bring a good price, but my objecting could cause him to forbid us entry. He spat. "One livre tax."

"One livre?" My ears felt like they were clogged. "Twenty sous? We must eat, too, Monsieur."

"Then charge more." He snapped his fingers. "Pay or get out of the way."

I reached into my apron pocket and fingered the coins. There would be just four sous left. I paid.

Étienne took the reins. I got down and guided the mare through the gate and into the rutted, stinking street. Following a wagon loaded with cabbages, I dodged a stream of waste from an emptied chamber pot, mounds of manure, rats as large as rabbits. Two men shoveled the filth, still steaming, into a heap. We hurried past to get a place on the other side of the square and pulled the cart next to a dark-skinned man who sold spices from barrels.

His green eyes were the shape of almonds. "Not seen you here before."

"It has been a few years. You do good business at this corner?"

He pushed out his lower lip and shrugged. "Beware the gendarmes. They steal your wares, and if you say anything, they take you for the thief."

I rubbed at the ache in my arms. "Thank you, Monsieur…"

He tipped his hat to me, "Fortis."

"I am Madame Chastain, and my son is Étienne."

From the back of the wagon, Étienne pulled a wooden board and crates. We stacked the crates and placed the board upon them for a table. Étienne walked around the wagon to unhitch the mare and feed her.

A gray horse, two hands higher than our plow mare, walked toward me. I tilted my head to look up at the rider. A gendarme.

He held out his gloved hand. "Permit."

"I paid the tax at the gate." I felt my heartbeat quicken. "The guard did not give me a permit."

"You pay *me* for the permit. Two sous."

I pressed the coins together in my pocket. "I do not have two, Monsieur."

"Then you will pay later." The corner of his mouth jerked up. "What have you got to give me now?"

His eyes were those of a hungry wolf. I reached into a basket, took a peach, and held it out to him.

He looked me over; his eyes lingered at my bosom. "Are your peaches ripe?"

I felt myself blush.

He leaned over the saddle. His gloved hand scratched my chest, delved into my bodice, and squeezed my breast. I choked and jumped back. His hand snatched the peach. I stood panting. He chomped down, juice streaming off his chin. Laughing, he tossed the peach behind him, dug his heels into the horse, and rode on.

Before I could reach the fruit, a tiny street urchin in a torn dress ran by and, without stopping, grabbed it and ate as she fled. The child was so thin and filthy, I was glad for her good fortune. I picked up a basket, rested it on the table, and unpacked radishes, leeks, carrots.

The spice man leaned over his barrels and whispered, "You were wise not to pay. There are no permits."

I gripped the table and stared.

"Leave early, before the market closes, before he returns for his bribe. Otherwise, he will accuse you of theft, although you have taken nothing, and drag you off to the Prison de l'Abbaye, just to see you fear him."

Peddlers set out their wares, laundresses hauled their bundles, maids and housewives made their daily rounds. A lace maker sat in front of a shop, tatting in a patch of sunshine. The clang of the blacksmith's hammer echoed in the street. People stood in line for baguettes. The smell of roasting meat made me miss my breakfast all the more.

As I reached for the last of the fruit, my finger sank into a peach. I felt the others: all bruised. I called out, "Étienne, you put the ripe ones on the bottom, now they are ruined. How can I sell these?"

He walked toward me carrying a box. "It was dark when we loaded the wagon." He shrugged. "How was I to know?"

"You could not feel them? You could not smell them? You should know; you helped your papa load the wagon for market since you were able to walk."

His eyebrows drew together shadowing his eyes. He looked beyond me.

I rubbed my neck. "If your father were alive he'd beat some sense into you."

"If Papa were alive, he'd be here and I'd be in school." He slammed the box on the ground. Peaches spilled and rolled about on the cobbles. He turned and ran through the crowd.

"Étienne, come back. You must help."

He was already beyond my view. I sighed, bent, gathered up the fruit in my apron, and returned to the table where two women stood examining the leeks and gossiping. I wiped sweat from my face. "What can I get for you?"

The younger, her cap crisp and white, asked, "Have you more peaches? For a tart?"

I nodded and bent to pick up the spilled fruit. A maid, I thought. Only nobles could afford the little sugar there was. I collected the peaches and began placing them into her basket.

The older woman, her cap frayed and singed, asked, "Your son, how old is he?"

I sighed. "Ten."

"Best to keep your eye on him."

"I do. As much as any widowed mother can." I stood tall. "He is old enough to take care of himself."

The young woman touched my arm. "You do not know?"

I turned toward the wagon to get more peaches, but the older woman grabbed my wrist. "Children are gone missing, and not just orphans, neither. They say gendarmes get bounties for them, so when they can't catch foundlings, they grab ours." She let go of me, gripped a celery root and shook it. "They say they bleed 'em for some prince's bath, got leprosy, the children's blood is supposed to be some kind of cure. Some say it is for Louis, the King himself! Can you imagine?"

The younger woman replied, "That is a tall tale." She leaned over the table and whispered, "Foundlings are sent to populate the colonies in America. Because the gendarmes are eager to earn the bounties, they care not if a child is an orphan, so they take children from their parents."

I gave a straight-lipped smile. "That, too, sounds like a tall tale."

The older woman leaned in. "Whether for blood or colonies, there's more than a hundred missing now."

The younger nodded. "Last month they got the rope maker's son at the Saint-Honoré market. How could you not know?"

"We live on a farm, three hours' journey from here, this is my first time at this market in ten years." My hands shook so that I almost dropped the basket. "How could I know?"

The older woman wagged her finger. "The blacksmith, in this very market, his son went missing last week."

A chill ran down my back. "Étienne!" I rushed to the front of the wagon, around the mare, and back. "Étienne!" I jumped onto the wagon, scanned the market, and yelled for him.

"Ah, dearie, let's hope they'll not be bleedin' your Étienne!" cried the older woman.

I blinked, willing my eyes to find him. Down by a stall hung with rabbit, pheasant, and quail stood Étienne, his head cocked back to stare at the bounty. My heart quieted. "Étienne!" He turned to look at me, shook his head, and walked farther away.

So stubborn, just like his father. I began to step down, but stopped. The chill inched down my back as I looked over the crowd. Across the square, the gendarme rode on his grey horse, parting the crowd before him. I fisted my hands. He stopped before the butcher's stall, his hand outstretched. The butcher's wife handed him a sausage, but the gendarme paid not a sou.

I climbed down and picked up one of the baskets. But something was wrong; I could not shake off the chill. I climbed back on top of the wagon and scanned the market.

The gendarme pushed his horse through the people. Where was my son? I called out for him again and again. My heart thumped louder than the sound of my voice. I watched as the horse stopped and pawed before a stall hung with bright fabrics and cords. Just beyond the horse, stood Étienne. I held my breath.

Étienne reached out his fingers and caressed a red ribbon.

The gendarme leaned down and snatched at my son. "Thief!"

I screamed, "No!"

Étienne yanked his arm away, but the gendarme was quicker. He grasped Étienne by the collar of his tunic and slammed him into the horse's flank. Étienne squirmed against the skittering horse.

I screamed, "Stop. He is my son!"

Merchants and shoppers paused and began to look about. Étienne twisted wildly as the gendarme tried to yank him up onto the saddle.

I thrust my fists into the air and screamed, "Stop that gendarme. He is taking my son!"

The gendarme hesitated; then, with both hands, he grabbed Étienne and heaved him over his saddle. He pressed his hand into Étienne's back, pinning him down, and yelled at the crowd, "He is a thief."

I lurched and wobbled. "No! He is not. Let him go!"

Market women began to flee, but men surrounded the horse. From the far side of the market, a woman screamed, "You were here last week! You took my son. Where is my André?"

From behind her, a red-faced blacksmith ran toward the gendarme, his hammer swiping the air above. Étienne pulled his foot to his chest and thrust it into the gendarme's stomach. "Let me go!" The horse reared. The gendarme slammed a fist into my son's chest and pinned him to the saddle.

I leapt down and slid across the cobbles. Pushing and shoving my way toward them, I screamed, "Stop him. He is taking my son."

The crowd parted. I stumbled, and a woman helped me to my feet. Ahead, a rotund butcher, arms as big around as hams, grabbed hold of Étienne's shoulders. "He's her son, do you hear?" His massive arms wrapped round my child as if Étienne were his own. The butcher wrenched Étienne from the gendarme, and held him to his chest, his hand protecting Étienne's head as if he were an infant. For a brief moment, instead of the butcher, I saw my husband holding Étienne. I sobbed and stumbled.

From the other side of the saddle, the gendarme pulled a whip and raised it. "I am the law! The child is a thief."

Étienne called out, "I did not take anything! Maman!"

From behind the horse, the blacksmith brought his iron hammer up over his head and bashed the uniformed back. The gendarme cried out and lost his whip. The horse whinnied and pawed the air. The gendarme slumped backward. The blacksmith raised his hammer again and shouted, "Where's my son?"

Men pushed past me, grabbed the horse, and attacked the gendarme with pikes and fishhooks.

The gendarme whimpered, "I am the law."

I shoved my way forward.

The butcher strode toward me with Étienne in his arms. I swore the man's head was surrounded by a halo. He rubbed my son's back, then put him on his feet. "Don't be leaving your mother, now. You don't want them to be taking you to the colonies, right? Not a bit of good meat to be had in those Americas."

I stood trembling, panting, gripping my son.

Étienne's face, white as a cloud, trembled. "Thank you, Monsieur." He bowed to the man, then turned to me and said, "I did not steal." Then, he fainted.

I flung myself to catch him, and we collapsed upon the ground.

The butcher laughed. I sat and cradled Étienne as I had when he was but a baby. I held my face to his blond curls and sobbed. I knew my tears were not only for my son but also for my husband. I held my son tighter to me.

The crowd pushed past. I wiped my face with my sleeve and looked up at the butcher. "Thank you, Monsieur. You are a true gentleman. Thank you."

His smiling face grew long. I followed his gaze and rose. Across the square, men had hog-tied the gendarme and were dragging him toward a street lamp. The blacksmith cried, "To the lantern!"

The gendarme struggled about like a fish on a riverbank. His shouts weakened, "I am the law."

Étienne awakened and looked about in the direction of the jeers. I bent and tried to keep him from standing, but he pushed himself up in order to see what the crowd was shouting about. I stood and held him against me.

The blacksmith's wife screamed, "Where did you take my André?" She hurled a stone, and the gendarme's head jerked back as blood gushed from his nose. He fell to his knees.

The old woman in the singed cap screamed, "There's blood for the King's bath. Not our blood—the King can have yours!"

The crowd cheered. The men toyed with the gendarme. Each time a rock hit its mark, they let him drop and pulled him up again. The gendarme gagged and tore at the rope. More stones flew. I felt nausea move through me, as it had the day the Baron forced us to watch my husband climb the steps to the gallows.

Étienne held onto my arms.

The blacksmith tied a noose round the gendarme's neck and yanked it tight.

My arms and legs felt limp, useless. I saw my husband's face, his clear blue eyes, his lips that were forever smiling, except for that last moment, with a noose wound around his neck. I kissed Étienne's head and tried to pull him from looking; I did not want him to be reminded of his father's hanging. He stood firm.

The gendarme's knees buckled. He slumped to the ground, only the rope around his neck kept him from falling completely. The crowd drew back. A laundress slapped a wet cloth across the gendarme's face to wake him to his fate. He moaned. Another man flung the other end of the rope up and over the lamp. More women picked up rocks. Men grabbed the rope and began to pull it taut. The gendarme dangled and bobbed like a desperate spider. The crowd chanted for his blood. Rocks flew.

The butcher held out a stone to Étienne.

I took it instead.

"He is not like Papa. He deserves to hang."

I felt the cold weight of the stone, the raw burn in my bosom, the pounding in my chest. I slowed my breathing, wiped at my face, and looked at my son. Sweat matted his hair. Blood crusted above his eyebrow. My child's eyes, pinched and dark, were no longer the wide and tender eyes of a sad boy who had watched his father die. He straightened his shoulders and held out his hand for the stone.

I put it in my apron pocket. Then I wrapped my arm around his shoulders and walked him back to our stall.

The spice man was hauling his barrels up onto his wagon. He turned to me. "You must leave here, before the gendarmes find their comrade hanging from the lantern."

Behind us the crowd continued their shouts for blood. I gripped Étienne's shoulder. "We have done nothing."

"They will be looking to take someone to the Prison de l'Abbaye."

I felt my breath leave me. "But we have no money. We must sell our vegetables."

"When they arrive, to whom do you think the mob will point?"

"We are innocent. It is the gendarme who is the guilty one." I gripped the stone in my pocket, and thought I would crush the skull of anyone who should try to take my son from me.

"The prisons of France are filled with the innocent." He pointed to Étienne. "And then what of your son?"

I wiped sweat from my face. "Étienne, harness the horse."

"Yes, Maman."

I ran to the baskets and threw them into the wagon. We would sell at the town market, at least there would be some money, I thought, as I pulled the boxes along the cobbles to the wagon and stacked them. I climbed up onto the wagon. The spice man picked up a box and handed it to me. "You can follow me to Marché des Enfants Rouges. I sell there during the week. They know me. They will allow you to use my stall." He picked up another box.

I swallowed against the tightness in my throat. Touching his arm, I whispered, "Not since the death of my husband has such kind—"

The sounds of shouts and horses' hooves came from behind us. We turned. A gendarme riding a horse entered the far end of the square. He pulled a sword and brandished it over the heads of the crowd. People began to scatter. A whip cut through the air, and the weapon tumbled. I followed the length of the whip and saw the blacksmith, who loosened the whip and cracked it again, this time slicing the gendarme's face. He cried out. A rock slammed into the back of the gendarme's head, and he toppled forward.

I whispered, "Mon Dieu, they will do it again."

The spice man grabbed my hand. "Leave the rest. Hurry." He jumped up onto his wagon and began to pull it in front of ours. He shouted and his wagon lurched forward.

Étienne yelled, "Maman, we must follow him."

I turned. Étienne stood at the wagon bench holding out the reins to me.

From behind us, and around the sides of our wagon, people came running; a tanner, maid, baker, chimneysweep, liveryman, a crew of stonemasons, the laundress who taunted the gendarme. I clutched the rock, but I could not make myself move from among the boxes on the bed of the wagon.

Étienne shouted, "Maman, we must go!"

We might run over these people.

"Maman!" Étienne dropped the reins, climbed over the boxes and grabbed my hand. He yanked me up to the bench and pressed me down to sit upon it.

He turned, grabbed the reins and snapped them. "Allez," he shouted at the horse. The wagon jolted. The mare shied. Étienne leaned forward and smacked the end of the reins against the mare's quarters. The wheels rolled and picked up speed. He smacked the mare and shouted, "Allez!" His feet planted firmly beneath him, he steered the horse toward the right. A box fell and shattered onto the cobbles. I gripped the bench and held on. His arms shook as he strained to turn the mare sharply through an alley. I prayed no one would open a door.

We raced out of the alleyway and across the cobbles of a wide street lined with shops, past merchants and aristocrats. A man dressed in striped waistcoat and tricorne hat ran from our path, turned, and shook his fist at us. I could not see the spice man anywhere.

"Allez!" Étienne shouted. The mare jerked the wagon and broke into a trot down the boulevard.

Tears blurred my sight. I cried, "Where is the spice man? We must sell the vegetables in Paris to make more money, or we will not be able to rent a room."

Finally, as we neared the city gate, he slowed the mare and sat next to me. "We'll go back to the town market."

I could not stop my tears remembering the gendarme grabbing my son.

"Do not worry, Maman. He patted my hand. "I will take care of you." His voice was deep and calm, so much like his father's.

Over the ensuing years, I worried that his anger over his father's murder and his own near-miss with the gendarme would change him into a bitter and vengeful man. But, he grew more and more like his father: helping neighbors, always offering a smile, doing other boys' chores in exchange for reading lessons. He brought home weathered pieces of wood to patch holes in our roof and never complained again of our lamb shed.

Then, throughout the countryside and in Paris, revolts erupted. Peasants began to fight against the feudal laws that had kept them starving and living in shacks not fit for animals.

Étienne led the neighboring farmers in sacking the Baron's château and destroying the records of servitude. Then he forced the Baron to watch, as they burned the gallows.

Our next story conjures up post-war Vienna, when the cold war was simmering and dark deeds are done among the shadows of night. Moral ambiguity is the stock and trade of spies, and everyone has a secret.

Mr. Tucher is the author of over sixty hardboiled short stories featuring Diana Andrews, a crime-solving prostitute. A novella featuring Diana, The Same Mistake Twice, was recently published by Untreed Reads. His story Hangman's Break recently appeared in Ellery Queen Mystery Magazine.

The Beethoven House

By Albert Tucher

"*Gratuliere*," I said. "Congratulations. Most impressive."

I was not lying. After years of chaos and obstruction, the pedestrian underpass was ready for its opening ceremony, just a few hours from now.

Baylor lurked unseen behind me, but I knew he was grimacing at my flattery. He needed to accept how things were done in Vienna. Kiss the hand, stab the back, and call it old-world charm.

He also needed to get over his problems with his boss. Me.

Inspector Hegyi held his reply. Seconds later a streetcar passed over our heads. Its rumble was faint, but after a lifetime in the city Hegyi was used to waiting for the noise to pass. He probably had the Viennese transportation schedules engraved on his brain, where they had survived even the interruptions of the war years.

"We are grateful that the American trade mission approves."

He never slipped up and said "CIA" to me. Or, probably, "KGB" to the Russians he dealt with.

"This afternoon we formally open the new *Opernpassage*," he said. "Tomorrow is the grand reopening of the State Opera. This is most inconvenient."

"Especially for him."

I nodded at the man sprawled on the stairs. He lay on his back in a position that I would have found unbearable, but he had the advantage of being dead. He had come to rest with his feet higher than his head, and the blood had followed gravity. His purple face had swollen until it looked ready to burst.

I had seen worse during the war, as had Hegyi, from his side of the hostilities. Baylor had missed it. That was part of what he held against me, but only part.

I recognized the dead man's tweed suit. Wolfi Stendl had thought it made him look English.

"Thank you for the call, Inspector."

I owed him for it. Austrian neutrality was tricky, and Hegyi was pressing the limits.

"I knew you would want to know about … an associate," he said.

I paused for some thought.

"How did he get in?" I said. "There was certainly a police guard."

Hegyi shrugged. "Policemen are poorly paid. I will investigate."

Had Wolfi bribed one of the guards, or had someone else done it and lured him here? And was the underground passage a meeting place, or a body dump?

I was standing on the floor of the passage. Hegyi's perch one step up brought him even with my six feet. He was a very Viennese type; short, dark, sleek. He turned away from me and climbed the stairs to the street level, where he tactfully pretended to examine the gate for evidence of tampering.

Baylor loitered close enough to Hegyi to join him, but typically, he ignored the charade. I caught his eye and jerked my head toward the street, where our car waited. It was childish of me, but I could not resist the prospect of five minutes without Baylor.

I crouched and began searching the dead man. From the breast pocket of the suit I plucked a wallet. I opened it and found an Austrian national ID under the name Wolfgang Stendl. That a few Schillings made up Wolfi's worldly goods.

His intangible legacy would last a little longer. The coffee houses would spread the news of his death, along with speculation about what it meant. I was the first to know, thanks to Hegyi, but the Soviets and every shady go-between in Vienna would be right behind me.

There was nothing more I could do there.

"I hope your ceremony can proceed," I said.

"It will. The underpass is too important to wait. We anticipate fewer pedestrian casualties. And of course, we get a brand new police station."

I had noticed a discreet door with "Polizei" lettered on it. The elegant shops in the new underground space would bring new opportunities for thievery.

"Wolfi's girlfriend," I said. "The police will notify her?"

"Eventually," he said.

Which meant I would have time to do so before him. I studied him, but he gave nothing away. Games within games were the Viennese way. There didn't even have to be a compelling reason for it.

I climbed the stairs and crossed the sidewalk to a black Mercedes that no one could trace to the embassy. Baylor sat behind the wheel.

"*Goldeggasse*," I said as I got in.

He gave me a blank look, which irritated me. He had been here long enough to learn the streets.

"Just get us to the *Favoritenstrasse* and keep going."

That he could manage.

Traudl Meinhofer lived in what had been the Soviet occupation zone just two months earlier. The Red Army had packed up and departed, but my nerves still gave me trouble when I traveled to their territory. The entire city belonged to the Austrians again, but old habits were hard to shake.

We took our time and arrived around eleven. I hoped it was too early for Traudl to have gentleman callers, but not so early that I would wake her and make her surly. She answered the door still in her dressing gown, but I knew that modesty was no longer part of her repertoire.

She was smoking, of course. Traudl no longer accepted cigarettes as payment, but she had kept the tobacco habit.

"Benjamin," she said. "You are naughty to have neglected me for so long."

She always spoke English with me, as if she could earn points toward emigration to America. I lacked the heart to explain to her that nothing could make up for her profession.

She ignored Baylor. Part of her disdain was a prostitute's mistrust of handsome young men, but in her mind I was still with the old, familiar OSS, while Baylor belonged to the upstart CIA.

"I'm afraid I have some bad news," I said "Wolfi is dead."

Her professional mask didn't slip, but she switched to German.

"*So ist's.*"

That's that.

"Shall we sit down, Traudl?"

I glanced at Baylor, and to my surprise he took the hint. He stayed behind at the apartment door.

Traudl turned and led me through the doorway into her living room, which was crammed with pre-war furniture. This block had somehow escaped significant bomb damage. Traudl pointed me toward an aging loveseat with a red and gold floral pattern. I left room for her to join me, and after a moment she did.

"Do you know who killed him?"

Not "how he died." His profession was more dangerous than hers, and she knew it.

"Not yet. The police are investigating."

"As are you, Benjamin."

"Can you tell me anything that can help us?"

"It might be about the tickets."

"What tickets?"

"To the opera gala. Two, at ten thousand schillings."

I did some quick arithmetic. That was roughly three hundred dollars each. They were not the most expensive seats, but they weren't the cheapest, either. For most Austrians they would be an unimaginable expense.

And yes, in Vienna some people would consider them worth killing for.

"How did Wolfi get them?"

"He said someone at the opera owed him big time. From the war."

She switched to English for the "big time."

"And he settled for opera tickets?"

"He said he was going to turn them into something even bigger. He thought it might improve his situation with you."

Only dumping Traudl would have accomplished that, but I saw no point in explaining.

"What else did he tell you?"

"Nothing," she said.

I was almost impressed. Wolfi had never been able to resist boasting to Traudl.

"I would have loved to go," she said in a small voice.

Ten years earlier I would have been surprised, but I had come to know the Viennese and their music. The opera house was to reopen with *Fidelio*, and Traudl could probably have discussed Beethoven's different overtures with any professor from the conservatory. No one would find that remarkable in a city that had a Beethoven residence on practically every corner.

It helped that the composer got himself evicted every three months or so.

So who had the tickets now? And had the same person or persons killed Wolfi?

As we descended the stairs to the street, Baylor asked me, "How do we know her?"

"We basically kept her alive after the war. She fed us little tidbits."

"How did she survive in this part of the city?"

The Soviets had not been known for gallantry toward Austrian women.

"She did better than most. She had a protector. A general, who made some interesting pillow talk."

I decided it was time for a bit of a showdown.

"She also kept us informed about our own men. And the French and the Brits. Your own side can hurt you more than the enemy."

I held his eyes as I said it. His face flushed up to his blond Ivy League crew cut, which was a tendency a CIA man should work to overcome, even when dealing with someone like me. Sometimes I felt like telling him that I knew what could go on in those all-male Princeton dorms.

"Anyway," I said, "Tomorrow night you get a treat. We're going to the opera."

<hr>

I felt like a penguin with an itch.

My cover story often required me to wear white tie and tails, but I disliked the stiffness and downright silliness of the get-up. And something, perhaps the local laundry soap, always made my skin itch ferociously under the stiff formal shirt. I knew I could forget about getting a good scratch until I undressed. And who knew when that would be?

Not that I could have raised my arms high enough to claw myself. The crowd of identically dressed men and gowned and jewel-encrusted women pressed in from all sides as we climbed the main stairway.

I knew the story. The night the bombs fell on the Opera, the wind veered at the last moment and saved the historic stairway. Now it felt like a sanctuary from the present. For as long as it took us to climb those stairs, the Emperor and the Tsar still ruled, and when it came to columns, arches, statues and rococo swirls, more was still better.

The old auditorium had vanished into the flames, but the new space evoked the past in a visual assault of red and gold.

I joined the crowd heading for standing room. Until the audience sorted itself, there was no way to distinguish the standees from the upper crust. Everyone had dressed as if for the most prestigious boxes. I leaned on the railing and watched the show before the show.

Ushers began examining tickets and directing guests with much bowing and fussing.

"*Bitte sehr! Bitte sehr!*"

More or less, "I beg you utterly."

The phrase was a typically obsequious Viennese way of saying everything while saying nothing:

Rank and file Austrians had spent as long as three days waiting in line for standing room tickets. The American embassy had preempted tickets for me and the three members of my team. Unfortunately, opera fanatics knew how to count, and they knew that the tickets had run out too soon. The whole city would be sullen tonight.

Something in the center aisle of the orchestra section demanded my attention. I scanned the crowd and spotted a familiar face. Klaus Fenstermacher was the best document forger in Vienna. I used him myself when I did not want to leave a trail of requisitions and supervisory signatures.

That settled it. This evening was worth the trouble. Until this moment I had not been sure.

He moved down the aisle like a luxury liner. His well-fed shape came from his aversion to hurry. An usher rapturously accepted Fenstermacher's schilling for a copy of the program and fussed with him over his seat. To the forger's left were a German oil importer and his wife. He greeted them with a handshake and an Austrian hand kiss.

Five minutes before curtain time no one had taken the aisle seat on Fenstermacher's right. Tonight of all nights, how could an orchestra seat go unused?

The lights dimmed. Could I be wrong after all? I had been admiring Fenstermacher's choice of rendezvous. Any two people in the city could meet in plain sight and claim that their encounter was a coincidence. And if they didn't already know each other, possession of the correct ticket would make the ideal password.

Or it would have been ideal, until Wolfi's murder confused the picture. Maybe the ticket holder had decided against taking the risk.

The auditorium was almost completely dark when a slender form strode down the aisle and slid into the empty seat. I saw the silhouette of a floor-length gown. A last glint of light showed me swept-back hair, blonde or perhaps white. The newcomer's youthful movements argued for blonde.

On any other evening she might have been the kind of young adventurer who lurked in standing room and then swooped down on an unoccupied seat, but that would not work tonight. She must have the missing ticket.

The postwar shortage of men made unescorted women less conspicuous, but she would still turn heads. That might account for her last-second appearance.

The orchestra tuned and then hushed. <u>Doktor</u> Boehm entered the pit and mounted the podium. The applause started. The noise from the orchestra seats was no more than polite, and it made me realize again the unfairness of letting outsiders overwhelm this occasion. The Austrians had waited ten years for this evening. It was up to the standees to welcome the maestro back. They did their best, and it was very good.

The overture began. In the past, I had dismissed German opera in favor of the Italian composers, but the first notes from this orchestra after ten years of silence changed my mind.

In the comic opening scene I seemed to remember how to laugh after years of mourning. Then the title character entered. Beethoven showed that he meant business, and so did the soprano, Martha Moedl. I forgot my feet, my itching, everything.

When the first act ended, I reluctantly recalled why I had come.

The lights came up on Fenstermacher and his neighbor, who was indeed a blonde. I watched in case they left immediately, but they stayed. It made sense. Empty seats would have drawn attention.

My neighbors in standing room tied scarves or other items to mark their places and went to promenade, and see and be seen. I kept watching.

A man stepped up to the rail on my right and rested his forearms. I glanced at him.

"Herr Paunov," I said.

We had a tacit agreement. I didn't call him "Colonel," his probable rank in the KGB, and he didn't mention the CIA. To the world he was a midlevel functionary in the Soviet embassy.

"Herr Lederer," he said.

We always used German in our encounters. KGB men of his rank spoke fluent English, but he never let me hear his. He was my height, with a trim build that evening clothes flattered. Stalin's purges had spared a few men like him, who could move in circles like this without looking like dressed-up thugs. I did not envy Paunov his life, waking up each morning and wondering whether this was the day the Comrade Secretary thought, "It's Paunov's turn," and sent the goons for him.

He had beaten the odds, but the evidence suggested that those men who had survived Stalin were now spending a lot of time explaining themselves. For some of them it was difficult.

"You have unexpected depths," he said.

"For an American, you mean. We do tend toward the practical."

I avoided looking at Fenstermacher and his contact, but the precaution was useless.

"You seem to have taken a fancy to one of the charming local ladies," said Paunov.

"Vienna is full of beautiful women."

He nodded. "More depths."

Meaning that his men had never observed me with a woman. Paunov was better at veiled threats than Baylor, but that was to be expected.

For a full minute we said nothing.

"I love this opera," said the Colonel. "As stirring as the second act is, I confess that I find it a letdown after my favorite moment in the first."

"Which one is that?"

"When the prisoners emerge from confinement and see the daylight for the first time in years."

That was a bit much coming from a representative of the purges and labor camps, but I refused to let him provoke me.

He held my eyes with a look that left me wondering about his depths.

"It's all new to me," I said.

"I'm sure this will be a memory to treasure. Good evening."

The standees returned precisely at curtain time, as if they had been practicing their part for the past ten years.

The second act picked up speed, and I began to understand the unique satisfactions of Beethoven. He made me think of the conventional wisdom, "Never let them see you sweat."

Beethoven stood the saying on its head. The musicians worked so hard that I wondered how they could keep it up.

As the curtain came down, I realized that I was shouting with the rest of the crowd. This was no way for a spy to behave.

Ovation followed ovation, but Fenstermacher and his neighbor appeared unmoved. I detected small movements of their shoulders and upper arms, as they exchanged something. The blonde woman left first. She held her evening bag close against her as she hurried up the aisle. I looked at two of my team and then at Fenstermacher, who sat and counted off the seconds before he could leave without appearing linked to the young woman. Two of my men extricated themselves from the standing room crowd and stood at the top of the center aisle, where they could intercept him.

Fenstermacher saw them but kept coming at his usual pace. He knew the rules, and he knew American muscle when he saw it, even in white tie.

That was handled. I turned my attention to the young woman. My other man and I let her pass and then fell in behind her. With the crowd around us we could stay close without warning her, but outside we would have to drop back.

I watched her from above as she preceded us on the main staircase. From that angle, the shape of her shoulders told me what I needed to know.

On the sidewalk I spared a glance at Fenstermacher, pinned between two powerful men. He was cooperating, as if he had a choice. A black Mercedes swerved to the curb and stopped, and one of my men reached for the rear door handle. He helped Fenstermacher into the seat and slid in after him. The other man opened the front passenger door and got in.

The car sped off. They would take him to one of the apartments we used to avoid the twenty-four-hour Soviet surveillance of our embassy.

I turned toward the shadows in the arcade along the side of the building. Baylor stepped into the light. I handed him my tailcoat and took the dark gray overcoat and Tyrolean hat that he held for me. If we proceeded on foot, I could take the hat off and put it back on as needed to vary my appearance.

But the young woman strode briskly to the curb, just as yet another black Mercedes swerved toward her. She opened the rear door herself and climbed in. The car took off.

I waved for the car I had in reserve. Baylor piled into the back, while I took the front passenger seat.

The Mercedes made an abrupt left turn off the Opernring, the broad street that encircled the oldest part of the city. We followed. It soon became clear that we were headed back to Favoriten.

The district had a number of late-night clubs of doubtful legality and reputation. The Soviets had found them convenient for many purposes that would embarrass their diplomats. The car we were following parked in front of one of the clubs. This time a doorman came forward to help the young woman out of the back seat.

"Drive past and take the first right turn," I told my driver. "Park where you can."

At the curb I climbed out of the car and pulled the rear door open.

"Give me my tailcoat," I told Baylor.

I changed coats again.

"I'll go in alone." I looked at the driver. "Go around to the alley."

I turned to Baylor.

"Give me fifteen minutes. If I'm not out by then, come in the front entrance and get me."

The driver kept his face expressionless. With a look I warned Baylor to do the same.

I walked around the corner to the club. My evening dress was actually a good disguise. I looked like the type of customer who enjoyed slumming in establishments like this. Vienna in 1955 wasn't Berlin in the 1920s, but today's Berlin wasn't its old self, either. This kind of club was the closest anyone could find to the pre-war days.

The doorman peered at me.

"Herr Lederer. It has been too long."

"Thank you, Leonhard."

I handed him a folded bill. He touched the brim of his hat and pulled the door to the club open for me.

Inside I saw a haze of tobacco smoke obscuring a crowd that was nine-tenths male. Only the performers on the small stage would be women, and not all of them. For occasional visitors the fun lay in guessing who was what.

I began scanning faces as discreetly as I could. Some men in places like this were quick to take offense, or to run. I recognized no one, which did not surprise me. The cast of regulars would change.

I saw no white evening gown, but I knew there were back rooms, an upper floor, and a rear exit.

A bead curtain hung across the doorway to the nonpublic areas.

I pushed through and looked to my left, where a stairway led upstairs. To the right a hallway disappeared into darkness. Beyond the gloom was the exit. I paused for a moment to decide. If my quarry had gone straight through to the alley, she was already gone. I would have to rely on my man outside to intercept her.

The only light spilled down the stairs from the rooms on the upper floor. I started to climb the stairs, sticking to the right as I went. I could see areas of shadow awaiting me at the top of the stairs. They could conceal anything.

Case in point. As my foot touched the top step, a form peeled itself off the right-hand wall and launched itself at me. Something struck me hard in the chest, and I toppled backward. My feet left the ground, and all I could do was wait for the impact.

It was even worse than I expected. I landed on my back, and my breath left me with a woof. At first nothing hurt, but I knew the respite would not last. I was right. Pain washed over me in waves. Footsteps passed by me, but I could do nothing about them.

Seconds or minutes later I managed to roll over through the pain and raise myself to my hands and knees on the bare wood. That was a good start. Next step, pull myself up to a praying position. Then I reached out for the wall and climbed an inch at a time to my feet.

I checked my watch. Five minutes of my fifteen were gone. I dragged myself by the railing up the stairs. The first room on the right was unpopulated. The light came from a makeup mirror with a fringe of low-wattage bulbs. The mirror shared a small table with a pile of women's clothing; a white evening gown, matching pumps, and a white-blonde wig. No handbag.

I wobbled down the stairs and continued past the beaded curtain toward the rear exit. I had to feel my way through complete darkness, but there were no more obstacles between me and a door that opened onto a malodorous alley. At the end of it I could see my car, with my driver leaning placidly against it.

"Did you get her?" I said.

"The blonde? Didn't see her."

"Did anyone come by?"

"Just a brunette in a red dress. Real looker."

"And you just let her go?"

"Nobody said anything about a brunette."

I said nothing more. It was my fault for not explaining.

"Was she carrying a bag?"

"Yeah, a little white one."

Baylor appeared around the corner. I climbed into the car and waited for the two men to join me.

"Let's go. The safe house."

I wanted to hold my aching head, but I didn't dare show weakness in this company. As it was, I caught a smirk from Baylor, which could have been about losing a fight, but more likely had to do with seeing me in my native habitat.

The current safe house sat on a small street off the Schotten-ring. Several times we doused the headlights and backed into an alley or side street to look for a tail, but we were clean.

Satisfied, we drove straight to our destination. Tradition called this another Beethoven house, but the provenance was weak. The authorities had not awarded it a commemorative plaque.

Seated at a bare wooden table, Fenstermacher looked as exhausted as I felt. Unlike me, he could afford to let it show. He had not had the wind knocked out of him, either. I took another chair across from him.

"So, Klaus," I said. "Tell us about your business this evening."

My use of his Christian name earned an old-world frown, but I wanted him to understand who was in charge.

"You can talk to us and go back to your affairs," I said. "We'll even keep throwing some business your way. Or, we can give you to the police."

He surrendered with a very Austrian wave of the hand.

"I have come into possession of some valuable articles."

I waited. It would take him time to overcome his habit of silence.

"Real Canadian passports. Ready to be filled in."

"And you were doing business at the opera?"

"I used to do much of my business there. It is a surprisingly secure venue."

"Okay, you acquired these passports."

"I spread the word that I was in a position to be very helpful to the right customer."

Vienna had a vigorous grapevine. Postwar neutrality had done nothing to interfere with tradition.

"I said I would sell to anyone who could meet my price and get me into the opera gala."

"How did you get the ticket?"

"It was to be left for me at the box office under the name Macdonald."

"The Canadian prime minister. Very droll. Weren't you afraid that someone would steal it?"

"Everyone knew that the ticket was, what is the current term? Radioactive. To be left alone."

"So you had no idea who would sit next to you?"

"None. That young man was a complete stranger to me."

Everyone exchanged mystified looks. Everyone but me.

Fenstermacher laughed. "Americans. You are so charmingly naïve. Have you never been to Berlin? Of course you have. But none of you is quite old enough to remember the Twenties and Thirties, when Berlin was famous for its transvestite performers."

He indulged himself in another laugh. "I do apologize," he said.

Which in Viennese meant that he didn't.

"What did he give you?" I said. "I saw something change hands."

"A down payment, of course. Half the price. And photos for the passports."

"I'll take those photos."

"You are putting me out of business," he said. "Customers give me these things in confidence."

"We won't tell, and these customers won't either."

I took the photos from him. One was of a young man, but I had no way to match him with my adversary at the club. The other I knew.

"And how are you to deliver the finished product?"

"We are to meet tomorrow afternoon at the Sacher."

It was my turn to laugh. "Only the best for you, Klaus."

"I endured much discomfort in my youth," he said. "The war years were worse. I will never go through that again."

I looked at him and felt one of the random twinges of shame that tug at a spy. Of the two of us, he was the more honest.

But I should be used to that by now.

"Don't get too comfortable," I said.

I used a different team to back me up in the Cafe Sacher. None of them would be recognized from the Opera. Five of my men occupied tables covered with coffee, cakes and newspapers. I also recruited several young women from the embassy staff to accompany the men, and help them blend in.

In the center of the room Klaus Fenstermacher had a table for four to himself.

There had been jokes, because the usual surveillance job involved standing for hours in the rain or snow. Everyone was comfortable, everyone but Baylor and me. We had to stay out of sight, because the young man from the opera would know me and might have seen Baylor. The only hiding place was the kitchen. We stood behind the swinging double doors and took periodic looks through the porthole windows. We did a lot of jumping aside for the waiters as they entered and exited.

We didn't have to wait long, which was just as well. The kitchen staff had been instructed not to see us, but they were still growing tired of us.

Then a young man came in. He crossed the room and took a seat across from Klaus Fenstermacher. That was our signal. In seconds my men had surrounded the table. I emerged from the kitchen and approached.

The young man did the smart thing, which was nothing. He sat still with his hands flat on the table.

"What is your name?" I said.

"Wiedner, Willi."

"You're quite the quick change artist, Willi Wiedner."

He said nothing.

"It's a shame I couldn't stay to see whether the show went on without you," I said.

Again he kept silent, and I felt a bit of shame at taunting him. I of all people should know what his life was like. I laid the photographs on the table in front of him. "Who warned you I was following?"

"I heard the beads. That's what they're for. No one had any business coming through that curtain."

"Where is he?"

Wiedner said nothing.

"Think," I said. "It's over. Your plan has fallen apart, and you can't go back to the way things were."

"Meaning," he said, "you won't let us."

"If you wish. We know, and we will use the information if we have to. It's our job."

Wiedner gave me a look of bleak hatred. "Let us not talk about how you know."

His words lay on the tabletop for inspection by anyone. Now I had to make this operation work, or doubts about me would surface again. I was doubly suspect, for being a holdover from the OSS, and for being me.

"He is upstairs," said Wiedner.

"What room?"

"Three Zero Five."

I had not bothered to inquire at the front desk. This man knew how to bribe or threaten hotel staff into letting him stay off the books.

"Let's go," I said.

We were through with Fenstermacher, and he knew it. He was already halfway to the door. I almost laughed. He could get his rotundity in motion when he had to.

The luxury hotel had seen much in ten years of postwar tension. A gang of men crossing the lobby attracted little attention. We climbed the stairs to the first floor, the second, and finally the third. At each landing we opened the door and eyeballed the hallway before continuing.

We reached room 305. I stood to the side of the door and motioned Willi Wiedner to knock He was reluctant, but I reminded him with a look that his choices were limited.

Colonel Paunov opened the door. He showed no surprise at the sight of us, but that meant little. After a moment he stepped back inside the room. I turned to Baylor.

"Go start the extraction protocol."

He nodded and left.

I followed the Colonel into the room. For a long moment we looked at each other. Our contest was over. One of us had won, and the other had lost. It could have gone the other way if he had been the one to catch me with my humanity showing. Either way there was nothing to celebrate, because we were professionals.

"I understand now what you were saying to me at the Opera," I said.

"I have received a summons back to Moscow."

In much of the United States his English would have attracted less attention than my Brooklyn accent.

"I can only assume that I have an appointment with a bullet in the basement of the Lubyanka."

"For being homosexual."

"For being a security risk all these years. Maybe if I had told them in the beginning, but I was ambitious. Sometimes I try to remember why."

His eyes held a warning for me.

"You could have come to us," I said.

"And be a useful freak? We wanted a life. A real life, not years of debriefings in safe houses."

"They would have found you."

"Possibly."

When a spy deceives himself, he does a flawless job of it. Otherwise Paunov would realize that the KBG never gave up on a defector. Even with the resources of the CIA behind him, he and Willi would always be in danger. They would not have survived a week in Canada.

"Why did Willi kill Wolfi Stendl? It can't have been you."

"Stendl made a deal, and then he decided to demand more money. I would simply have paid him, but Willi is not a professional. He let his temper get the better of him."

"You should have aborted the operation."

"We were committed. There was no going back."

I checked my watch. "It's time to go downstairs. First we will get into a car. Follow my instructions exactly."

"I know how it is done."

We descended to the street. My men spread out from the hotel entrance. Another Mercedes signaled with its headlights and swerved to the curb. We surrounded Paunov and Willi as we hustled them into the back seat of the car. I closed the door on them, and signaled the driver to pull away. A second car took the place of the first at the curb. Baylor and I would follow the first and guard the rear.

Baylor lingered on the sidewalk and stole glances to the right and to the left.

"Move," I said. "What does the Agency teach you these days?"

He took a step toward the car, but he kept looking for the cavalry to arrive. Inspector Hegyi would enjoy that comparison. Europeans love cowboys and Indians.

I got into the rear seat and left the door open.

"He's not coming," I said.

Baylor's attempt at a blank look annoyed me. He couldn't even lie well.

"Hegyi. He's not coming."

Baylor climbed in beside me with as much enthusiasm as if I planned to send him to Moscow in Paunov's place.

"One thing you should always remember," I said, "is how far east Vienna lies."

This time his mystified look was real.

"The Viennese like to say that Asia begins at the city gates. I think they're more Asian than they realize."

He kept staring at me.

"Let me guess how it went. Hegyi listened and nodded, and you thought you had a deal. That's the American way, but this is Austria. It's not the way things are done here. You thought he would show up and grab Paunov, and the Austrians would expel him to Moscow. Then you could tell the Agency I had lost him."

I let him think about that.

"Relax. You just helped bring a KGB Colonel in. It should do wonders for your career."

The prospect did not seem to console him.

"And next time, remember what I said. It's your own side that can hurt you most."

The American West is the setting of our next story. Dewey's the sheriff of Red Lodge, in the Montana Territory, a man who would prefer to find a peaceful solution to a problem, but if that isn't possible, a man also good with a gun.

Mr. O'Leary comes to writing mysteries after a career in the cutthroat world of advertising. His non-fiction book, Warriors, Workers, Whiners & Weasels, explores the modern workplace, and his literary fiction may be found in such journals as Lost River Review and Mulberry Fork Review.

The Purification

by Timothy O'Leary

"Sheriff?"

Dewey jumped at the interruption, then glanced in annoyance at the thin head framed in the doorway. The clatter of boots on the wooden sidewalk or the loud whining of handcuffed drunks normally served as an angry knock. He wasn't accustomed to youngsters visiting his office.

He was immersed in the new Sears & Roebuck catalog, fingering the bedding section with careful consideration, as he imagined plopping his head on thick feather pillows. Thirty-nine cents each. Not cheap, but since his horse spooked, any relief to his sore neck would be worth the price He'd been riding near Twin Lake, investigating Tommy Dillon's report of a bad-tempered grizzly absconding with his brother while they were poaching deer. Tommy had barged into Dewey's office, bloody and bruised and looking like he'd rolled down the canyon, spouting a wild tale about a psychotic bear that knocked them down, ripped off one

175

of his brother's arms, and dragged the body by its gushing neck into the ravine. Tommy, not the bravest man in Carbon County, had hightailed it out, figuring nothing that big would be dissuaded by a Winchester 30-30.

Knowing the Dillon brothers, Dewey suspected the tale was born in the bottom of a bottle but figured he'd take a ride out anyway. Belle wasn't normally skittish, but they'd both been surprised by the roaring form, huge and brown as a barn, exploding out of a thicket of cottonwoods. Belle reared, catapulting Dewey onto a wide-felled pine. He feared he'd look up just in time to see yellow teeth spread wide for his neck, but the animal ambled off, satisfied to create a little non-lethal carnage. Dewey felt fortunate his spine hadn't snapped. But ever since, the pain felt like he was wearing a ten-pound hat.

He glanced curiously at the boy, his body still hidden by the door, a top-notch of dirty red hair poking through.

The kid looked at him with wide feral eyes.

"Come in, boy. What can I do you for?" Dewey puffed his smoldering cigar to life as the door swung open.

The boy was slight, five two or three, but with enough sinewy muscle Dewey knew he was slim from hard work and not lack of food. He looked to be thirteen or fourteen, dressed in a stained white shirt and the rough woolen trousers favored by the Mennonites. His boots and pants were splattered with the sandy red mud that formed Red Lodge's side streets, telling Dewey he'd avoided the cobblestone thoroughfares. His right cheek mushroomed angry purple, blood crusted near his ear lobe, like someone had taken a log to the side of his head.

The boy looked at the floor nervously, one hand picking at the other as if he intended to rip skin from a knuckle. "Uh, Sheriff, I'm surely sorry to bother you, but I got no other place to go, and I was hoping maybe you could maybe lock me up."

"Lock you up? You do something wrong?" The kid looked familiar, but there was something odd about him, not necessarily in a bad way, but he had a *sheen*. Aside from the bruise, he could be an actor from the movie theatre that had just opened up the street. More pretty than handsome, a face that would be equally pleasant on a man or woman.

"Not sure I did anything wrong, but my Pa seems to think so. He took after me yesterday. Beat me hard. He does that sometimes, but not like yesterday. He aimed to kill me and drop my body down one of those old mine shafts up Rock Creek. Send me to hell, he said, and I tend to believe he means it. He tripped while he was going for an axe, and I ran out. Otherwise, I'm pretty sure he'd of chopped my head off. I spent the night in the woods, but I can't survive out there by myself. Not for long anyway, so I came to town. I got nothing to pay my way, but Pa said the Sheriff was hired to protect folks."

"Why in the world would your Pa want to cut your head off?" Dewey frowned, blowing a billowy line of smoke, thinking he probably knew the answer. The hills around Red Lodge were chock-full of angry men: dust-covered miners working worthless claims, drunks cutting a little timber to support shiftless lives, reprobates and crazies that enjoyed taking their frustrations out on the women and children that sometimes wandered into their lives.

The boy seemed embarrassed. "He says I'm wrong in the head. There's evil in me. I'm a tempter and a pox. Said Satan sent me down to confuse men and drag them off to hell, and by killing me he'd help save mankind."

Dewey tapped an ash, and snorted in disgust. "Who might your father be?"

"Canner Shultz." The boy announced the name as if introducing a political candidate. "He works a claim near Soda Butte. You might know him. He sure knows you. Told me you killed Lester Andrews and his brother. Called you a real old-time gunfighter, like Wyatt Earp." The boy brightened at the mention. It amazed Dewey, the different ways an old story could be retold.

Canner Shultz. Not a name Dewey cared to hear, but it made sense. He now remembered seeing the kid in town with Canner and his wife two, three years earlier, the boy just a pipsqueak.

He'd heard that Canner's wife had since died with her second in childbirth.

Canner arrived in Red Lodge representing himself as a preacher, spouting his own brand of angry religion that folks found anything but comforting. In fact, Canner's God seemed a sadistic son-of-a-bitch. Somehow he'd met a woman, Dewey recalled she was from Bridger, and after they married, he gave up the Jesus business and moved out of town to strike it rich mining. After his wife passed Canner sometimes came to Red Lodge mumbling to Jesus, as if tragedy afforded him a direct line to the Lord. Apparently, Jesus told him to drink, as he was known to tear up a saloon from time to time. In fact, he'd spent more than one night in this very building, sleeping it off behind bars. And whenever Canner got out of control, Dewey knew to send at least two deputies and avoid the scene himself, feeling too old these days to engage in barroom antics, especially with a man of Canner's dimensions and disposition.

The boy had inherited Canner's red hair and long Germanic nose, but not yet his size. Dewey himself was a big man, 6'2" and stout, but Canner towered over him, probably 6'5", tree trunk legs, and knotted arms hardened by years of sluicing. Dewey wasn't inclined towards fear, but he always approached Canner with caution.

He peered at the youngster as he moved into the room. Dewey raised a hand towards the boy's chin, who recoiled, then moved forward when he understood Dewey meant no harm. "Nasty bruise," Dewey said, turning the boy's head, examining the red rivulet below his right ear. "Can you hear OK?"

The boy nodded. "Yeah, it's sore, but I hear fine."

"You hurt anywhere else?"

The boy blew a long sigh, shaking his head an unconvincing no. "Does this mean you'll lock me up?"

"This isn't a hotel. The jail is for criminals, and you don't appear to be breaking any laws. Now your Pa; that might be a different matter." Dewey traced a bruise that began at the base of the boy's skull and disappeared somewhere south of his collar bone.

"You can't go after my Pa. You do that and he really will kill me. I don't want to get him in no trouble, I just don't want him to catch me. I can sleep anywhere, and I can help out. I'm good at cleaning," he said, motioning at the wood stove, "And I could keep the stove stoked. I make fine coffee too. Even cook a bit. Not fancy, but Pa likes it. I won't be any trouble, and soon as I figure out how to make some money I'll be on my way. Maybe get a job over in Billings. I'm mighty strong for my size."

He winced when Dewey's hand dropped to his shoulder. "Son, take your shirt off."

The boy shook his head, moving towards the door. "Probably I shouldn't be here. I don't want no trouble."

"Take your shirt off," Dewey said firmly. He fought back a gulp when he saw the boy's naked torso, the rope-like scars on his stomach and across his back, some healed clean, but others hanging bits of bloody dried skin.

"Good God, what did he do to you?"

"He purifies me sometimes," the boy said in a whisper.

"What do you mean, purifies?"

"He gets drunk, ties me up, and brands me with the fire pokin' rods. Sometimes I pass out. Claims they're signs to rid me of Satan. Cleanse me of the sin that lives in me. But last night he said it was too late, that the Devil had me for good."

"Jesus Christ. Did he do this anywhere else on your body?"

The boy nodded. "I'm like this all over. My legs, my behind, even the top of my feet. That hurt the worst."

"Let me see."

The boy dropped his pants. He was wearing rough home-made underwear that hung to his knees, his calves and feet a mass of scars. Dewey lowered the shorts a couple inches, revealing long crosses branded into his buttocks.

"How long has he been doing this?"

"It started a couple months after my Ma died. Sometimes I'd wake up, maybe because I could smell him. He smells mean. Sour. He'd be sitting on the side of my bed staring at me. He'd touch me, at first kind of soft, but then he gets angry. And then the beatings, and after a while...." The boy drifted off and traced a finger across a scar on his abdomen. "The purification."

"Christ," Dewey said, and signaled the boy to get dressed. "What's your name?"

"Jacob. Jacob Schultz. Named after my Ma's father."

Dewey gently grasped his hand, removing his finger from the scar. "Jacob, I'm going to take you to the doctor to get fixed up. We'll figure out a place for you to stay. Someplace nicer than the jail. And let me tell you something. Nobody, not your father, *nobody* is ever going to do anything like this to you again. Understand me? You're safe." The boy nodded, and Dewey could see how desperately he wanted to believe him.

After the incident with Belle and the bear, Dewey upgraded his mode of transportation. Bouncing on even the gentlest horse made his neck ache even worse. Surprisingly, the Carbon County Commissioners hadn't objected when he requisitioned a new 1915 Model T, the first real actual police car within five counties. Dewey was popular in these parts, a bridge between the violent, saloon-laden mining town that didn't want to grow up, and a more progressive contingent that wanted to see Red Lodge become a real city, so the Commissioners tended to give him what he wanted.

Over the last fifteen years Dewey had made the Carbon County Sheriff's Department into one of the best in the State of Montana. The previous year his deputies even started wearing uniforms, all except Dewey, who preferred his Levis and Pendleton shirt. He also made sure his men were equipped with the most modern firearms, Colt 1911 automatic military pistols and Springfield pump-action 12-gauge shotguns.

He'd moved to Red Lodge in 1899, fresh from the Army fighting the Spaniards in Cuba. He'd come to Montana to work in the coal mines, but discovered that profession short-changed him in a couple ways, lifespan and pay, and he quickly took a job as a Sheriff's Deputy. Red Lodge was out of control, ragged mean miners stumbling between twenty saloons, law enforcement content to mostly watch and help mop-up blood.

Six months into the job, Dewey's life changed. He was walking down the alley behind the Merchant's Bank when the back door burst open, and a major commotion poured out. Lester Andrews and his brother Butch had been drinking for the better part of two days. When the money dried up from their tiny bit of gold, they decided to make a cash withdrawal. Not criminals, more just hardened alcoholics, Dewey normally could have taken a fist to the side of their heads and they'd have come peacefully. But Avril Thompkins, the Bank's Vice President, fired off a couple shots from the puny .22 he kept in his desk drawer. The Brothers hadn't anticipated any resistance, and hightailed it out the back when the shooting started, Lester firing a couple times into the ceiling to slow Avril down. Followed by a half-assed shot at the deputy when they saw him in the alley, the bullet whizzing five feet above his head. Dewey drew his revolver, hoping the boys would accept their predicament peacefully as he yelled, "Put them down." But he saw a wildness in Lester's eyes that led Dewey to take aim and drop him. Butch Andrews, stumbling drunk and shocked by the smoky hole in his brother's chest, grabbed for Lester's gun, forcing Dewey to cap him too with a single shot to the forehead. No great feat of marksmanship, as both men were only five feet away, but it allowed Deputy Sheriff Dewey Mansfield to take his place in Western lore as the last gunfighter in Montana, with the story growing more heroic with every telling.

What people didn't know was that Dewey puked into the bank's rain barrel when he saw what he'd done, and shook so badly that for fifteen minutes he could hardly walk. He'd never shot a man before, at least none that he knew of. Everyone he'd fired at in Cuba had been running through trees at a distance. But no matter. He was a shoe-in for Sheriff in the next election—every town wanted a legendary gunfighter as their sheriff—a position he'd held for fifteen years. Luckily for Red Lodge he was good at his job.

Jacob gasped when Dewey led him to the car. "Never been in one of these," he said, carefully sliding into the passenger seat as if it might break. His eyes widened as Dewey pulled a U-turn and headed east, and he rubbed the leather dashboard with light fingertips. Cars were rare enough that people turned to stare, and Jacob waved, all smiles, as if he were the star of a parade.

Doctor McBride lived across the street from the new hospital in a white Victorian that had originally belonged to one of the Carbon Coal Company owners. Who's your friend?" he asked when he answered the door.

"Morning, Doc. This fine young man is Jacob Schultz, and my guess is he would love one of those tasty rolls you keep around. And maybe some bacon and milk, as I don't believe he's had his breakfast yet." They led Jacob to the kitchen, and Doc put out a spread for the boy, leaving him to eat as the two men exited to the converted examination room.

"And how did young Jacob come to be here?"

"You know his old man, Canner Shultz?"

Doc nodded. "Big crazy German? Used to stand in front of the café and holler at everyone about hell and damnation?"

"That's him. I need you to examine the boy. Looks like Canner brutalized the kid pretty good. Burning, beating him, plus I fear Canner's a diddler. Never seen anything quite like it. Make you sick to your stomach. Jacob says Canner intends to kill him, and until I have a talk with the bastard we need to keep the boy out of sight. Said he spent the night in the woods, so he'll probably sleep once he's fed and you get done looking him over. Can you put him up for a few days?"

"I'll stow him in the back bedroom."

Dewey nodded and thanked his friend. "You can update me this evening," Friday being their standing supper night.

On Tuesdays Dewey attended the Kiwanis luncheon at The Pollard Hotel. He had no idea what Kiwanis even meant. A few of the local businessmen had opened the first charter in Montana a few months earlier, and it seemed important to spend time with the movers and shakers. Plus, it was a free lunch. As usual Dewey was cornered by the Main Street merchants, who groused about two whorehouses on the edge of town. Dewey suspected the men's wives made them complain, as he knew at least a couple of their husbands were patrons.

Dewey was talking to the mayor after lunch when Dan Plummer approached. Dewey's right-hand deputy was deceptively crafty for his size and age. Most men weren't intimidated by a rotund five-foot-six inch lawman pushing sixty, but of course, they'd never witnessed Dan's talents with the baton that swung from his belt. That morning Dewey had told Dan to keep an eye out for Canner.

"Sorry to interrupt," Dan said, "but I wanted you to know your friend's in town. At The Lincoln, probably on his fifth beer by now."

The Mayor, always anxious for gossip, perked up. "So, there's going to be some action?"

"I doubt it," Dewey said, shaking his hand goodbye. "Just a little annoyance is all."

Canner Schultz was sitting in the rear of the saloon, rolling a cigarette and chattering to nobody in particular. From a distance he looked harmless enough, drunk and shaking. But as they approached Dewey recognized the same look he saw in Lester Andrews' eyes all those years ago, right before he put a bullet in him.

"Afternoon Canner. What brings you to town?"

Canner glanced up to acknowledge Dewey. He'd lost weight, still huge, but his skin the yellow tint of a sickly man. "Sheriff.

Afternoon." He tilted his head, and said, "Come for supplies, and to look for my boy. Hoping he might've wandered into town."

Dewey nodded. "Or he might've run off, afraid for his life?" He pulled back a chair and sat down in front of Canner as Dan moved behind. "Maybe he's trying to get away from a father that beats him. A sick son-of-a-bitch that tortures him and tries to cut his head off."

Canner flashed red, but stayed contained. "You know where he is?"

"Canner, child beating is against the law. Trying to kill a boy, even your own blood, that's against the law. Serious enough that you could spend the foreseeable future in Deer Lodge."

Canner snorted. "How I discipline him is my business. He's mine, and I'll do with him what I please. You just tell me where he is, for starters, and let's see what transpires from there, shall we?"

"You're not understanding the situation." Dewey leaned in. "Jacob's safe now, and you're not going to touch him. I'm this close to locking you up, maybe send you away until Jacob is full grown and might decide to take a beating to his Pa for old time's sake."

Canner rose, but Dan pushed his baton hard on his shoulder, forcing him back into his chair. "You'd do best to hold your temper," Dewey said, "Dan here senses the tiniest threat, he'll snap your damn neck with his stick. Believe me."

Canner simmered, but stayed silent.

"You got a couple choices, "Dewey said. "You can get up, go back to your place, mind your claim, and leave the boy alone. Or you can cause trouble, and maybe we'll stop by the hospital to get you fixed-up before we lock you up. Might even forget where we put you, though I wonder who'd be seeking you out anyway. Your choice. Either works for us, given we don't care much for child beaters."

Canner slumped, rage draining. "Sheriff, you don't understand. The boy ain't right. He's got the devil in him. He's a

The next morning Dewey saddled up Belle for the first time in several weeks, the horse frisky, high-stepping at having a job to do. The Model T wouldn't make it where he planned to go, the road up Beartooth Pass a jagged trail six feet too narrow for a car. He had a plot map that clearly showed Canner Schultz's claim, which he calculated to be a two-hour ride.

Forty minutes into the trip he vacillated between cursing Canner Shultz to hell, and pledging to order those Sears pillows. By the time he reached Canner's stake the throbbing pain in his neck was blurring his vision. He tied Belle to a tree a hundred yards from the smoke rising in the clearing, checked to make sure his 12-gauge was loaded, then worked his way through the thicket towards Canner's cabin.

"Canner. Canner Schultz. You here?" Dewey yelled as he reached the clearing. There was a tiny cabin, garbage strewn all around, two wooden chairs facing a fire pit in front of the structure, a small corral with Canner's horse maybe a hundred feet off. Dewey blanched when he saw the iron rods propped near the fire pit, wondering if they'd been used on Jacob.

Canner came around the side of the cabin wiping his hands on a dirty rag. "Sheriff. Sure didn't expect to see you all the way up here. What is it you want?"

"Well, I'd start with hello and the offer of some coffee, if you're feeling hospitable. It's a long ride." Dewey motioned at the pot sitting on a grate above the fire.

"Before I welcome travelers, I like to know they mean me no harm. You carrying that shotgun makes me wonder. You here to arrest me?" Canner balled the rag, threw it down, and widened his stance.

"No, I'm here to talk, hopefully straighten things out. We both know how you can get rambunctious, and I brought this along to make sure things don't get out of hand. If you pledge to control yourself I'd be happy to set it down, as its heavy and I'm tired."

Canner peered at Dewey, then motioned at one of the chairs. "I'll get you a cup. But I warn you, not everyone takes to my coffee. Tends to be a bit thick."

"I'm sure it'll be fine," Dewey said, and set the shotgun down as he took a seat, then reached back to rub his neck.

The coffee was the consistency of the sludge Dewey drained from his Model T's crankcase, but somehow comforting. The two made small talk about mining and the canyon, then Dewey got to the point. "I'm not in the business of breaking up families, but I also can't stand still and see the boy brutalized."

"Sheriff, a man knows his own blood, knows their soul. I'm trying to save Jacob. That's my responsibility. Satan is dirty business, and it's my duty as his father, and as a Christian. You got to trust that I know what I'm doing."

"Well, Canner, I don't have any children that I know of, so I'm not one for parenting advice. But I want you to take it easy. You damn near killed him, and he don't deserve that." Canner dropped his head and didn't say a word. "Can you keep in control if I allow him to come back?"

Canner nodded. "Sheriff, I'll do what's best for the boy. You have my word on that."

"The law doesn't allow me to split up a family, but it's against my better judgment that I'm going to trust you on this. Remember, I'll be keeping an eye on you. Saddle-up and I'll take you to him, long as you pledge to treat him better."

Canner looked up, surprised. "He's in town?"

"Nope. I sent him to stay with the Hughes family yesterday, over near Twin Lake, less than an hour from here. They've got a passel of kids, said one more wouldn't make much difference as long as it wasn't permanent. You know Joseph Hughes?" Canner shook his head. "No matter, I'll lead you to where they live and let them know it's OK for Jacob to return with you."

Canner and Dewey spent the next hour riding in silence. As they neared the lake, Dewey stopped to let Canner pass. "I have to stretch my knee and take a piss." When he remounted, he followed ten feet behind. Five minutes later he recognized the tangle of trees where he'd been thrown.

"They live right on the lake?' Canner said, and turned with a confused look. "I've fished here, and never seen a house."

"No, their place is just over the bluff. A new homestead, nice piece of ground." Dewey quietly unholstered his Colt when Canner faced front again. "Canner, something I'm curious about, you being religious and all. Just how *does* God feel about you buggering your own son?" Canner jerked his horse to a halt, and reared around to face Dewey's raised gun. "Don't go doing anything crazy now. Big fellow like you makes an easy target."

"What in the hell are you saying? And pointing a gun at me?"

"I'm just trying understand a man that rapes, tortures, and damn near kills his own son. Learn what makes a sick son-of-a-bitch like you tick."

"Where's my boy?" Canner demanded.

Belle skittered, and out of his right eye Dewey saw bushes rustling fifty feet away. "Canner, I've had to spend a lifetime thinking about men like you. Men so sick in the head they rape children without the least remorse. Hell, I had a father that was that kind of man, so I don't hold much tolerance for your type."

Canner grew pale. "Listen, Sheriff, I…"

Dewey interrupted. "Like your boy, I got the hell away from home before my Pa could kill me. Left at fourteen and never looked back. Found the army, and that saved me. But I dreamt about him. Still do. And you know what haunts me the most?"

Canner eyes darted, looking for an escape route, and finally shook his head.

"That I didn't just kill the bastard. Put an end to his foolishness. Even as a kid I could have stabbed him in the heart while he slept, or caved his head in with a rock. But a father has a particular power over a son, so I ran."

"You didn't bring me here for Jacob, did you?" Canner, terrified but resigned.

"No," Dewey said as he fired into Canner's chest. The blast knocked Canner backward, horse rearing, his right foot catching in the stirrup as he fell, body dragging as the animal raised-up. Dewey grabbed the reins and settled the horse, then dismounted to free Canner's foot, smoky air acrid with gunpowder and blood. Canner's body spasmed, the fist-sized hole below his throat bubbling dark red. Dewey stared at him curiously, with none of the revulsion he felt when he shot the Andrews brothers.

Both horses whinnied as a low-pitched vibration rumbled from the trees. Dewey mounted Belle and grabbed the reins on Canner's horse, steering up the trail. He turned midway at the grizzly's roar. The bear had clamped onto one of Canner's legs and was dragging him into the trees, leaving a wide red stain.

Back in Red Lodge he rode straight to Doc's house, tying both horses to a post at the back. "That god damn automobile of yours broke again?" Doc said, motioning at the horses.

"Not exactly. I had some official business that couldn't be navigated in my fine Ford."

"And it took two horses?"

"Well, the one here is for Jacob. Figured he might need it. How's the boy today?"

"He's fine," Doc said, looking curious. "I got him doing a little cleaning at the hospital to help pay his board. He's a good worker. He's feeling better, got his strength back. How'd you come across another horse?"

"Belongs to Canner," Dewey said. "I rode up to have a chat with him, but he was nowhere to be found. Didn't want to leave the animal on the off-chance he wasn't coming back. Too fine an animal to starve to death, and I figured I'd give it to Jacob to take care of, at least until Canner shows up. If he does shows up."

"*If* he shows up," Doc repeated slowly. "You think something might've happened to him?"

"You never know. Lot of grizzly action in those parts. A dangerous proposition to be up there all by yourself. Anyway, I have to check in at the office, make sure there hasn't been a crime wave hit Red Lodge since this morning. Maybe we can catch up later for a beer?"

"Sure," Doc said as his friend walked away. "Dewey, you OK?"

Dewey squeezed the back of his neck, then realized with a smile the pain was almost gone. "Yeah, Doc, I actually feel the best I have in a long time." And right then the thought occurred to him that he might not need those new pillows after all.

Another frontier features next, the wilds of the Caucasus, back when Russian Cossacks used pistol and saber to settle matters of honor, and deceit and deception were currency. In this story, an itinerant peddler weaves a delicate path between rival factions, with death never far away.

Mr. Lawton is a past member of the MWA National Board and has close to a hundred stories published, many of them in Alfred Hitchcock Mystery Magazine, and ten mini-mysteries in Woman's World Magazine.

A Private Matter

by R.T. Lawton

When a long shadow cast itself across the floor of my hut, I turned slightly toward the entrance to see one of the Cossack elders standing there. Daddy Bohdan, in his loose white shirt, baggy trousers, cracked leather belt and worn black boots, had come for me. He filled the open doorway, grinning, cap in one hand and long grey beard clutched in the other.

"Armenian, the Russian Lieutenant sends his respects and requests the honor of your presence."

In my business of trading goods on both sides of the Terek River, such flowery words spoken in my direction were seldom heard... unless a person wanted something special. Usually, this something consisted of a low price for a much desired item. Maybe a silken kerchief or silver trinket for his mistress, his *little soul* as the Cossacks so aptly called them. Or perhaps something only for himself, such as an ornate dagger of tempered steel from forges in Turkic lands to the south. But this, this sudden show of respect had a different feel to it. This was not for trinkets.

I turned my head fully in his direction to watch his face.

"Which Russian Lieutenant? There seems to be several of them quartered in the village these days."

Bohdan leaned his shoulder against the doorframe. "It's Vassili Ivanoff, the one come down to us from Petersburg, up near the Baltic."

I tried to wait the old Cossack out for more information, but he appeared content to stand there in silence.

"And what does Lieutenant Vassili want with me?" I finally inquired.

"There's to be a duel—" he began.

"Ah, but the General forbade his officers to engage in duels amongst themselves," I interrupted, hoping to avoid any fateful involvement with the Russian masters of this frontier settlement. "He needs all his men to be healthy for his summer campaign into the wild country below the Terek this year. Anyone breaking his command is to be severely punished."

"You heard truly, Armenian, that's why this little disagreement will be settled on the right bank of the Terek, at some distance from our military cordon."

"On the Chechen side of the river?" I asked.

"It's a point of discretion already agreed on by both parties," replied Daddy Bohdan as he stroked his beard. "In this manner, if one or more of the Russian officers should happen to be injured or killed, such an incident will then be blamed on a raiding party of Abreks come north from the hill tribes. The General will never know the truth."

I thought on this for a quick moment. It seemed that the minds of men often schemed to get around rules imposed upon them, especially if strong emotions drove them to an end. This appeared to be one of those times, but why include me in their deception?

"The Russians can go kill themselves without my presence," was my response. "As you can see with your own eyes, I'm packing to leave in the morning. There are other villages where I must take my goods."

"That is one of the reasons why Vassili chose you as his second."

I handed the last of my trading stock to the little Nogai boy who acted as my servant and then stood erect.

"He wants me as his second?"

"To help make all the necessary arrangements not yet agreed on," said Bohdan, "nothing more on your part."

"I know little about being someone's second in a duel. Tell him to pick another for that questionable honor."

The old Cossack shrugged, yet his grin remained with a hint of slyness to it now.

"He can't. This private matter is set for tomorrow morning and must be kept small in numbers. Already too many may have heard of the challenge and acceptance. The rest must be done in as much secrecy as possible. And, if you are to leave immediately afterwards, then that is one less person for the General to question, should he somehow hear rumors and become suspicious. I, myself, have planned a hunting trip and will be gone for several days."

Daddy Bohdan was deliberately leaving something out in his telling of this affair, but I had yet to know what it was. I would need to ask more questions and hope to find the missing piece for myself.

"How many are to be involved?" I inquired.

Looking now at the splayed fingers on his left hand, the Old Cossack used the tip of his right index finger to tick off each name as he recited the list, starting at his left first finger.

"There's me, then there's Lieutenant Vassili Ivanoff, there's Lieutenant Aleksei Petrovich Maksimovich," He paused before pointing at the tip of his little finger. "There's Sub-Lieutenant Grigori as Aleksei's second,"

He paused again. The grin was gone. He'd run out of fingers.

"Ah, of course," he finally said pointing at his thumb, "and then there's you as Vassili's second. Five of us makes for a tight little group. Easier to keep a secret that way." He closed his fingers into a fist.

"And why should I risk incurring the General's displeasure by becoming Vassili's second?"

Daddy Bohdan's sly grin was back.

"Some in our little group put our heads together about this situation. It seems that Lieutenant Vassili owes you a sizeable debt, does he not? A debt he promised to pay as soon as his rich, merchant father sent one of his twice-annual stipends by courier from Petersburg. However, it also occurs to us that you may not be able to collect all those rubles owed to you if Vassili suffers a grievous wound tomorrow morning."

The old Cossack had keenly utilized his strongest argument in our short conversation. Whereas others in this world concerned themselves with glory, or love, the acquisition of power, or even their own concept of honor, I worked hard to make a profit on my trading goods. Money was my way of keeping score, and uncollected debts ended up on the wrong side of the ledger. It might serve me well to at least find out more about this situation before I decided on any course of action.

"What disagreement led to this, this affair of honor?" I hesitated to call it that, but surely this was how both parties involved would see the matter before one of them found a bullet lodged in his chest.

"Come," said Daddy Bohdan and took my arm in his calloused grasp. "It's a long story and I will tell you as we walk. After all, they are expecting us at Vassili's hut."

If there were to be five of us involved and two of us were now walking towards the hut, which Vassili rented from one of the local Cossack families, then I could only guess who of the remaining three *they* were.

"As you well know," began Daddy Bohdan, "our Lieutenant Vassili's family is from that new class of rich merchants in Petersburg, while Lieutenant Aleksei comes from an old line of nobility in the Muscovy area. This matter of one's heritage has been a constant source of friction between the two."

"They're willing to die over a distinction of birth?" I muttered in a low voice. This made no sense to me, but then I had always preferred to use the brains that God had given me rather than try to settle any conflict with personal violence on my own part.

"It has become more than a matter of class," replied the old Cossack. "Aleksei has the arrogant manner of his lineage, thus the way he treats others can soon wear on a man. And, it's true he's not well liked, even by the other Russian officers. But also lately, one of our local girls has come between them."

Now we were getting to the final cause of friction. Slights of class might be endured for the sake of one's military career, but raw emotions from the heart prompted many an unwise action. Untended graves in the Wild Country south of the river gave mute testimony to this fact.

"Each lieutenant courted the same young woman in our village," continued Bohdan. "She is a lively thing and fair to look upon. Long black hair, dark eyes and skin the color of almonds." He smacked his lips in appreciation. "No doubt these were a birth gift from her mother who was taken in a raid on the Turks by one of our bold Cossacks many years ago."

I knew the girl he mentioned. She had a certain beauty and, like many women, she used her beauty to great advantage. I wondered if she knew what other results might be produced from her actions of playing one headstrong young man off against another.

We had only a short distance left to go. As evening darkened the sky with shades of purples, pinks, and fading yellows on the horizon, boisterous sounds of village girls bringing their family's cattle in through the front gates of the stockade reached my ears. Some girls whistled to move the cows along the dirt street, while others bandied gossip and traded good-natured jests. Already, I could see trails of golden dust roiling up from the cattle's hooves, while clouds of gnats and small swarms of black mosquitoes hovered over their broad backs. Soon, Daddy Bohdan and I would have to step to one side in order to avoid the crush as small individual herds plodded past, the girls reaching out with long switches to guide each beast into the correct yard for the night. Low wattle fences surrounded the raised house of each family, with some houses built close enough to the road that a young Cossack on horseback paying suit to a lover could merely lean over to knock on the window and exchange a few quick words before riding on.

Daddy Bohdan took up his telling again.

"Vassili threw small parties for the girl and her close friends, with sweet pastries and bottles of *chikhir*, our strong wine. He bought her trinkets from your store goods, silk headscarves in bright patterns of reds and greens, and a pair of earrings made of Turkic silver among other items. You probably know the full tally better than I, since it's you he owes the money."

True. I knew exactly how far into debt Vassilli was to me. The question now on my mind was what would I have to do to ensure he was alive long enough to pay off this debt? I was soon to find that other minds were already searching for a solution to this problem.

As we stepped through the small yard gate, I noticed two men sitting on a rough wooden bench on the front porch of a rented hut with its reed thatched roof and roughly carved gables. It was Lieutenant Vassilli and Sub-Lieutenant Grigori with their heads close together whispering. Apparently, they were discussing the impending duel and had no wish for their voices to carry to others who might bear tales to the General's ears. At least they were being discreet.

We crossed the worn grass yard and moved halfway up the porch stairs. Now, the old Cossack and I were standing eye level with the other two, who quit their whispering and moved slightly apart.

Grigori was the first to speak.

"Ah, good end of day to you Armenian," he said in a friendly manner. "Nice of you to come as Lieutenant Vassilli's second. Now we can conclude our arrangements for this private matter."

I glanced momentarily at Vassilli, but his face showed me nothing and no words were forthcoming, only a nod to acknowledge my presence. Very well, I would see what Grigori had to say as Lieutenant Aleksei's second. Perhaps there was reason in this man and we could avoid this predicament altogether.

"Is it possible," I began, "that cooler heads will be able to prevail? Perhaps you and I can persuade these two gentlemen from meeting each other in a duel."

A serious look crossed Grigori's face as if he were contemplating this possibility. Then he shook his head slightly.

"Unfortunately, no. I've discussed cancelling the meeting across the river tomorrow, but both parties feel their honor is at stake. Even though we have tried to keep circumstances quiet, there was at least one other junior officer present during the confrontation. No doubt by now he has told others of his same rank, and word has spread." He gestured at the old Cossack standing beside me. "Daddy Bohdan here is also privy to this information, but assures me he has told no one. It appears the duel must go forward else reputations will be lost."

"Exactly how did this confrontation come to pass?" I inquired. Perhaps a way out might be found in the details.

Grigori looked to Vassilli, who nodded his permission, and then back to me.

"It seems," said Grigori, "that Vassilli was giving a party at a young woman's house, someone in whom he has a great interest. He had invested the last of his coin in vodka and sweetmeats for the girls. All were laughing and dancing and playing kissing games, having a festive time, when another person rode up on horseback and knocked on the window. The young woman went to see who was there. She stayed at the open window for a long while, talking, some say flirting, with the person outside. Unhappy with her extended absence, as the story was told to me, Vassilli soon appeared beside her in the window frame and saw it was his rival, Lieutenant Aleksei, on horseback in the street. Words were exchanged and Vassilli gave Aleksei a personal insult."

Grigori paused in the telling, crossing his right leg over the other at the knee. One brightly polished cavalry boot now hovered a few inches above the wood plank porch. "At that point," Grigori continued, "Lieutenant Aleksei felt compelled to uphold the honor of his family. In the heat of anger, he issued a challenge."

"And then," I prompted him for more.

"Vassilli accepted. As the challenged party, it was his right to choose which weapons were to be used." Grigori cast his eyes in Vassilli's direction before finishing his statement. "A wise move on his part."

"How so," I inquired.

Grigori removed a leather pouch from a side pocket of his coat, extracted a clay pipe from the pouch and began to tamp shreds of loose black tobacco into the small pipe bowl as he spoke.

"Amongst the Russian officers, Lieutenant Aleksei has a fierce reputation with a saber. As I see it, Vassilli here would have stood little chance in any meeting with swords."

Grigori placed the pouch back into his coat pocket while holding the clay pipe by its bowl with his other hand. He turned his head slightly towards Lieutenant Vassili.

"No offense," he told him. Then he directed his attention back to me.

"By holding his temper enough in check for Aleksei to be the one issuing the challenge, Vassilli was able to choose pistols as his weapon of choice, which gives him a fair chance of winning. However, I also think that the selection of pistols provides us with a solution to this situation."

Here, he paused as if to ensure he had our full attention.

He definitely had mine. I, for one, would accept almost any solution which removed the risk of violence and bodily harm.

"Since high spirited young men are known for exchanging insults in the heat of a disagreement, words they may regret after their tempers have cooled," Grigori continued, "it has become acceptable these days for both parties to quietly agree in advance as to the outcome of their duel."

His right boot swung back and forth in small arcs over the wood planks.

"Under this type of agreement, both parties face each other with loaded pistols. Upon command, each man raises his pistol above his shoulder and discharges his round into the air. Having thus withstood fire from his opponent, so to speak, everyone's honor remains intact."

He uncrossed his long legs.

"However, I'm sure there are some small details which will still need to be negotiated. Details…such as the insult given to Lieutenant Aleksei's family…before he would be willing to join this type of agreement. I will let you gentlemen discuss those possibilities among yourselves while I find a light for my pipe."

With that, Grigori stood up and made his way into the hut. I watched him go. In front of the brick and porcelain tiled stove, he selected a long thin twig and opened the oven door. He soon had a small flame on one end of the stick to light his tobacco.

I knew the Cossacks did not like for their lodgers or guests to smoke inside their huts, but I figured Grigori would yet stay away long enough for us three outside on the porch to conduct our business. And in truth as it turned out, it did not take much persuasion from me for Lieutenant Vassilli to give his agreement to Grigori's offered solution. For much of our time, Vassilli seemed to stare off into the distance and speak as few words as possible. No matter, he was probably contemplating the events of tomorrow morning if these discussions did not work out. But, if all conflicts could be resolved this easily by a simple agreement, then the world would be a more peaceful place.

As our mostly one-sided conversation wore down, Daddy Bohdan gave a cough.

Grigori must have taken this as a signal our discussion had concluded. He strolled back onto the porch and resumed his place on the bench.

"Lieutenant Vassilli agrees to your proposal," I stated, "as long as he is not required to apologize for anything he said at the window this afternoon."

Grigori frowned as if he had expected this particular problem.

"However," I quickly interjected, "he *will* agree to take back the insult." This had been Daddy Bohdan's offered compromise when Vassilli and I had appeared to reach an impasse in our discussion. Fortunately for everyone involved, Vassilli had readily agreed to Bohdan's idea. At least now we could move forward to the next obstacle.

Grigori nodded his approval. "Aleksei might agree to this compromise, however the proposal will need to be presented to him by someone who can be very persuasive with words. That's where you come in, Armenian. You are seen as impartial to both parties involved, plus we all believe you to be an honorable man. Yes, you are the right man to present this final proposal to Aleksei."

As I pondered his statements, Sub-Lieutenant Grigori rose from the bench and moved towards the stairs.

"Come. I will go with you and we will see what Lieutenant Aleksei Maksimovich thinks of the arrangements you have made on his behalf."

I was not happy with being drawn into this little deception these Russian officers had come up with, but I saw no harm in the proposed agreement. It was better than a death or injury and then having to foster a lie as to how either of these had occurred. I would go along with their solution, and in the end my ledger books would balance. So be it.

I was up long before dawn, skipping my morning tea and any early repast. Much was still on my mind for this morning's happenings. In short time, my little Nogai helper and I had the riding horses saddled and my trading goods loaded onto the backs of our pack animals.

Thick dew clung to blades of grass and dripped from tall weeds in the yard as I mounted. In the sky, a waxing moon near full beamed down on us as clouds of mist from the river drifted through the damp dirt streets. Cattle in their yards were lowing, anxious to reach their grazing fields outside the stockade, but few lights showed yet in windows of the nearby Cossack houses. The boy and I started our ride silently through the mist, packhorses following in single file.

I saw by torchlight that the Middle Gate was already open. The guard leaned back against the log wall as if he had been recently roused and was now trying to go back to sleep standing up at the end of his watch. He stiffened slightly at our approach, until he saw it was only a trader of goods and his Nogai helper, no officers to worry about, then returned to his position of rest. We left the village without a word, only the slow plodding of horses' hooves and the creaking of saddle leather.

A couple of *versts* along the road, I pulled rein to the right near a long dead Plane tree, its bone-white trunk scarred from a past summer strike of lightning, yet still it stood towering over the land. Daddy Bohdan waited for us here on horseback. This morning, he was dressed in a tattered white Circassian coat with his musket strapped across his back. Several of the individual cartridge pockets sewn vertically on the front of his coat rounded out with charges of powder and shot wrapped in tubes of waxy paper. His cap was set at an angle and his face was hard as if he had serious business to attend.

"You are slow, Armenian. We need to be across the river before people are about. The crossing is behind me."

He wheeled his horse about and we fell in behind him. After a few hundred feet through the woods, we descended into a small ravine that came out at the river's edge. Without hesitation, Daddy Bohdan plunged his mount into the slow moving, turgid flow of the Terek. Dark water swirled up past my stirrups before we were halfway across. My little Nogai helper quickly encouraged the packhorses forward.

We rode up on shallow sandbars on the far side, splashed once more through knee-deep waters, then moved carefully into the reeds and onto solid ground. We were now on the right bank and the beginning of Chechen country. In this grey-wolf hour of morning, as the sky grew lighter on the horizon, the mist acquired a silver sparkle as it drifted along with us in rising wisps. Birds called out on the riverbanks behind us. Then it grew still except for the blowing and snorting of our mounts.

Three *versts* or more into the Wild Country, the rolling grassland in front suddenly dropped into a long shallow area. I saw three saddled horses with their reins on the ground while they grazed quietly on the tall grass. Two men stood to the left of them while a third stood apart to the right. I recognized Lieutenant Vassilli Ivanoff as the one standing alone.

Stopping my horse well back from the others, I dismounted and handed the reins to my little Nogai helper. He acknowledged my instructions to keep a tight control on our horses as they might shy at the pending discharge of firearms between the duelists and try to bolt. Then I strode over to where the others were now gathering.

Upon my arrival, Sub-Lieutenant Grigori produced a wooden case of well-polished walnut and had Daddy Bohdan hold it across his upturned palms. Grigori opened the case. Inside lay two flintlock pistols, a metal flask of powder and a small leather bag containing several lead balls.

"These," he said in a measured voice, "are a set of dueling pistols which belonged to Lieutenant Aleksei's great-grandfather from his time spent in France many years ago." He looked at Vassilli. "Do you find these acceptable?"

Vassilli nodded.

"Very well. Armenian, if you will bear witness, I will now arm each pistol with powder and shot."

I glanced at each combatant. Both appeared to be calm. Knowing that there existed an agreement between them, one which I had helped arrange the night before, I quietly inquired, "Do we need a lead ball to be inserted into each pistol?"

"But of course," replied Grigori, "as a matter of honor, each man must be able to say in all honesty that he withstood deadly fire from his opponent."

I stepped back and watched him load the weapons. The same amount of powder and one lead ball was carefully tamped into each pistol barrel. At least Grigori was not favoring one pistol over the other. When finished, he offered both weapons to Vassilli.

"Since these are Lieutenant Aleksei's dueling pistols and you are the challenged, you have first choice."

Vassilli waved him away.

"I give my opponent first pick."

Grigori turned to his left. Aleksei chose the one closest to him. Grigori handed the other to Vassilli.

To some degree, I was comforted with their open display of sportsmanship, even though I had no wish to be here. Had there been another way to guarantee Vassilli's payment of his debt to me, I would not have found myself caught with a nervous shiver running over the surface of my skin on this cool morning.

"At a distance of twenty paces apart," said Grigori in a solemn tone, "I have marked positions for each opponent. You will take your places and face each other, each man with his pistol raised above his shoulder. Upon my command, each of you will discharge his weapon into the sky."

He looked from one officer to the other.

"Gentlemen, are there any questions?"

"None," replied Aleksei.

Vassilli shook his head slightly in the negative.

"One last item," continued Grigori. "To ensure that each of you follow the full letter of the agreement you both made with the Armenian last evening, Daddy Bohdan will shoot any party breaking that agreement."

We all looked at the old Cossack in his white Circassian coat as he slipped the long musket off his shoulder and cocked it. That sly grin I'd seen on his face the day before had returned.

"Understood," said Aleksei.

"But of course," replied Vassilli. His face appeared cold white in the early morning light.

Grigori motioned to the front and off to each side of himself.

"Then, Gentlemen, take your places and await my command."

As patient as I could make myself, I watched the two Russian officers stride off to their designated spots in the grassy hollow, turn and raise their pistols to shoulder level.

Grigori glanced quickly at each in turn until he seemed satisfied.

"Gentlemen," he bellowed out into the still morning, "Ready your firearms." Then he paused long enough until we heard two metallic clicks before he ordered, "Discharge your weapons."

My eyes were focused on Lieutenant Aleksei. He gave a haughty smile of boredom and fired up into the air.

But I only heard the one shot.

Quickly, I turned my attention to Lieutenant Vassilli in time to see him also smile, but his was in triumph, not in aristocratic boredom. He leveled his pistol and pulled the trigger. Flame and smoke belched from the barrel.

Aleksei took a half step to the rear as the ball caught him square in the chest. His leg buckled and he pitched backwards. His upraised arm flung sideways, throwing his pistol out into the grass.

I turned to Daddy Bohdan, expecting one more shot in this rapid turn of events.

The old Cossack slowly uncocked his musket and slung it back over his shoulder, then looked at me.

"I had no love for that man, Armenian. Only last month when I took him hunting for boar, he shot my best hunting dog and refused to pay me recompense. Said she was a nuisance and got in the way of his gun. I loved that bitch like one of my own children; she knew how to hunt. The world won't miss one more arrogant Russian, will it now?"

As I stood there in stunned silence, Grigori took my right hand in his left, turned my hand palm up and placed a leather pouch of clinking coins into it. With his right hand, he closed my fingers over the pouch.

"Lieutenant Vassilli wishes to pay off his debt in full," he said. "Our business here is finished. You had best be on your way." He turned and walked toward the fallen man.

I looked for Vassilli, but he was already mounted and riding off toward the Terek without a word or backward glance.

Daddy Bohdan loaded Aleksei's body across the saddle of the horse the Lieutenant had ridden to this place, while Grigori retrieved the empty dueling pistol from where it lay in the tall grass. When finished, the old Cossack mounted his own horse and waited.

From my side of the hollow, I saw Grigori toss a small leather pouch to Bohdan who caught it with one hand. I heard no muffled clinking from this distance, but knew it had to contain Rubles or silver coins of some country or other.

As the grey-beard Cossack cantered past me, he swept off his cap and bowed in the saddle. "Good day to you, Armenian. You have been a great help in this matter." Then he galloped on, singing a lusty ballad as he rode. The sound gradually trailed away.

Lieutenant Grigori was now mounted, with the lead rope to Aleksei's horse in one hand. He glanced once in my direction, then rode off at an angle to avoid any further conversation.

I was left here in the stillness of the coming day with Judas coin in my hand.

The Nogai Boy and I rode for several days, deeper into the Wild Country, headed for a Chechen village near the Blue Mist Gorge where I hoped to trade. After all, making money was my business. For all those days, I rode in silence, speaking scarce a word to my helper. It gave me time to reflect.

Vassilli, Grigori and Bohdan had all made me their fool. And, their scheme had worked for each man's desired aims. Bohdan got revenge for the loss of his favorite hunting dog and the insult of not being paid recompense, while Vassilli had found a way to work out his dark feelings of jealousy and that irritating difference of class. No wonder Vassilli had been so tight-lipped that evening on the porch. His mind had been filled with getting rid of his rival, and thus feared something he might say could give away the plot if he spoke too much.

Grigori was the one who had fooled me the most though. It was he who had obviously come up with their scheme when opportunity presented itself, and also the idea of involving me so as to make the agreement appear legitimate to Aleksei. As Daddy Bohdan had said when he came for me the night before, Aleksei's arrogance could wear on a man. Grigori, being a junior officer under Aleksei's command, must've been worn through to the bone over time. And, by paying me the Judas coin, those three hoped to tarnish me as a fellow conspirator and ensure my silence.

It was a good plan and it had worked. They knew that upon my return to the Cossack village a few months from now, I could say nothing to the General, nor anyone else as to the true facts without exposing my own actions in this matter.

As for business, my ledger books on trade goods would balance. In the future, however, no Russian officer would be allowed to purchase on credit. No more of that.

What my mind worked on now was another ledger, a debt ledger I kept only in my head. Those Russian officers and the old grey-beard Cossack had deliberately placed me in a precarious position. Eventually as time passed, through drunken bragging or an indiscreet act of ego, even if they didn't elaborate on all the details, one or more of them would let it be known that I could easily be deceived. In this violent land where a man's reputation preceded him and sometimes protected him, such a poor reputation could make me a target for all. This would not do if I were to survive on both sides of the river. It was now necessary that three balance entries be written in blood. It might take a while to make special arrangements as circumstances became available, but then many things happen on Chechen soil, south of the Terek River, and I am a patient man when it comes to this sometimes needed side of business. Using my brains, not personal violence done by my own hand, has long been my way of life in this treacherous land.

Those three in my debt would soon be travelling deep into an already dangerous land during the general's summer campaign. Death would be a common companion. What were three more untended graves in the Wild Country?

Our next story takes place in the rigidly formal daily life of the landed gentry of Navarre in the thirteenth century. A young woman learns that deceit and trickery is not constrained by elevated social standing. A shorter version of this story was previously published by Tales of Old.

Ms. Csernica's historical fiction has appeared in Weird Tales and These Vampires Don't Sparkle, along with the upcoming Clockwork Alchemy anthology, Twelve Hours Apart. Under the name Elaine LeClaire she has published Ship of Dreams, a novel of pirate romance.

Cunning as a Serpent, Innocent as a Dove

by Lillian Csernica

In Anna's mind, the coming of Spring and the coming of Sieur Phillipe and his entourage were one event. How marvelous to have guests after the long, dull winter. The snows had melted, clearing Roncesvalles Pass. Pilgrims would soon throng the *camino francesco* bound for Santiago de Compostella. Sieur Phillipe was wise to make his journey early, before all manner of travelers crowded the *camino* in the sweltering summer heat.

Anna waited nervously just behind Doña Esperanza, her aunt. The great lady of the *castillo* stood calm and elegant, the long sleeves and high collar of her dove gray bliaut suiting the scooped neck and trailing skirt of her emerald cotehardie. Anna wished she possessed even a little of Doña Esperanza's poise. Many hoofbeats thundered into the courtyard, bringing a whoop of delight from Anna's cousin Francisca. "They're here! *Madre, los Frantzes están aquí!*"

Doña Esperanza tidied a fold of Francisca's linen wimple, smoothing it along her cheek. "*Mija*, calm yourself. You are a lady of Navarre."

Lucky Francisca. Anna was just a poor relative from Castile, dressed in a blue bliaut and wine-red cotehardie borrowed from Francisca. Anna and Francisca had the same long black hair and dark eyes, but Anna was shorter and fairer than her wayward cousin. Anna squared her shoulders. She would be brave. If all went well, Sieur Phillipe might offer to take Francisca to Santiago de Compostella, perhaps even to Paris itself. From all Anna had heard of Paris, it had to be the very center of the world. She longed to see it, even if it meant going along as Francisca's maid.

The great hall's massive oak doors stood open, allowing the sunlight to stream in and make a broad golden carpet on the flagstones. Gatito, the Cook's tabby cat, lay sprawled on the doorstep, sunning his white belly while he licked his paws. Don Augustín strode through the doorway, making Gatito scurry off toward the kitchen. At fifty Don Augustín was still a handsome man, his black hair and beard scarcely touched by gray. He'd thrown one arm around the shoulders of Sieur Phillipe who now carried the title of le Compte de la Croix as a reward for his part in the recent Crusade. A genuine Crusader! Anna studied him, burning into her memory every detail of his appearance.

Sieur Phillipe was a tall, stocky man with hair like thinning cornsilk. Over his chainmail byrnie Sieur Phillipe wore a velvet surcoat, the left side scarlet and the right bright yellow. He made Don Augustín's brown houppelande with its voluminous sleeves and embroidered panels seem quite drab. Despite the grandeur of his attire, Sieur Phillipe looked worn and haggard, his gray eyes reddened from lack of sleep.

Behind them walked an older woman. Her bliaut was scarlet, her cotehardie butter yellow, her wimple the finest immaculate lawn. Her golden girdle was set with red jewels, surely garnets or rubies. Age had added a few fine lines to the lady's face, but her blue eyes were sharp and clear. Treading a few respectful steps behind her was a girl little older than Anna herself. Her colors were more subdued, her bliaut wine red and her cotehardie a deeper shade of yellow. The girl kept her eyes down and her hands primly folded.

Sieur Phillipe bowed to Doña Esperanza. *"Bon soir, cher madame.* May I present my sister, Madame Lysette de Coubertín."

"Soyez la bienvenu, Madame." Doña Esperanza made a deep curtsy.

Madame Lysette smiled. *"Merci beaucoup,* Doña Esperanza. You have a charming home."

Anna and Francisca traded a look of delight. The great hall blazed with color. To welcome the French pilgrims, all the banners had been taken down and beaten, ridding them of a winter's worth of dust and soot. Garlands of wildflowers hung over the doorways. More twined along the rail of the wooden staircase that led to the private chambers above. A dozen fresh roses from the *castillo's* garden adorned the head table. Doña Esperanza had put Francisca and Anna in charge of gathering all the flowers.

Madame de Coubertín reached behind her to take the girl by the wrist and gently draw her forward. "This is my niece, Isabeau de Rochefort."

"The daughter of my younger brother," Sieur Phillipe added.

Isabeau was beautiful, fair-skinned, her eyes like sapphires, her lips rosy. To Anna she looked like Guenevere herself. Isabeau made Doña Esperanza a curtsy in return. The swish of her skirts stirred up the strong scent of lavender. To Anna it was like a breath of Heaven.

"Allow me to present our daughter, Francisca." Don Augustín nodded to Francisca, who promptly stepped forward and made her curtsy. "And our niece, Doña Anna Innocencia Sanchez y del Muñoz."

The seeming grandness of her name pained Anna and made her shyness that much worse. Doña Esperanza gently urged her forward. Anna curtsied. Madame Lysette gave the girls a warm smile, but Sieur Phillipe acknowledged them with the barest nod.

"You are most welcome," Doña Esperanza said, holding out her arms to encompass them all. "Let me offer you some wine."

"*Merci, Doña.* Perhaps later." Sieur Phillipe made another bow, not a gesture of thanks but a dismissal.

Doña Esperanza's back stiffened. Francisca's mouth tightened. Anna was astonished. To push Doña Esperanza's hospitality aside, and in such a blunt way!

"Don Augustín," Sieur Phillipe said, "you must tell me how things stand between Peter the Cruel and the pretender, Henry Trastamara. Their feuding may affect the safety of our journey."

"Of course, *mon ami.*" Don Augustín came to Doña Esperanza and took her hands, murmuring in Castilian. "*Por favor, mí corazón,* have pity on him. He can think only of his wife. She is so ill."

"*Sí, mi esposo.*" Doña Esperanza put on a bright smile and turned to Madame Lysette. "Perhaps, Madame, you will permit me to show you to your rooms."

Doña Esperanza led Madame Lysette, Isabeau, and their maids up the stairway. Anna came last, following behind Francisca. Gatito scampered up beside Anna, rubbing against her ankles and almost tripping her. She scooped up the small bundle of warm fur and scratched behind Gatito's ears.

"Come, Augustín." Sieur Phillipe beckoned Don Augustín. "I have something you'll want to see."

"Doña Anna?"

A sharper note in Doña Esperanza's voice made Anna turn around so quickly Gatito dug his claws into her shoulder. Doña Esperanza and Madame Lysette now stood at the head of the stairway with Francisca and Isabeau a step below them.

"Sí, Doña?"

"The pieces are in the ivory box on the Moorish table. And put that cat down before he tears your silk."

Doña Esperanza meant the game of *castilio* kept on the table near the hearth. Anna nodded and hurried back down the stairs. She was good at *castilio,* beating Francisca nearly every time. Perhaps, if she was careful to lose to Madame Lysette, the great French lady might like her enough to invite her to join the pilgrimage.

As Anna passed the head table, Sieur Phillipe's voice boomed out.

"I have only daughters. I love them, God knows, but I need an heir!"

Startled, Gatito dug his claws dug into Anna's arm. Wincing at the pain, she froze, praying no blood stained the blue silk.

"I need a miracle," Sieur Phillipe said. "For Marie-Therese's sake, I would crawl to Santiago de Compostella on my knees!"

Don Augustín patted him on the shoulder. "All things are possible with God, *mon ami*. He will surely hear your prayers."

Sieur Phillipe reached inside his surcoat and withdrew a small bundle of pure white silk. He unrolled it to reveal a silver box as long and as wide as his middle finger. Delicate floral designs covered the mirror-bright surface. Tiny jewels adorned the center of each flower, glowing like sparks of colored fire. A sweet, dusty fragrance filled the air. Anna tiptoed closer.

"A reliquary." Sieur Phillipe stroked the silver box with his fingertip. "I had it made, then filled it with frankincense I brought back from Jerusalem. Only such a lavish offering might persuade the church officials to grant me a relic, even the tiniest scrap of the rag Santiago used to clean his boots."

Gatito chose that moment to leap from Anna's arms onto the table. He walked right across the white silk and sniffed at the reliquary, then sneezed three times.

"*Morbleu!*" Sieur Phillipe roared, snatching up the reliquary and rolling it back into the silk. "Get that animal away from me!"

"*Pardonnez-moi, mon seigneur!*"

Anna caught Gatito and backed away from the table, trying to keep her grip on the squirming, sneezing cat.

"Doña Anna." Don Augustín gave her a stern look. "*Vete al Doña Esperanza.*"

"*Con permiso, mi tío.*" Trapped in a misery of embarrassment, Anna forced herself to speak. "Doña Esperanza sent me to fetch the *castilio* pieces."

Don Augustín strode over to the little table, grabbed the ivory box, and held it out to her. With Gatito under one arm and the ivory box under the other, Anna made a wobbly curtsy then fled up the stairs.

In the hallway above, there stood Isabeau, wreathed in that divine scent of lavender.

"Oh, poor Doña Anna! I couldn't help overhearing *mon oncle*. He can be rather loud at times."

Isabeau reached out to pet Gatito's head. His ears flattened. He hissed.

"Gatito!" Anna cried. "*Gato malo*! I'm so sorry, Mademoiselle…"

Isabeau waved away Anna's apology. "It is nothing, Doña Anna. I am a stranger to him, that is all." She looked Anna over, her expression pained. "A word of advice, Doña. If I were you, I would take care not to appear before *ma tante* Lysette in such *déshabillé.*"

Struggling to control Gatito had left Anna's girdle crooked and her wimple askew. At least her sleeve was free of any stain or tear. Even so, she couldn't possibly join Doña Esperanza and Madame Lysette in this condition.

"But—" Anna winced at the rising note of panic in her voice. She struggled to hold on to her composure. "Doña Esperanza told me to bring the *castilio* set to her."

"I will deliver it." Before Anna could object, Isabeau plucked the ivory box from beneath her arm. "Hurry along now. It would not do to keep Madame Lysette waiting."

Anna watched Isabeau sweep down the hallway. The sight of such *elán* compared to her own disarray made Anna's heart sink. She dashed into Francisca's room and dropped Gatito on the bed. Gatito pawed at his nose, still snorting.

"*Gato estupido!* See if you get any more milk from me!" Anna threw herself on the bed and buried her face in the pillow. "Now they'll *never* take me to Paris with them!"

She would not cry. She would not! Bad enough Madame Lysette would hear of her silliness from Isabeau. A red nose and puffy eyes would only make things worse.

Gatito curled up against Anna's hip, licking his paws again and again as he scrubbed at his nose. Anna ran her hand over his short thick fur, stroking the stripes on his side. She shouldn't blame Gatito. Sieur Phillipe was the one who couldn't behave himself. With a sigh, Anna tidied her clothing and resigned herself to an evening spent playing *castilio* very badly.

A voice like elegant thunder woke Anna. She lay perfectly still, not daring to breathe. The voice went on and on, shouting and demanding and complaining. Now and then a quieter voice spoke.

Francisca rolled over, yawning. "*Su Majestad Boca Grande* is up early."

Anna giggled. Only Francisca would dare call Sieur Phillipe "His Majesty Big Mouth."

"What could he be so angry about?"

Francisca shrugged. "He's French. Poor Juana told me she and two other maids nearly wore their arms out carrying hot water for his bath." She yawned again. "I suppose we should be thankful he did bathe. When they first arrived, even La Belle Isabeau reeked of sweaty horse."

"You don't like her?" Anna asked.

"Should I?"

"She seems so kind…"

"*Dios mio!* She wouldn't even play *castilio* with us. She said she had to embroider more linens for her *trousseau*." Francisca pronounced the last word with a scornful drawl.

The door swung open hard enough to slam against the wall behind it. Doña Esperanza hurried over to the bed and pulled down the blankets. "Get dressed, both of you!"

"*Por favor, Madre!*" Francisca sat up, eyes wide. "What has happened?"

Doña Esperanza seized Francisca's wrist and dragged her out of bed. "The longer you make Sieur Phillipe wait, the more furious he will be!"

Her distress was enough to silence even Francisca. The moment both girls had finished dressing, Doña Esperanza hurried them ahead of her out the door.

Down in the great hall, everyone in Sieur Phillipe's retinue had assembled shoulder to shoulder facing the *castillo's* servants. Sieur Phillipe paced up and down between them. Don Augustín sat at the head table. Just as Anna reached the bottom of the stairway, Doña Esperanza's hand on her arm made Anna pause. Doña Esperanza put her hand to her mouth to hide a discreet cough.

Sieur Phillipe spun around. His face, already flushed, turned an even deeper shade of red. "There she is!"

He stormed toward Anna. She cringed back against Doña Esperanza.

"Sieur Phillipe!" Don Augustín's tone halted Sieur Phillipe in midstride. "You will gain nothing by frightening my niece."

"On the contrary. I may gain everything." Sieur Phillipe glared at Anna. "Speak, Doña. Tell me where I might find my reliquary. The one your cat so admired."

"*Mon seigneur*," said Doña Esperanza, "what makes you think Anna knows anything about the matter?"

"My niece told me she caught a glimpse of Doña Anna in the hallways last night, creeping around with that cat in her arms."

Anna answered Sieur Phillipe's glare with a shake of her head. "*Pardonnez-moi, mon seigneur.* I don't know where your reliquary is."

Sieur Phillipe scowled. "I left the reliquary in my chamber for a brief time while I bathed before supper. The servants tell me you quite disappeared after you left us last night. Where were you, Doña?"

Anna clung to Doña Esperanza's waist, her heart thudding with shock and terror. Sieur Phillipe hadn't misplaced his reliquary, he thought she had stolen it! Her hesitation only angered him further.

"Answer me, *ma fille!* At once!"

"Sieur Phillipe." Don Augustín's voice bristled with formality. "You are a guest in my home, but that does not permit you to speak so harshly to any maiden under my protection."

Sudden awareness of his breach of chivalry doused Sieur Phillipe's temper like a bucket of cold water thrown in his face. He stepped back and ran one hand over his mussed hair. Don Augustín stood up and held out his hand to Anna. With great reluctance she stepped away from the safety of Doña Esperanza's protection.

"Doña Anna," Don Augustin said. "Do you have any idea where we might find the reliquary?"

"No, *mi tío.* I only saw it there, on the table, before Sieur Phillipe put it away."

"You're sure?"

"*Sí, mi tío.*"

"Where did you go last night, after you left the great hall?"

"I took the *castilio* set upstairs, *mi tío*, as Doña Esperanza asked me to do."

"*Es verdad, mi esposa?*" Don Augustin asked. "She was with you the entire time?"

Doña Esperanza started to speak, then paused. "After she came back, *sí*. But—"

Anna closed her eyes, whispering a prayer.

"—she was a long time returning to us."

Don Augustín translated the Castilian into French for Sieur Phillipe, whose lip curled in a triumphant sneer.

"Just as I thought. Doña Esperanza, was it not Isabeau who brought you the game pieces?"

Doña Esperanza nodded. "*Oui, mon seigneur*, she did."

"Did you not wonder why she brought them, instead of Doña Anna?"

A faint blush colored Doña Esperanza's cheeks. "Isabeau told us about the Cook's cat and your reliquary, *mon seigneur*. I assumed poor Anna must have hidden herself somewhere."

Sieur Phillipe glared at Anna. "So I am to believe she hid herself away out of shame?"

"*Oui, mon seigneur*. My cousin is a shy little mouse." Francisca stepped forward. "Has anyone asked Mademoiselle Isabeau why *she* was wandering around last night?"

"Francisca!" Doña Esperanza frowned.

"Tell them, Anna," Francisca said. "Mademoiselle Isabeau did more than just see you!"

Made brave by Francisca's boldness, Anna nodded.

"Mademoiselle Isabeau met me as I came up the stairs. She offered to take the *castilio* set to Doña Esperanza for me so I could do as Mademoiselle Isabeau said and make myself more presentable."

"That does not answer the crucial question, Doña Anna," Sieur Phillipe said. "Where were you, *after* you left the great hall and *before* you joined Doña Esperanza in her chambers?"

Anna bowed her head. The truth would shame her further, but there was nothing else to say. "I hid in Doña Francisca's room, *mon seigneur.*"

"Was anyone else in the room?"

"Only Gatito, *mon seigneur.*"

Hearing his name, Gatito appeared from beneath the head table. He rubbed his head against Anna's skirts.

Sieur Phillipe threw up his hands. "Perhaps the cat will tell us the truth!"

"Phillipe! What is all this shouting?" Madame Lysette came down the stairway, graceful as a queen in her crimson and yellow attire. Isabeau followed, poised and perfect in her amber bliaut and garnet cotehardie.

"The reliquary, *ma soeur*. It is gone!"

"Gone? But how?"

"That is what I am trying to discover. Last night I left my room just long enough to take a bath. Only Doña Anna cannot prove where she was during that time."

Madame Lysette frowned. "Phillipe, you are too hasty."

Sieur Phillipe shook his head. "It must have been taken from my room. I would sooner forget my armor than allow that reliquary to be misplaced. I *must* find it!"

"Mademoiselle Isabeau," Doña Esperanza said, "there appears to be some confusion over the events of last night."

"I have told *mon oncle* all I know, Doña Esperanza," Isabeau said. "What is in dispute?"

"Anna tells us you met her in the hallway above and took the ivory box from her," said Don Augustin. "You told Sieur Phillipe you only caught a glimpse of her in the hallways. Which statement is true?"

Isabeau blinked her wide, innocent eyes in a gesture of pretty helplessness. "Forgive me, *mon oncle*. I did speak to Doña Anna."

"Why were you there in the hallway?" Francisca asked. "Why did you leave Doña Esperanza and Madame Lysette?"

Isabeau's eyes narrowed. She made no reply.

"A reasonable question," said Don Augustín. "Mademoiselle Isabeau? Your answer, *s'il-vous plait?*"

"But of course, Don Augustín. I wanted my basket of needlework."

"Why didn't you send one of the maids, Mademoiselle?" Anna asked, genuinely puzzled. "You didn't have to walk all that way yourself."

"That's true," Doña Esperanza said. "There was no need to put yourself to such trouble, Mademoiselle."

"*Con permiso*, Papa. I have remembered something." Francisca very nearly bounced up and down with excitement. Anna's heart leaped with hope so intense it was painful.

"Go on, *mija*," Don Augustín said.

"When Madame Isabeau first arrived," Francisca said, "her clothing smelled like a whole field of lavender. Isn't that right, Doña Anna?"

As she spoke, Francisca tilted her head toward Isabeau. Bewildered, Anna took the hint and moved a few steps closer to Isabeau. Drawn by her movement, Gatito chased after her. He raised his head to sniff at the air, then began sniffing at Isabeau's skirts. Anna took a deep breath, and then she understood.

"*Mi tío.*" Anna turned to Don Augustín. "Now Mademoiselle Isabeau smells like something else."

"*Incroyable!*" Isabeau snapped. "*Mon oncle!* Am I to stand here like some peasant on trial while this little country goose chatters about how I smell?"

"Isabeau!" Madame Lysette cried. "You will apologize this instant!"

"It is I who am owed the apology, *ma tante!* What does it matter which floral essence I wear?"

"It is utterly beside the point," Sieur Phillipe said. "Doña Anna is clutching at straws. Let me say again—"

"Phillipe, be still." Madame Lysette made her way down the stairway, bestowing on Isabeau a glare that promised trouble later, then laid her hands on Anna's shoulders. "Doña Anna, you say Isabeau's scent is different now. Can you tell us what that new scent is?"

Anna took another deep breath, praying for some revelation about whatever Francisca meant. Prayer. Church. Incense. "The inside of the chapel! That's what she smells like!"

Gatito pawed at the broad band of embroidery newly sewn round the hem of Isabeau's gown, then let out an explosive sneeze. Isabeau swatted at him with her skirts, trying to shoo him away.

"*Mon oncle!*" she screeched. "Get this rat-eating beast away from me!"

Isabeau stumbled backward up the stairs and lost her footing, landing hard on her bottom. Sieur Phillipe seized Gatito by the scruff of the neck. Gatito's furry little body shook with sneeze after sneeze. Sieur Phillipe snatched the dagger from his belt.

"No!" Anna ran to grab Sieur Phillipe's wrist and hang from it, using all her weight to drag his arm down. Sieur Phillipe dropped Gatito and rounded on Anna, his face nearly purple with fury.

"So! You would save your accomplice!"

The great hall thundered with shouts and screams. Strong arms closed around her from behind. Holding Anna tight against his chest, Don Augustín spun around, putting his own body between her and Sieur Phillipe.

"*Halte!*"

Sieur Phillipe's mouth opened.

"Silence, Phillipe!" Madame Lysette's cool voice cut him off. "You've caused enough of a scene for one morning."

"I believe I know where to find the reliquary." Don Augustín drew his own dagger and started toward Isabeau.

"What—what do you mean to do?" she asked.

"The hem is ruined, *mademoiselle*. A little more damage will not signify." Don Augustín knelt at Isabeau's feet. Using the point of his dagger, he opened what stitches remained along the hem of Isabeau's skirt. Metal struck metal with a soft plink. "*Voilà!*"

Don Augustín held up the reliquary. A stray shaft of sunlight struck it, making its tiny gems flash and sparkle. The sudden hush in the Great hall was broken only by the sound of Gatito licking his rumpled fur.

When Sieur Phillipe spoke, his voice was hoarse. "My own blood. My brother's child. Why did you do this?"

Bitterness soured both Isabeau's tone. "For my father's sake."

Sieur Phillipe shook his head. "Child, are you that ambitious?"

"With no offering to barter for the saint's blessing, you would have no hope of an heir." Isabeau got to her feet. "My father would inherit your lands, *mon oncle*, and I could have my choice of husbands. I would do the choosing, instead of being bartered away like some little ivory figure in a game."

"The game!" Francisca cried. "While we sat there playing *castilio*, Mademoiselle Isabeau was busy sewing the reliquary into her skirt!"

Sieur Phillipe closed his eyes. "Don Augustín, would you have somewhere appropriate we might confine my niece until I can make arrangements for an escort to take her back to France?"

Anna gasped. Isabeau was to be jailed for her crime! Francisca smiled, nodding with satisfaction.

"I do, *mon ami*," Don Augustín said. "And I will provide her with a maid, so none of her own are too tempted by their loyalty."

Don Augustín beckoned his seneschal. Sieur Phillipe raised a weary hand to call two of his men forward.

"Take Mademoiselle Isabeau where Don Augustín directs you. She may have food and drink, books and needlework, but nothing and no one else without my leave."

The seneschal led the way upstairs as Sieur Phillipe's men escorted Isabeau to the room that would now serve as her prison cell. Sieur Phillipe watched them go, then turned to Don Augustín.

"A thousand apologies, old friend. Mere words cannot express my shame."

"Please, *mon ami*. A little shouting is nothing."

Sieur Phillipe shook his head. "I have slandered your niece. Lay a penance on me. My conscience will not let me rest until I have made amends."

Doña Esperanza came to Sieur Phillipe and took his hands in hers. "You acted out of love and fear for your lady wife, *mon seigneur*. When it comes to holy things, we cannot be too careful."

Sieur Phillipe's anguished look softened into a smile. "You are most gracious, Doña Esperanza. I thank you for your charity."

"There is one more apology owed." Madame Lysette untied a small pouch of crimson velvet that hung from her golden girdle. She opened the pouch and withdrew a paternoster, a rope of one hundred delicate amber beads. "Doña Anna, allow me to present this to you in the hope that you will forgive us the distress we have caused you and keep us always in your prayers."

Anna held out her cupped hands to receive the treasure. "*M-merci beacoup*, Madame."

"You have a good heart, *ma petite*." Madame Lysette smiled. "Truly, you did not have to lose every game."

Bern, Switzerland at the turn of the previous century is the setting of our next story. A young patent clerk with his mind focused on mathematics discovers the sinister truth behind a set of seemingly random slayings.

Mr. Palumbo's name will be familiar to many readers. After a successful career as a screenwriter (My Favorite Year) and television writer (Welcome Back Kotter), he became a psychotherapist and author. His work has appeared in major markets, including The Strand and Ellery Queen Mystery Magazine. He's also the author of the Daniel Rinaldi mystery novels (Poisoned Pen Press).

A Theory of Murder

by Dennis Palumbo

My friend Albert Einstein unwrapped his sausage roll, then looked up at me with frank, dark eyes. "Tell me, Hector, what is the secret to living in harmony with a woman?"

I shrugged inside my thick overcoat. It was cold out there in the dawn mist, beneath the wintry mantle of holiday snow. We sat, as we did every morning before work, on a bench overlooking the Aare River.

"I know less about women than you do," I answered, sipping my tea. "At least you've managed to marry one."

"I prefer to think that Mileva married me. For my money, perhaps?"

"It can't be for your looks," I said.

He smiled, and then bit into his steaming roll, chewing as carelessly as he did most things.

Below us, the river flowed stubbornly around islands of scrabbly ice. Traversing its treacherous surface was a sleek racing scull rowed by the university team, undaunted by the frigid conditions. I could just make out a half-dozen broad-shouldered students, encased in thick coats and heavy blankets, urged on by their coxswain.

We ate in a familiar, comfortable silence. I became aware of the rolling of cartwheels on icy cobblestones, the flap of shop windows opening to the new day. Cool morning light poked through the haze, revealing the shapes of old, weathered buildings—relics of a past that young men like Albert and I had long since shrugged off.

We were the new generation, like those students on the water. The men of the future. It was the year 1904.

We finished our meager breakfasts and trundled down the snow-draped streets. As it was two days before Christmas, we passed several small clusters of religious folk, in gaily-colored mufflers and hats, ringing their bells and collecting for the poor. Guilt made me dig into my own relatively poor pockets for some change.

Albert had said little as we made our way through the growing, early-morning throng. He'd seemed quite distracted these past months, though whether due to marital problems or his struggles with his arcane physics papers I couldn't be sure. Whenever I asked about them, he'd merely say they weren't ready for publication yet. I confess I doubted whether they might ever be.

At last, Albert and I arrived at the patent office. Inside, we found our employer, Herr Hoffmann, his thick mustache stained with coffee. A copy of this morning's *Gazette* was in his hand.

"Have you heard the news?" he said, more agitated than usual. "Have you?"

"Are the planets still holding to their prescribed parabolas?" Albert asked mildly.

"Are they *what?* Honestly, Herr Einstein." Hoffman shook his head, and raised the folded newspaper like a flag.

"The most horrible of all," he said gravely. "Just last night, not five blocks from this very room. And during Christmas, for the love of God."

"More murders?" I said, stunned. "Like before?"

"Worse. An entire family. Husband, wife, three children. Murdered in their beds. Slaughtered like cattle."

I took the paper he offered, my hands trembling as I read the horrible details.

"You must see this, Albert," I said. "It's unnatural. A crime unlike any in history."

"Now that, dear Hector, I sincerely doubt. I trust you've heard of the Boer War. The massacres on the African coasts. Certain penal colonies in the Australian continent."

"Yes, yes," I said irritably. Truly, Albert could be maddening at times. In such moments, I didn't envy Mileva her choice of husbands.

"My point, Albert," I went on coolly, "is that a monster is afoot in Berne."

"Exactly!" Hoffmann sputtered. "We have a Jack the Ripper in our midst."

Albert opened his eyes, at once penetrating and leavened with sadness. "Yet one far less discriminating. The Ripper chose his victims from among the women of the streets. This killer seemingly chooses them at random. That, I suppose, is the great bafflement. How he chooses his victims, or why."

Hoffmann nodded. "That's what the police say. There appears to be no motive." He pointed to the paper in my hands. "You see, they've listed the deaths so far. The watch-maker, stabbed in his shop. The knifing of the elderly couple. Three seminary students, hacked to pieces. Now this poor family."

"No recurring pattern," Albert mused. "So unlike the universe, when you think about it. Or the habits of most men."

"Except for one thing," I said. "He always uses a blade of some kind. A scissors for the watchmaker, a knife for the old couple, a thick cleaver for the students. Appalling."

"And inefficient," Albert said. "Unless the killer's trying different approaches to discern the most effective. Trial and error. Hypothesis and experimentation. The scientific method."

I stared at him. "The man's obviously deranged! And you talk of methods?"

Hoffmann clucked his tongue. "Sometimes, Herr Einstein, I worry about you."

"I'm touched, Herr Hoffmann."

"Exactly. That's what I'm worried about." Hoffmann laughed at his own wit and shuffled over to his desk by the front door. "However, should you feel inclined to join the rest of us in the real world, I'd appreciate the schematics of the Beringer application by first post."

As I turned to my own work, I caught sight of Albert once again leaning back in his chair. He seemed to be staring at a spot on the ceiling. Or perhaps *through* the ceiling, and the sky beyond, to the very edge of the universe.

I hated to agree with Hoffmann, but Albert's mind did usually seem everywhere except in this real world of brick and soil and sausage rolls, of yearning and sorrow and sudden, horrible death.

My odd friend Albert. So secretive about his as-yet unpublished physics papers, yet so casually sure that they'd stun the world. At times as playful as a child, at others sober and introverted.

Especially today, since hearing the gruesome news about the murdered family. Albert and I had exchanged not a word, cloaked in a thick silence broken only by the shuffle of drafting papers, the scratching of pens, the muffled ticking of the wall clock.

Until lunchtime arrived, along with Inspector Kruger of the local police, who entered stamping snow from his boots.

Herr Hoffmann stood, mouth agape, as the tall, slender Kruger pulled his gloves from his hands and saluted.

"Just routine police work," Kruger assured us. "We have these murders, you see. The whole Department is engaged."

"Of course." Hoffmann rubbed his hands nervously. "It's a comfort, knowing our police are on the job. Berne is a peaceful town. We've never known such brutal events before."

Kruger smiled. "Calm yourself, Herr Hoffmann. Men must be strong. It is our duty." He turned to me. "Actually, I'm here to ask Herr Franks to come with me. To headquarters."

"Me?" Like an idiot, I actually pointed to myself.

Albert rubbed his nose inoffensively. "Is Hector a suspect in these killings, ludicrous as that sounds?"

Kruger tightened his jaw. "I can't say more."

Albert's own jaw tightened. He'd never handled authority very well, he told me once. I could plainly see that now.

"I suggest I accompany you, Hector," he said at last. "As your second."

Kruger looked as though he were about to respond, but then merely shrugged. He ushered us out the door.

<hr>

The police wagon, wheels rattling, turned onto Aarstrasse. I frowned at Kruger, wedged between Albert and myself in the rear. "This is not the way to police headquarters."

Kruger shrugged. "We must make one stop first."

We pulled to the curb before a rambling, two-storied house shadowed by ancient firs thick with snow. A squad of uniformed policemen milled out on the lawn, hugging themselves against the cold, smoking brown cigarettes. As we climbed out of the wagon, the men came quickly to attention.

Beside me, Kruger merely grunted his displeasure and led me up the icy porch steps and into the foyer of the somber house. I heard Albert's steady shuffle behind us.

The first horror awaited us in the drawing room. Splashes of dried blood covered the carpet, the arms of chairs, the gilt-edged picture frames, even the still-hanging Christmas tinsel and carefully wrapped presents under the tree.

The Inspector pointed to an obscene black stain near the hearth. "Herr Gossen and his wife were killed there."

I couldn't find words, but I heard Albert's quiet voice behind me. "The children?"

Kruger nodded to the staircase. "Upstairs."

He led the way up velvet-lined steps and into the first of two bedrooms. Toys, stuffed animals, and colorful downy blankets attested to the ages of the children. Twin boys, I recalled from the *Gazette*, not yet five.

Kruger drew our attention to the little beds. Blood-soaked. Sheets a tangle. "Murdered as they slept," he said. "Perhaps it was a blessing."

I found my voice. "But why are you showing this to us? To me? I don't understand."

Kruger stirred. "You will. In the girl's room."

He led us to the second bedroom, evidently that of a girl in her teens. Soft, feminine. I saw the glint of a blond hair in the afternoon sun, where it adhered to a blood-stained pillow.

I took a breath, then felt Albert's reassuring grasp on my arm. It was he who questioned the Inspector this time.

"I don't see the reason for bringing us here," he said.

In reply, Kruger took a folded cloth from his pocket. Within lay a heart-shaped gold locket, smeared with blood.

"It was found clutched in the dead girl's hand," Kruger explained. "Which was severed from her body, and lay a few feet away."

"No!!" I cried. It took both of them to keep me upright as I swayed, gasping. "It… it can't be…"

"So you recognize the locket?" Kruger stared at me.

I nodded dumbly. How could I not? It had once been mine.

"It was a cruel act," Albert was saying to Kruger, as we sat in the Commissioner's office at police headquarters. "And unnecessarily theatrical."

"Perhaps." Kruger's bald head shone in the wintry light from the windows. "But I thought it might be effective."

"For what? Extracting a confession from Herr Franks? You can't possibly suspect Hector of these heinous crimes?"

I sat in silence on a padded bench at the far end of the large, wood-paneled room. I felt disembodied. Adrift in a nightmare from which I couldn't awaken.

Until I was startled from my melancholy by the arrival of a slender young girl, in the company of a police matron.

"Mina!" I said, leaping from my seat. Upon seeing me, Mina froze in her tracks, face turning pale as chalk.

She was as beautiful as I remembered, luminous eyes now red-rimmed from recent tears.

Kruger rose, and turned to Albert.

"This is Fraulein Mina Strauss," he explained. "She was a school-mate of the late Fraulein Gossen."

Mina's voice quavered. "Poor Katie. She was my best, my truest friend. We---" She burst into tears, hands covering her face. The stoic matron idly handed her a

handkerchief.

"Fraulein Strauss is also known to Herr Franks," Kruger said, finally looking at me. "Isn't that so?"

"Yes, I---" I looked at the floor. "I loved her once. Some few years ago."

"Love?" Mina's eyes found mine. "It was an infatuation, Hector. I was only sixteen, and even I had the wit to know that." She turned to Kruger. "Hector worked for a summer for my father. He flattered me with his attentions. But I never returned his affections. Even after he sent me the locket."

Kruger pointed to the gold locket on the table next to us, still nested in the folded cloth. "This locket?"

Mina nodded, miserable. "I shouldn't have kept it, I know. But it was so pretty. Perhaps I'm vain. Perhaps---" Her smile back at me was kind. "I'm sorry, Hector."

Albert took a step forward, hands in the pockets of his loose trousers. Old pipe ash flecked his sweater.

"Might I ask how the locket came into the possession of Fraulein Gossen?"

Mina gazed warily at Albert's careless appearance. I could sense that she found him…unimpressive.

"I gave it to Katie," she said carefully. "As a token of our friendship, our bond. We shared a special kinship."

She looked at me for a long moment, then away, as though having decided I wouldn't understand. Her voice dropped to a whisper. "Now my world is over. Finished."

I found her words perplexing, and glanced over at Albert. But his expression was unreadable.

A heavy tread sounded in the doorway. It was the large, imposing figure of Commissioner Otto Burlick. In his wake came a sturdy-looking young man wearing rimless glasses and a crisp college uniform beneath his winter coat. He had the same thick, dark features as the Commissioner.

Behind him, lounging in the doorway was another college youth, though he had the sullen look of a street ruffian.

Burlick lumbered over to his desk, rummaging hastily through the top drawer until he pulled out a checkbook.

"Won't be a minute," he said to the room, exasperated. "My son Jeffrey is in need of a loan."

"It *is* a loan," Jeffrey, the first boy, protested. He glanced neither at me, Mina, nor the Inspector. "I'll pay it back."

"Don't grovel, Jeffrey," said the boy in the doorway. "It's disgusting."

Jeffrey whirled at this, face reddening. "Do shut up, Hans. If it wasn't for you, egging me on---"

Hans laughed sourly. "So now it's my fault you bet on the wrong rowers?"

Burlick looked up from his desk, bristling. "Hans Pfeiffer? I've heard Jeffrey speak of you. You think you're some kind of tough character. No doubt you'd benefit from a good hiding."

He turned to his son. "As for you, Jeffrey. Gambling on athletic events? Is this what they encourage at your university? I shall have to speak to the Chancellor."

Jeffrey gasped, mortified. "Father, don't!"

Burlick returned to his checkbook. Jeffrey, seemingly at a loss, swept the room with his eyes. Then, with a forced casualness: "Hello, Herr Einstein."

Albert registered a mild surprise. "Do I know you?"

"I've seen you around the campus," Jeffrey said easily. "A real scholar, I'm told. Not like me. You wouldn't want to hear about my difficulties with mathematics."

Albert gave him a rueful smile. "I can assure you, young sir, mine are far worse."

The sound of Commissioner Burlick ripping a check from his book drew our collective gaze. He gave it to Jeffrey, glowering. "Now go! And, by God, look to your studies."

Jeffrey nodded, stuffed the check in his pocket and sauntered out. Hans turned to follow, but not before giving Mina a leering wink that made her look away.

An embarrassed silence filled the room. Then the Commissioner settled into his chair and smiled gamely.

"Sorry about the interruption. With children, one does what one can. After that..." He shrugged, and then turned his attention to Mina. "So, Inspector, have we taken the young lady's statement?"

"Yes, Commissioner." Kruger sniffed. "It was Fraulein Strauss who gave Katie Gossen the locket we found. As a gift."

Albert cleared his throat. "Excuse me, but how did the police know the locket had originally belonged to Hector?"

Kruger laughed shortly. "Because we are not incompetent, Herr Einstein. The locket is inscribed on the back with a serial number and the name of the maker, Gerd Oberlin, on Marktgasse. We checked his records and found it had been sold to one Hector Franks, and at whose instructions it was sent by post to Fraulein Mina Strauss."

Albert nodded. "And from whose hands it then passed to the murdered girl. But I don't see how Herr Franks is further involved."

"Perhaps he learned his gift had been unappreciated by its recipient," Burlick said officiously. "That, in fact, it had been given to another. Driven by jealousy and rage, he stole into the Gossen home to retrieve it. There, surprised in the act, he was forced to---"

"Butcher the entire family?" Albert chuckled.

The Commissioner looked at him sternly. "I have seen stranger things in the course of my career, young man. And I don't appreciate Jewish impertinence."

Inspector Kruger seemed embarrassed suddenly, but by what I couldn't tell. At any rate, he was quick to usher Mina, Albert and myself out of the Commissioner's office, and into the bustling corridor beyond.

"Am I free to go?" I said to Kruger, trying to sound indignant. I had somewhat found my feet again.

"For now. But keep yourself available to us." He turned to Mina. "The same for you, Fraulein Strauss."

Mina nodded, then turned and allowed the matron to escort her briskly down the corridor. She never even glanced in my direction.

And I knew, as one knows these things, that I should never see Mina Strauss again.

I sat in my rooms that night surrounded by discarded newspapers. The murders had gripped the imagination of the Continent. The killer's reign of terror was recounted in explicit detail, including wild theories of genetic insanity, religious sects, and political anarchists gone amok.

I poured myself an unaccustomed second brandy and sat, sleepless, in my chair by the fire. I couldn't imagine sleep. Not after what I'd seen that day.

And Mina? Seeing her again after all these years. Learning what had happened to the locket. How could she have been so callous as to give what I had offered her to another?

I was stewing in this self-pitying broth till almost four in the morning, when a pounding at my door broke me from my reverie. I glanced at the mantel clock. At this hour?

I pulled open the door to find an equally exhausted-looking Albert Einstein, bundled in a thick wool coat.

"My God, Albert, do you know the time?"

"More intimately than most, I promise you." Then, with uncharacteristic urgency, he brushed past me into the room and began looking about. "You'll need a warm coat, of course. And boots. You don't happen to own a revolver?"

"A revolver? What are you talking about?"

"All will be explained." He stared at me, impatient. "Well, are you coming or not?"

The pre-dawn chill was like a cloak of ice. It had snowed again during the night, leaving two-foot-high drifts that impeded our progress toward the boathouse.

Beyond the long, wood-framed structure were the venerable spires of the university, which lay under the gloom as though crouching for warmth. The only sound was the distant tolling of Yuletide church bells for the morning's first service.

As we carefully approached the silent building, I could hear the river lapping gently at the dock. Out on the frigid water, silent as ghosts, the rowing team propelled their boat smoothly through the mist.

Albert led us to the near side of the boathouse, and then to a position beneath a window. We peered through the smudged pane at an empty room, warmed only by the light of a huge cast-iron stove. At the far end of the room stood a large water keg.

I turned to see Albert nodding to himself. "Of course, the drinking water! I *wondered* how he planned to subdue them. Some kind of soporific in the water. Then he could..."

"I swear, Albert, if you don't tell me what's going on---"

"It occurs to me, Hector, that I might be putting you in harm's way. I did leave a note for Inspector Kruger, but I doubt he'd take me seriously." He frowned. "Not that I blame him, given my gross stupidity about these murders."

By this point, I merely stared at him.

"It was so obvious, I couldn't see it," Albert went on. "There *is* a pattern. Prime numbers. Divisible only by themselves and one. Perhaps a mocking reference to his own troubles with mathematics? Who can say with such a man? One who kills so ruthlessly.

I recall reading Buhler on the subject of compulsions, Atwood on multiple murderers. Mileva has some interest in psychology, and keeps many books on—"

"Wait! Prime numbers?"

"Yes. 1,2,3,5,7, etcetera. *One* watch-maker, *two* old people, *three* seminarians, a family of *five*, a rowing team—"

"Of *seven*!" I exclaimed. "Six oarsmen and the coxswain."

He nodded. "Where better to find the necessary seven victims than at his own university? He's familiar enough with the sport to gamble on it. And there has to be at least one more murderous act for the pretense of a killing spree to be maintained."

"Pretense?"

"To hide the real motive for the crimes, and the real—and only—intended victim. Katie Gossen. The killer knew her murder would inevitably lead the police to his door, unless it was merely one in a series of brutal, senseless deaths. Part of an insane pattern based on prime numbers."

A sudden noise from within the boathouse silenced us. Footsteps against creaking floorboards. Muffled, secretive.

Carefully, we once again peered into the shadowy room.

A figure in a black overcoat and gloves was leaning over the water keg. On the bench beside him was a thick-handled axe, its blade glinting dully in the half-light.

I felt Albert's restraining hand on my arm, but I risked another look. The man lifted the keg lid and poured in a powder. His face shone in a pale shaft of light as he leaned over the barrel.

I sank back next to Albert, stunned. "But I thought it was---I mean, you saw what kind of creature Hans Pfeiffer is. The way he winked at Mina."

Albert nodded. "Yes. Coarse, familiar. But how could he not take notice of Mina Strauss? An uncommonly beautiful girl. Yet Jeffrey never gave her a glance. I thought that was odd, unless he knew her. Unless he purposefully ignored making eye contact. Because Mina knew him—or, at least, *of* him—from hearing of his unwanted attentions to her friend Katie."

"How in God's name do you know of this?"

"I asked around at the campus," Albert replied. "Jeffrey was hopelessly enthralled by Katie, and she spurned him. I thought something like that might be at the core of this, thinking of how Mina had likewise rebuffed you."

I stiffened. "Thanks very much."

He ignored this. "I'm sure his advances were crude and improper. He has a reputation for violence and drink. A loutish, aggressive type, under which lies an even darker, murderous nature. He finds being thwarted in his desires intolerable. Emboldened by his father's wealth and position, thinking himself above the laws of God and man, he's driven to murder. But to disguise the motive, he embeds the killing of Katie Gossen in a series of brutal slayings---seemingly the work of a madman, following some absurd, fanciful pattern."

I struggled to absorb his words. "So you guessed that he needed at least one more to make a convincing picture. The seven members of the rowing team. But how did you know?"

"Imagination, Hector. The unheralded seed-bed of all theory." A wry smile. "I simply imagined what I would do in his place."

Another squeak of floorboard from within drew our eyes to the glass. Jeffrey was moving back against the far wall, axe in hand. Melting like a wraith into the lattice of shadow.

"Now all he need do is wait," Albert whispered. "The team will be returning any moment. After a vigorous workout, they will doubtless drink from the water keg. Jeffrey knew there were too many to handle unless they were incapacitated."

I nodded. "So after the drug takes effect, he can move in for the kill. Unless---"

Where this sudden flush of courage—or foolishness—came from, I cannot say. But suddenly I was barreling as fast as possible through the snow, around the corner of the low-slung building and through the opened double doors.

"Hector!" Albert called out, but I'd already crossed the threshold into the room.

Jeffrey Burlick turned at the pounding of my footsteps, and rushed from the shadows to confront me. I leapt at him, hands outstretched, a cry bursting from my lips.

We landed in a heap on the floor, Jeffrey awkwardly tried to bring the axe to bear. I saw the horrible glint as its blade sliced down toward me. I saw my own death.

Then I saw Albert, face red with exertion, struggling with both hands for the axe. But the burly young student merely flung Albert to the floor.

Winded, scrambling to get up on our elbows, we looked up at the glowering face of a demon. Jeffrey hefted the axe as though it were weightless, raising it high.

"You two thought you could stop me?" he cried. "Two penniless patent clerks? No one can stop me!"

"You must stop!" I gasped. "Even *you* must see that killing these men avails you nothing. You've had your revenge on Katie, you've ended her life. Why must you end these others?"

"Revenge? On Katie?" His eyes narrowed to dark slits. "She's nothing! She means nothing to me. The design is all. The purity, the immutable beauty."

He paused then, regarding me with bemusement. "Something a man like you could never understand. Bound by your pathetic, bourgeois pieties."

He tightened his grip and raised the great axe once more to strike—

Another voice shot through the room. "Not as pathetic as you, Jeffrey!"

Burlick froze where he stood, as the tall, ramrod figure of Inspector Kruger stepped through the doorway. He held a police revolver pointed at Jeffrey's chest.

"Put down the weapon, or I'll be forced to fire."

Jeffrey wavered, glance darting from us to the Inspector.

"I assure you," Kruger said sharply, "I don't care who your father is. I will shoot you where you stand."

A strange, anxious smile played across the young man's lips. "My father? With his rules and regulations, so rigid, unbending. The unspeakable hypocrite! You don't know what he's really like, what he did to me." His voice caught. "*He's* the monster."

His eyes blazed now as he turned to stare at Albert. "And yet powerless against the march of mathematical inevitability! Surely, Herr Einstein, you must understand. If no one else, surely *you*..."

Then suddenly, in two brisk strides, Kruger was at the killer's side, the revolver pressed hard against his ribs. Jeffrey Burlick gave the Inspector the merest look before letting the axe fall to the floor with a clatter.

Albert rose beside me and smiled at the Inspector.

"I see you received my message," he said. "I'm surprised you gave it any credence."

"I'm surprised that anything surprises you, Herr Einstein. Not after this."

He nodded at Jeffrey, who, to my utter incomprehension, stood calmly with his arms folded, as though waiting for a train.

"No." Albert was shaking his head. "I miscalculated. Your arrival here was an unexpected variable. A random occurrence. If I didn't know better, I'd think perhaps God plays dice with the universe after all."

I struggled to my feet, my fear rapidly being replaced by irritation. I hated when Albert talked like this.

"Forget your theories, for the love of heaven!" I snapped at him. "We were almost killed this morning."

"*I* wasn't the one who seemed intent on heroics. Honestly, Hector, that was perhaps the most amazing surprise of all."

In a matter of minutes, a police van had arrived, and Jeffrey was bundled away in restraints by two stout officers. Inspector Kruger followed them out.

Alone with Albert in the eerie stillness of the boathouse, I gave voice to my thoughts. "Young Burlick must suffer from a diseased mind. It's the only explanation."

Albert looked off, in that way I'd become accustomed to.

"No, he's not mad. He knows the difference between right and wrong. I saw that clearly. He just doesn't care."

"But that's unthinkable! To butcher innocent people without remorse? Without a conscience? Believe me, Albert, I doubt there's a word for such pathology in your wife's scholarly books."

"Perhaps not." He gave a sad smile. "But I fear one day soon there will be."

***

Another gentle flurry of snow had begun to fall outside, and I realized with a start that tomorrow was Christmas Day. Though, admittedly, such holiday thoughts were far from my mind at that moment.

Albert and I stood with Kruger, watching as the rowing team, oblivious, began making their way to shore. From the dock, I could hear the sounds of another pair of policemen, dumping the keg of drugged water into the river.

Another sound, that of boots scraping heavily against frozen earth, made us turn. Jeffrey Burlick, shackled hand and foot, was being led to the rear of a police van. As the door was held open for him, he paused and looked directly, nakedly, at us. Then, showing a small, tight smile, he turned and stepped into the van.

As it rumbled away in the blur of morning light, Albert looked gravely at Kruger.

"He's the Commissioner's son. This will cause a scandal."

"Not my concern."

Their eyes locked. "I am curious why you believed me," Albert said quietly.

"Let's just say, not all of us share the Commissioner's prejudices, Herr Einstein."

Then, with a curt bow, Kruger went to join his men.

Albert watched him go, before brushing himself off and heading in the opposite direction. I followed him.

"That's quite enough adventure for me," he said. "Now it's back to my physics papers."

"No," I said. "It's back to the office, and the Beringer patents. We work until six, even on Christmas Eve, or Hoffmann will dock your pay."

He grimaced. "And Mileva will be furious."

Then, smiling, Albert Einstein put his arm around my shoulder. "Ah, Hector, the mathematics of love. Compared to it, physics is but child's play."

On the way back to work, we stopped for a sausage roll.

The final story in our collection takes place during the coal mining strife of the late nineteenth century, when mine owners brought in Pinkerton enforcers to combat the Molly Maguires. One man finds that it is time to take a stand.

Mr. Murr has lived on every continent except Antarctica, and currently resides in the Netherlands where he writes crime stories. Publications credits include Beneath Ceaseless Skies, Chizine, and Noir Nation.

The Mercy of Men

by Joe L. Murr

After ten hours in a lantern-lit coalmine, Olli shielded his eyes against the afternoon sun and hawked up thick sputum. He hated to think what his lungs looked like. At least he was still in good health, unlike Sean, wheezing beside him. Though both men were in their early thirties, the years had been much tougher on Sean.

Sean said something that Olli couldn't quite hear over the voices of the other miners. His ears still resounded with the din of picks on rock and the constant churn of steam-engine pumps.

Olli leaned in. "Say again."

In his heavy Irish accent, Sean said, "The wife was feeling poorly this morning. D'ye have any of your fever medicine left?"

"No, but I can make new batch." He spoke English in the monotone cadences of his native Finnish. "I go pick herbs."

"Grand." Sean gripped Olli's shoulder, smiling, but then his eyes flicked away, hardening. Olli followed his gaze. A gentleman in a suit stood ahead of them, a dark figure against the blazing colors of the autumn hills. He wore a revolver on his belt.

"A Pinkerton man," Olli said.

"A messenger of death, he is." Sean's voice was taut with anger.

The Pinkerton agent had gray muttonchop whiskers and a ruddy complexion. His sharp eyes surveyed the miners. Three mine guards stood close-by, eager to enforce order with fist and baton.

The agent raised his hand. "Halt. Which one of you is Sean Gillick?"

Sean muttered an obscenity under his breath, but didn't announce himself.

"He's a suspected Molly. We want to question him."

This was a death sentence. Any man suspected of being a member of the Molly Maguires – a secret organization of militant labor activists – was liable to find himself hanging from a rope, guilty or not.

"Step forward, or we'll punish every single one of you," a guard shouted.

A miner pointed at Sean. "That's him."

Sean elbowed his way out of the crowd, tried to run. He didn't get far before the guards caught him. Sean punched one of them in the face, but the other two wrestled him to the ground. The third, his nose bleeding, started kicking. The smug Pinkerton agent watched, hands on his portly waist.

Olli saw his future split into two paths. Do nothing and let his friend be hanged without a trial. Or help him and damn the consequences. So be it. He'd had enough.

Olli rushed the agent, jabbed him one-two in the kidneys. The agent gasped and reeled. Olli relieved him of his revolver, cocked it.

The three guards turned to him, shock in their eyes.

"Let him go," he said.

Cursing him, they backed away and let Sean rise to his feet. Olli kept the gun trained on them until Sean was by his side.

"You might as well drop the gun, son," the Pinkerton man said. "There's no place you can hide."

"You follow, you get bullet."

Olli and Sean ran for the storage field. Here the coal stock-piles were like black hills. Pressure and heat buildup made them smolder, an acrid reek in the air. It was ten acres of hell.

They clambered up a scree slope at the far end, boots slipping on loose stones. Once in the woods, they caught their breath. Sean sat on a carpet of fallen leaves. He gasped for air, his lungs ruined by coal dust.

"You shouldn't have intervened. They'll hang you for that, they will."

"Better than slow death in mines." Olli cast a glance down at the storage field. As yet, he could see no signs of pursuit, but the guards would be coming soon. "Is it true? You are Maguire?"

"Yes. I'm a Molly."

"Why didn't you tell me?"

"I wanted to, you're like a brother to me, but the others wouldn't have it. You're not Irish, or even Catholic."

"I don't agree with Maguire methods, but I'm with you now." Olli heard the baying of hounds. "They're coming. Follow me."

The Pennsylvania woods engulfed them. Olli knew the lay of the land well. He often hiked in the forest to get away from the filth and noise of the mining town. Sean pushed himself in spite of his coughing fits. Soon they arrived at a swift river some thirty yards from bank to bank.

"We lose them here," Olli said.

They hauled a fallen log into the river. Olli took off his boots and looped a lace through the trigger guard of the revolver. Then he tied the laces together and hung his boots around his neck. Sean did the same. They waded into the river. Though the day was warm, the water was ice cold. Olli hung onto the log, crooking his arm around a sturdy branch. Sean held onto the other end, his teeth chattering.

The two men kicked deeper into the river. The current seized the log. Olli heard dogs howling, close. Too close. Something moved deep in the trees.

"Stay still," he whispered.

He let the river carry the log, praying that it would not get caught on a rock. A bloodhound broke out of the undergrowth, tiny at this distance, and the Pinkerton man came on its heels. Olli and Sean kept their heads down.

Not a moment too soon, the log swept around a bend. Olli didn't think their pursuers had seen them.

"How long?" Sean said, gasping.

"Few miles. Hang on."

The river narrowed, ran faster. The log bobbed along at a terrific speed. Rocks flashed by them. Something slammed against Olli's ribs. He grunted with pain, but managed to hold on with his cold-numbed fingers. He knew they would hit whitewater soon. They would have to get out now. Kicking hard, they headed for the opposite bank of the river.

Sean sat in silence on the rocky shore and looked at some faraway point. "Thank you, Olli. Now go. Run. I have to go back. I can't leave my wife behind."

Olli considered this for a moment. "They won't expect us to return. I help you."

They wrung out their clothes and hung them to dry. The sun was low when they set off upriver, clothing still damp. Three, four miles and then it would be dark and safe enough to cross, Olli figured. The terrain was easy and Olli hiked slower than he would've preferred so that Sean could keep up without exhausting himself.

He thought about their situation as they walked, the unknowable future stretching out ahead of them.

"Sean, can your Maguire brothers help us?"

"No. I can't risk being seen with them anymore. They'd be found out. Someone would snitch."

"We won't last long without money. I have saved little, but not enough." His wages were less than two bucks a day and the mining company's general store charged inflated prices for necessities. It was a vicious cycle – he worked for meager pay and the company got almost all of it back. Thinking about it made him furious. "We need more."

"And how'd you propose we do that?"

"We take what's owed to us."

Sean frowned. "I'm no criminal, Olli."

"You are now. They take your life from you. You take it back. I came to this country because there isn't enough work in my own country, not enough food. I came to live, not die slow death. Now we live, and if we die, we die quick death."

Sean mulled this over. "We'd never be able to break into the payroll office. It's got walls four feet thick."

"That isn't what I had in mind."

"What then?"

"You leave problem of money to me. You get wife."

At dusk, they lashed together a raft for their clothes, and swam across the river.

As they walked toward the mining town, the temperature dropped fast, the chill of autumn in the air. Sounds of drunken laughter and song carried from the shacks at the edge of town. They descended into the storage field, rubbed their faces black with coal.

Olli adjusted the revolver in his waistband. "Meet me one mile north from railway station, in burnt-down shack. If I don't come by dawn, leave."

"What do you intend to do?"

"Going to get compensation."

Olli walked a half mile to the mine manager's house. It was a colonnaded mansion with ornamental eaves and surrounded by vast and well-tended lawns. He made a full circuit of the perimeter, keeping to the dark woods.

No dogs, fortunately, but two guards with rifles sat out front, and a third on the back porch. The threat of Maguire violence made them vigilant. The Mollies had resorted to kidnapping and even murder in their efforts to intimidate mine owners and supervisors.

An elm stood a short distance from the rear of the house, the perfect hiding place. Keeping the tree between him and the guard on the back porch, Olli proceeded at a crouch and climbed into the leafy boughs. From here he had a good view of the interior through the large windows. He saw brass and crystal, fine velvet drapes and lace. Two men smoked cigars in the oil lamp-glow of a study. The first was the mine manager, a lanky fellow in his mid-fifties. A lampshade obscured the other's face. Presently the man rose to help himself to a drink, stroking his muttonchop whiskers. The Pinkerton agent. In the corner, Olli saw what he'd been hoping to see – a combination safe.

Nothing to do now but wait.

Eventually the mine boss and the agent called it a night. Olli had expected the detective to leave, but now realized that he was staying as a guest. This complicated matters. He considered aborting his plans. This was much too risky. But they needed money. And – more important – Olli wanted payback. The urge to strike back had hardened inside him like a diamond.

The guard on the back porch rose to his feet and walked toward the far railing. Heart hammering, Olli climbed down. He approached the porch fast, revolver in hand.

The guard urinated, whistling out of tune. The porch creaked under Olli's boots as he closed the gap. The guard turned his head. Without hesitating, Olli slammed the butt of the gun against his temple, just above the ear, and prepared to strike again. One blow was enough. The guard collapsed, out cold. Olli took off the man's shirt and tied him up with it, then entered the house.

The mine manager slept upstairs. Only one way to find out in which room. He climbed the stairs. Squeaks echoed through the house. Someone coughed in the dark.

There were four doors at the top landing.

The first creaked as he opened it. Muttonchop whiskers gleamed gray in the murk. The agent mumbled in his sleep. Olli backed away, eased the door shut.

The next door was the correct one. The mine manager was curled up under his blankets. Olli sneaked to him, gun at the ready, hoping he wouldn't have to use it. He clapped his hand on the man's mouth, held firm. The eyes snapped open, then focused on the barrel of the gun.

Olli whispered, "No sound. Or you die. Nod if you understand."

He did.

"We go to your safe. Come."

Olli led him to the downstairs study. The boss picked up a box of matches, but Olli shook his head, gestured at the safe with the gun. Meekly, the manager kneeled and entered the combination. The safe opened with a clank. There wasn't much inside – a stack of ledgers, a few bundles of banknotes and a velvet pouch of jewelry.

"Don't kill me. That's all I have here."

"How much?"

"Just over four hundred dollars."

"You owe me that. For two years of work."

Olli stuffed the bills and jewelry in his pockets and then tied the man's arms and gagged him with his own nightshirt.

"This is how it feels to be at another man's mercy. Remember this."

As Olli walked out of the study, the mine boss kicked his desk. A glass tumbled to the floor and shattered, sounding as loud as an explosion.

"What was that?" someone said outside.

The guards would come in any second now.

Olli dashed for the back door. From the corner of his eye, he saw shadow massing on the stairs. The Pinkerton man was descending, a revolver in his hand.

Olli turned and fired twice. Darkness blossomed in the man's gut. Olli went through the door and across the yard, zigzagging. A bullet whizzed by his ear. He was almost at the treeline.

Something slammed into his calf. He tumbled, rolled, pain searing his leg. He forced himself up and kept going. More bullets zipped by him. He reached the woods, took position behind a tree, and returned fire, forcing the guards into cover.

He inspected the wound. The bullet had gone clean through, missing the bone. He'd been lucky, but he wasn't sure how much longer he could keep running. Once the rush of action wore off, he'd be in a world of hurt.

He ran, knowing they would soon follow, bloodhounds on his trail. It was over a mile to the burnt-down shack where he was to meet Sean and his wife. He pushed himself on, his wounded leg cramping.

The shack emerged from the night, a gray shape in a black field. He limped to it, entered the charred doorway. Sean stared at him, a two-by-four raised over his head. His wife was pale and shivering from both sickness and fear.

"Thank God," Sean said.

Olli pressed the money and jewelry into his hand.

"This is yours. Go. Leave now."

"Surely you're coming with us."

"No. I shot Pinkerton man. They won't rest until they catch me." Olli raised his hand to silence Sean's protests. "Winter is coming. Alone, I have chance. I can live in mountains. You stay with me, we all die."

Sean exchanged a look with his sick wife.

"We'll pray for you," she said.

"Go as far as you can," Olli said. "Make a new life for yourself."

And with that, Olli headed into the woods, leg throbbing with agony. A savage joy filled him. With every painful step, he was breaking free. Now he would live or die on his own terms.

Hounds howled in the distance. He howled back.

Acquired:
Waltham pocket watch, 1
Silver cow creamer, 1
Carved ivory napkin rings, set of 8
Regards,
The Fox
Wilder
Rumors
A Lewis Wilder Mystery
MOLLY MacRAE

About This Book

The typeface in this book is 11.5 Garamond and Helvetica (for the headings). It was laid out using Adobe InDesign software and converted to PDF for uploading to the printing facility.

About Darkhouse Books

Darkhouse Books is dedicated to publishing entertaining fiction, primarily in the mystery and science fiction field. Darkhouse Books is located in Niles, California, an inadvertently-preserved, 120 year old, one-sided, railtown, forty miles from San Francisco. Further information may be obtained by visiting our website at www.darkhousebooks.com.

www.ingramcontent.com/pod-product-compliance
Lightning Source LLC
Chambersburg PA
CBHW031232120726
47905CB00002B/560